DEAR GOD, NEVER AGAIN

Memoirs of a Different Child Soldier:
Reclaiming the Dreams of a Forgotten Nation.

DEAR GOD, NEVER AGAIN

DR. EWA UNOKE

TATE PUBLISHING
AND ENTERPRISES, LLC

Published by Tate Publishing & Enterprises, LLC
127 E. Trade Center Terrace | Mustang, Oklahoma 73064 USA
1.888.361.9473 | www.tatepublishing.com

Tate Publishing is committed to excellence in the publishing industry. The company reflects the philosophy established by the founders, based on Psalm 68:11,
"The Lord gave the word and great was the company of those who published it."

Book design copyright © 2015 by Tate Publishing, LLC. All rights reserved.
Cover design by Jim Villaflores
Interior design by Jimmy Sevilleno

Published in the United States of America
ISBN: 978-1-63418-884-5
Biography & Autobiography / Personal Memoirs
14.12.08

REPUBLIC OF BIAFRA

Biafra (White Area of Map) Courtesy: Eric Gaba

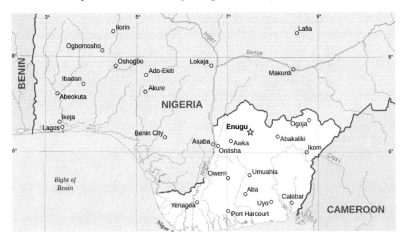

Biafra, unofficially the Republic of Biafra, was a secessionist state in southeastern Nigeria that existed from 30 May 1967 to 15 January 1970, taking its name from the Bight of Biafra (the *Atlantic bay to its south).* The inhabitants were mostly the Igbo people who led the secession due to economic, ethnic, cultural and religious tensions among the various peoples of Nigeria. The creation of the new state that was pushing for recognition was among the causes of the Nigerian Civil War, also known as the Nigerian-Biafran War. (Wikimedia)

The opinion expressed above is not necessarily that of the Biafran nationalists. Biafra still exists as a sovereign nation-state in international law, having been officially recognized by Gabon, Haiti, Tanzania, Zambia, and Ivory Coast.

The Vatican, American public, Jewish council, Ireland, and France also gave implied recognition to Biafra. But Nigeria, with the use of force, annexed and blocked Biafra's admission into the United Nations. Like Nelson Mandela's African National Congress, ANC, the Republic of Biafra's diplomats and government-in-exile operate from Europe and the United States.

MEMORIES

To MY FATHER, "Ogom" Ogbuinya Chi-ukwu Unoke Ekirika, the Adakaogu warrior who had the audacity and wisdom to save my life from my kidnappers,

To my mother, "Nwadam" Aliuwa Unoke, the iroko woman who bore the pain of a son's captivity, torture, and imprisonment,

To Anayo, Aloy, and Emeka, my three kid brothers, who, like us, loved life, but who were deliberately starved to death by the military junta with the inhuman strategy that "starvation is a legitimate weapon of warfare,"

To the "Lost Children of Biafra," who the adults betrayed. "Even a blind man can tell when he is walking in the sun."

UBUNTU

Ubuntu is a Zulu word which means, "I am nothing without you. You're nothing without me. We're nothing without each other."

On July 19, 2014, both family and friends made the journey to the Gate of Heaven mausoleum. When the dirge ended, we all went home without Isabela E. Gibson, the eternal traveler who dared to give her "baby" to marry an ex-child soldier.

At the age of nineteen, Lady, Slim, and Finegirl (as I fondly call her) innocently married an ex-teenage BOFF commander without knowing the implications. But as it turns out three decades later, Melody is my soul mate. Life would be meaningless without Lady and our two adorable Mgbom princesses, "Adaewa" Aliuwa and "Adakaogu" Jamike. This story is for them to know their Biafran and Igbo roots and what life has taught me as a village lad.

I wrote this story, but the Tate Publishing team professionally gave my narrative its aesthetic value and enduring image. I salute them: acquisitions editor, Jeff Foster; project manager, Cindell Pilapil; editor, Wendell; and cover designer, Jim.

Davies Sitenta, my Zambian mentee, worked on the manuscript for three semesters. Zambia recognized Biafra and his contribution to my story has a nostalgic significance. Vivian Thomas, my Puerto Rican work study student, spent several months typing the handwritten script. On several occasions, I stumbled into Vivian silently weeping. As she explained, she felt my childhood pains and suffering. Finally, Debra Belt, an adjunct faculty and friend, edited the initial manuscript. I am eternally indebted to my friends Joe Grasela and Jared Hill for their research, library, and technological skills, without which there would be no memoirs and memories. It has taken me five years to tell this story since the UN Undersecretary General for children in war asked me to write my memoirs as a Biafran child soldier. I am grateful to Radhika Coomaraswanmy and all of you my partners in letting the sun shine again on Biafra.

Nkiruka! Tomorrow is greater!

CONTENTS

TIMELINE

2005

Ewa, can we schedule you to tell our college community about your improbable journey as an African child warrior and Igbo prince who overcomes the odds to become a professor?

—Prof. Melanie Jackson-Scott, Director,
Intercultural Center, KCKCC, Kansas City, Kansas (2005)

2009

Have you thought of writing a book about your life as a Biafran child soldier? The world needs to hear your story, especially, now when children are so much abused in many global conflicts. [Think of the abduction of the Nigerian school girls by Muslim jihadists]

—Radhika Coomaraswanmy,
United Nations Under-Secretary for Children
in Armed Conflicts, Dole Institute, University of Kansas,
Lawrence, Kansas (2009)

2011

I found this story very truly inspiring. As I read the story, tears came to my eyes, and I wept… quietly for him, for his family and for his people. Ewa Unoke is proof that people who have suffered horrific things can accomplish great things. His life is a testimony of the inner strength that we all carry within, and with the right motivation nothing is out of reach for anyone.

—*Tonia Harmon, Author, "A Life Opened" (2011)*

2013

I am excited to hear that you are writing your memoir. We need such eye-witness books from people like you who actually experienced the crisis. As a child soldier in that Civil War, your account will not only be original and authentic but also insightful and culturally relevant. The Unokean truth may be bitter to swallow for Nigerian plutocrats and combative tribalists, but it is the necessary medicine for cure of the nation's illness. It is a book I intend to use in my future classes. Meanwhile, I want the publication of *Never Again* soon. Let's complete the book in 2013!

—*Prof. Kenneth Butcher, University of Missouri,*
Kansas City, MO, USA

2014

When typing the book, it made me shed tears, thinking about the pain he had to go through. I felt his pain and how hard it was for him to survive and become a professor today. Something must be done about this injustice. And, this is a book that should be read by everyone because we all have much to learn from it.

—Vivian Thomas, KCKCC student (2014)

On July 18, 2014, Dr. Matlotleng Matlou sent me this email:

> As we remember Rolihlahla Mandela on his 96th birthday; may his soul rest in peace and the world become a better place. We also celebrate a co-celebrant Ewa Unoke who shares the same birthday with Madiba. Many many happy returns. Grow and grow and transform the world. Knowing you has enriched my life and many more around the world; keep up the good work.

Sharing the same birthday with Nelson Mandela has not been an easy task because his shoes are so big while my own are so small in continuing his work: fighting for human rights, freedom, and justice.

INTRODUCTION

My students and friends in the United States ask me:

- As a former child soldier, did you amputate people's hands and legs?
- As commander of BOFF, what atrocities did you commit?
- Is it true Biafran children were deliberately starved to death?
- Like the Nigerian jihadists, did you kill or kidnap school girls during the war?
- Can you tell us your childhood pains and pleasures?

My response usually is, "Wait until you read my memoirs."

In sparking the memories of Biafra's triumphant and tragic past, we will never forget what happened to us in Nigeria. The pain of those we lost never goes away. It is now four decades since our sun stopped to shine. It is now forty-four years since the world turned its back to Biafra and to justice. When the moral world refused to grant recognition to Biafra or to stop the Muslim jihadist genocide against the Christian Igbo people four decades ago, the seed of anarchy and terrorism was sowed. Since then, the culture of beheading, kidnapping, and violence never stopped in northern Nigeria. The result is the seemingly unstopable kidnap-ping and selling of innocent children in the same northern states where over thirty thousand Igbo citizens were massacred in 1966.

Today, it is sunset in my ancestral homeland. Yesterday, it was sunrise in my fatherland. But tomorrow, the Biafran sun might rise and shine again. This is because of freedom's audacity and Igbo spirit. We're Igbo. Igbo people are from the land of the ris-ing sun. In Iboland, we do not surrender to fear. We're lions and leopards. We're the descendants of the original warriors of West Africa. However, our story as an ethnic nation is pregnant with pride and prejudice. The Igboworld is a world of dualities and oxymorons, as we say in Igbo: *osondi owendi*.

The kidnapping of Nigerian school girls tagged, "Bring Back Our Girls," global campaign has its roots in the unfinished nation of Biafra. Something must be done to remedy the historical injustices of the past. Otherwise, durable peace and sustainable security will remain elusive worldwide with dire consequences.

In the fight against terror, how can you make peace with peo-ple who believe in beheading "others" who are different from themselves? How can you make peace with people who believe in death while you believe in life? How can you make peace with somebody who believes in war while you believe in peace? Yet diplomacy is still possible in the twenty-first century.

Biafra's Declaration of Independence was the best of times and the worst of the times. When we could no longer tolerate the political culture of chaotic existence, beastly beheading, kidnap-ping, and violence, we said, "Ozoemena." Never again. In Biafra, we, the teenage freedom fighters, stood together in solidarity with our military leaders in proclaiming that, "Divided we will stand and united we would fall apart." Nigeria was too fragmented to stand as one nation, one people, with one destiny. After almost five decades of incessant terrorism, my views have not changed. In Nigeria, we are different people with strong loyalty to our different ethnic nations, but if the denmocratic experiment succeeds, this multicultural state is positioned to become not only a great nation but a global superpower.

Dear God, Never Again is about the audacity of freedom. As a political memoir, it is not only about my role as a child soldier. Rather, it is also about what life has taught me as teenage freedom fighter, Igbo prince, and professor. This is the story of a different child soldier that begins with the difficulty of imagining those we call "others" who are different from us. The remote and immediate causes of the current terrorist attacks in Nigeria, United States, and worldwide are rooted in this dilemma of imagining "others" who are not like us.

1

THE DANGER OF IMAGINING "OTHERS"

Life is not a fairy tale.

ON THE MORNING of February 24, 1959, our bold and fearless village mayor, Chief Nwiboko Obodo, was hanged by the colonial British government. Earlier, the colonial court had ordered that fifty-nine other members of the Odozi Obodo society (committee of peacemakers) should also be hanged. Nwiboko and the peacemakers were "suspected" of killing one of Nwiboko's thirty-three wives and other alleged victims. If Nwiboko and the villagers truly committed murder, then hanging them is justified. But let's assume the colonial government had wrongly executed Chief Nwiboko and other innocent victims. For example, how could fifty-nine villagers and Nwiboko, at once, kill one woman?

While the British colonial administration believed that Nwiboko was an evil man, many Abakaliki people still think their leader was falsely convicted and hanged because he was a daring and powerful opponent of British colonial rule. Nwiboko audaciously opposed the British "taxation without representation" policy which exploited his fellow Izzi villagers.

How should the long-oppressed Igbo people deal with the injustices of the past and the present? Should the perpetrators of historical wrongdoings be punished or pardoned and forgotten? *Transitional justice,* as a postconflict healing approach, is concerned with such past injustices.

On August 04, 1959, *Time Magazine* described Nwiboko's Abakaliki society, which is also my homeland.

In the vast British tropical colony of Nigeria, the backcountry people of the Eastern Region have long been a troublesome lot to [British] officialdom. Mostly halfnaked farmers, they take unusual delight in staging bloody campaigns against vaccinations, and in setting schools on fire. Each time the [colonial] police must come in to restore order. But of all the assignments that the police have undertaken, none has produced such eerie results as the search of the house of Chief Nwiboko Obodo.

According to *Time Magazine*:

> For months reports had poured in of a high homicide rate
> around the tiny town of Abakaliki, about 50 miles from
> the Eastern Region capital of Enugu. Men would go to
> their farms in the morning and simply disappear; women
> went to market and never came home. Police found evi-
> dence that since 1954, there had been more than 100 mur-
> ders in Abakaliki. But it was not until they raided Chief
> Obodo's house that they found the reason why.

The article concludes,

> Inside, they discovered rope, leg irons, and swords, as
> well as an assortment of juju charms bearing the warning
> that all men and women in the 14 villages around *must
> respect me and do whatever I say*. It soon turned out that the
> chief was a member of a secret cult that inappropriately
> bears the name of Odozi Obodo, the Committee of the
> Peacemakers.

Is the above speculative evidence sufficient to convict Nwiboko
of murder? What the *Time Magazine* article failed to explain
was why the British administration should forcefully and ille-
gally dispossess Abakaliki citizens of their land, their money, and
their dignity. Why should alien invaders force rural kids to attend
colonial schools, force Igbo youth to forget their own culture and
learn colonial culture, force adult Abakaliki men to marry only
one wife, force Igbo children to be vaccinated, and force our parents to pay taxes to a colonial government which did not provide
them any protection or services?

What the colonial British empire did not know was that
Abakaliki was a warrior subnation in Igboland. Strangers do not
tell us how to live our lives. Our proud parents asked, "Who are
you to tell adult Abakaliki men how many wives they ought to
marry or what tools they should have in their homes?"

Most of the things found in Nwiboko's home were typical items used for farming by the average Abakaliki farmer. My father had ropes, leg irons, swords, and dane guns for hunting, as well as an assortment of juju charms for spiritual security. Leg irons were precious ornaments which young Abakaliki girls wore on their ankles as sign of elegance and beauty before marriage. The ropes and swords were used in yam barns, agricultural work, and to protect the family.

The hanging of Chief Nwiboko and the fifty-nine members of the committee of peacemakers was an example of the danger of imagining others who were different from us. The colonial government imagined our traditional leader as an evil man in order to kill him. This human rights violation was an act of war.

TAXATION WITHOUT REPRESENTATION

Before Chief Nwiboko was hanged, the major security threat to the three clans that made up Abakaliki province (Ezza, Izzi, and Ikwo) was the brutal destruction of our people's dignity by the colonial administration over late payment of *hut-taxes* and *hut-rates*. Every market day, our parents and uncles were ambushed, arrested, and tortured for failure to show receipts of tax payment. In my childhood memories, I witnessed grown-up Ezza men arrested, handcuffed, flogged, dumped into lorries, and taken to Abakaliki maximum prison for nonpayment of taxes. During my childhood, I began to *imagine* and dream of another society in which our parents could be free from colonial rule and taxation.

One day, my father travelled to Izziogo market to sell his metal wares to Izzi farmers. He was an Ezza blacksmith and metallurgist. In the evening when the market was over, people returned to their homes except my father. Papa had been arrested, tortured, and taken to Abakaliki prison when the *kotma* (colonial court messengers) raided the market. As a child, I said to myself, "Colonial injustice has drilled a hole in my head. And I must fight to set my father, Abakaliki, and myself free." This was my first battle cry.

Such was the time during Chief Nwiboko's arrest. In defense of the much abused native people, Nwiboko Obodo had established a parallel government to British rule. The colonists considered him a threat. But many times Nwiboko paid taxes in block for the poor Izzi farmers while such people paid him back in installments to avoid imprisonment. Sometimes, Nwiboko intervened and released the poor farmers held in colonial jails. Such was the time. The colonial rulers considered Nwiboko a daring enemy who should be silenced.

In my Abakaliki homeland, the British could not see anything good about our people. They *imagined* Igbo-Abakaliki as half-naked, timid, and nonpersons. Likewise, while our people could not see anything good in British people. We *imagined* British rulers as lawless invaders without morals, who scammed and extorted taxes from innocent native people. At first, I thought Britain was incredibly racist, but then I realized it could be due to the country's own unintentional ignorance. There was no logical way to make sense of colonialism.

The "rain began to beat" *Ndigbo* (Igbo people) from the period of British colonization until today. That was when our trouble began. Britain did not trust Igbo and the Igbo people did not trust the British. It will be difficult to understand why the British government supplied the undemocratic Nigerian military dictatorship with war planes, arms, and ammunitions to kill Igbo children and their parents in an unjust war unless one understands our uneasy history. Given the British–Nigerian example, the postcolonial state has not rebuilt the moral foundation necessary for diverse ethnic citizens to live together in democracy and peace. But, despite rampant colonial injustices of the past, Igbo people themselves have also committed serious historical wrongdoings which contributed to Igbo-phobia and hatred in Nigeria. But the day of reckoning will arrive unexpectedly.

LIFE HIDES IN THE PAST

The seed of our present life hides in the past, where we
may look for understanding in the face of trouble.

—Harold Klemp

Before the war, the ethnic Igbo nation was polarized between
"wawa Igbo" and "ijekebe Igbo." The former comprised the politically excluded, poor, and less-educated people from Abakaliki,
Awgu, Enugu, Nsukka, and Oji River. The latter group comprised the more "civilized," more educated, and wealthier Igbo
people primarily from Awka, Onitsha, and Owerri. Most schools,
churches, and businesses were owned and run by the Ijekebe
or Agbenu Igbo, who constantly humiliated the less privileged
"wawa" people. In particular, Abakaliki, Ezza, Izzi, and Ikwo citizens were treated as nonpersons. I am wawa. Wawa Igbo had no
urban homes, no good schools, no transport, no professions, no
jobs, no roads, no water, no electricity, no hospitals, no welfare,
no social security, and no representation in colonial and postcolonial governments. For too long, we have remained a voiceless
and politically excluded society.

Abakaliki is a Puritan-like society. In Igbo language, *Odozi*
Obodo means exactly what it is, "committee of peacemakers," not
committee of half-naked murderers as the colonial British Empire
misinterpreted the village vigilante slogan. Most Abakaliki villages still have such committees today for community development and peace building.

The Igbo people's attempts to come to terms with their unpleasant past have failed. There are new calls for the prosecution of
perpetrators and the establishment of truth commissions to deal
with the injustices of the past. The effects of postcolonial conditions and human rights violations of the indigenous Abakaliki
people compel us to seek redress. But such redress must focus on
the crimes committed by the colonial British empire, Nigerian

Muslims, the Nigerian military government, and the January 1966 Igbo coup plotters who killed the Muslim politicians.

The case of Nwiboko Obodo is an unfinished human rights issue. There is a growing desire among the youth to address the long history of colonial wrongdoings in the former Eastern Nigeria, later known as the Republic of Biafra. The outcome of a retrial of Nwiboko's case will help my Abakaliki homeland to heal, to forgive, and to reconcile with Britain.

Today, the human rights community is shocked to hear about the hanging of over sixty Abakaliki farmers in 1959. This political injustice represents the turning point in Nigeria's struggle with its history, freedom, and justice. In reckoning with the past, Britain and Nigeria must deliver an official apology to the victims of colonialism and human rights abuses of Biafran children and their parents before, during and after the war. An apology will open the door for healing and reconciliation.

The human rights abuses perpetrated against Chief Nwiboko, his Odozi Obodo peacemakers, and Abakaliki taxpayers were injustices which still cry out for justice today. Such was the time, memory, and my homeland's turning moments.

2

TURNING MOMENTS

Life is a series of turning moments.

MY FRIEND, KEVIN Olsen, a humanitarian pastor with the Zion United Church of Christ, and I had our last monthly luncheon before he left to take up a new position in Colorado. "Why is life so difficult to understand?" I asked Kevin. "Many of my students consider me an inspirational college professor, but once in a while, one is bound to encounter a very difficult student who is not yet ready for college education."

"Ewa, it is all in the scheme of things for you, for me, and for all humankind," Kevin responded. "It is all in the master plan of our destiny. Providence or Spirit or God wants us to face both the good students and the difficult ones. In each situation, there are lessons for us to learn. So, both situations have very important lessons and values for our growth, mission, survival, and wisdom here in the physical universe.

Kevin further explained that there is something we call *moments* in our lives. "Many people believe in the biblical miracles that occurred since two thousand years ago. But miracles, for lack of a better term, have continued to occur in our individual lives, without our really noticing them as such. Can you remember any important incident or unforgettable event in your life? At the very *moment* when the event occurred, you were at one with the *Universe*, *God*, *Spirit*, or any other name you may choose to call this inexplicable phenomenon which most of us experience many times in our lifetime." Although such *moments* could be good or bad, we do not forget such moments—for example, the hanging of Chief Nwiboko Obodo by the British empire and numerous human rights violations during the colonial era.

However, Biafra is the most unforgettable *moment* in my political life. The Republic of Biafra was born out of the clash between freedom and power politics. But after nearly five decades in captivity, the surviving nationalists are determined to reclaim their long-forgotten freedom. The world has forgotten that Biafra was recognized as a sovereign nation-state under international law, but forced to rejoin the Nigerian federation after defeat in war.

The current revolutionary movements, terrorist attacks, and kidnappings in Nigeria reveal the danger in ignoring past human rights abuses in the postconflict and postcolonial society. The jihadists' anger which provokes killing and kidnapping of innocent people is linked to the unhealed wounds of the colonial past which forced the Muslim north to merge with the Christian south. Nigeria's past has not healed because past governments and society do not know how to do justice, forgive, punish, or reconcile. Yet the victims of war continue to hope and dream.

3

CHILDHOOD

Believe it, dreams are real.

WHEN I REFLECT on my childhood "moments," Nwoja Awoke's dream remains etched on my mind.

"Ogbuinya itehu (Ogbuinya, good morning)! I have come to tell you the dream I had last night about you and your wife."

"Itehu kwa *Nnem* Nwoja (Good morning, Mother Nwoja)," responded Ogbuinya. "I dreamed that despite your futile efforts to have a child in your ten-year marriage, the time has come for you to have a son. In my dream, your would-be son sneaked into your residence at night and silently surveyed each hut in search of a peaceful hut to be born into. When the spirit boy entered some of the huts, there was too much anger and children were crying for food.

"In the third hut, which is your first wife's hut, the spirit boy sneaked in after listening for a while. There were happy children, laughing and eating peanuts, coconuts, fruits and vegetables. The dream boy joined them. In my dream, the spirit boy could see everybody, but nobody seemed to notice his presence. He was invisible. In my dream, I heard the boy say, 'I will come into this family through this kind and caring woman.' Just then, the cock crowed and announced the dawn of a new day."

In the Ezza ethnic nation, dreams are real. Everyone knows it. Shortly after the dream, Aliuwa got pregnant during the year of the eclipse, and she gave birth to the spirit boy in Nwoja Awoke's dream.

More dreams began to pour in. This time, the messages were conflicting.

In the current dreams, the fight is between Ekirika Chita Effia and another Mgbom ancestral hero and warrior. The reason for the quarrel between Ekirika and the ancient Mgbom warrior had to do with the naming of the baby boy. To resolve a conflict of interests between the living and the dead (spirit) is a delicate issue, which no man has the power to resolve. Therefore, the proud father consulted a local mystic (*nwajibia*) to resolve the issue.

The spiritual verdict was to name the boy after the family's war hero, Ewa, and not my grandfather. This is the story of my journey into this world as Ewa Unoke. Ewa means "reincarnation" or "renewal" or "return of the ancient sage." If there is something in a name as Ezza people would say, then my own name is a scary one. It comes with an enormous responsibility. How could I ever live to demonstrate our ancestral bravery and courage in life? Yet, I did not choose the name. Ewa was the nwajibia's choice.

Whether people believe it or not, our ethnic Igboworld believes that dreams are real. My own life's journey, as discussed above, began in a dream state. I have since learned to dream big because dreams do fulfill. Igbo people dreamed of freedom. And, from dream, Biafra became a reality. Igbo people dreamed and fought for Nigeria's freedom and it became a reality. When Nigeria used guns to force us back into the Nigerian federation, our freedom dream turned into a nightmare. However, freedom dreams cannot be caged forever. We call it the audacity of freedom.

FAMILY

The man who gave me his genes.

At a very early age, she was betrothed to another boy in the neighborhood. Such was the tradition—early marriage. It was time to test the boys' wisdom. "Your sister will soon get married. According to our culture, you boys will have to decide how you want her dowry paid by the husband's family. Would you like the dowry paid to you with a calf or by cash payment?" asked the elders.

As the family elders waited for their decision, the two orphan boys said, "We want the little cow; we don't want cash." The next day, the lone calf arrived and Nwekewa and Ekirika were happy with their new friend.

Over the years, the wise choice of a cow dowry payment instead of cash has made a difference in their lives. The lone cow has continued to give births until now. The *owoko* (cow barn) is filled up with over fifteen cows.

One of the boys, Ekirika was my grandfather. This was the foundation of my grandfather's wealth, which we inherited. From a very early age, therefore, I learned from the wisdom of "Ogom" Ekirika to think *big* in life, and to make plans for the future despite life's turning moments. Before our revolution, therefore, we lived in abundance as compared to other ordinary villagers.

IKPENYI AND JIOKE

Of all my father's cows (inherited from my grandfather), the two most notable were Ikpenyi and Jioke. While Ikpenyi was black, beautiful, and adorable, Jioke was brown, deviant, stubborn, and wild. During my childhood, ownership of cows was a sign of abundance and wealth in our villages. On many occasions, poor villagers would come to our home to complain about Jioke's constant destruction of their farm, fences, cassava, and yam tubers. Sometimes, my father apologized; sometimes he paid for the cost of the damaged farm products; and sometimes, the complainants would end with threats to kill Jioke the next time it broke into their farms. And many times Jioke would break away stubbornly out of line and strike again and again.

One day, all the cows returned without Jioke. We smelled trouble in the air. This had happened before, so many times. Later, Jioke would be found. But this time, things were different. After a search for the lost cow that lasted from one Eke market day to another Eke market day, Jioke was found gravely wounded. An aggrieved and unknown farmer had shot a spear into Jioke's left belly and ruptured its intestines with the deadly spear sticking out of the cow's stomach. Young men from Mgbom filed out to bring Jioke home for treatment. For two more weeks, our family's young men battled to remove the spear in order to save its life. After a short while, as Jioke's life was coming to an end, my father sharpened his nkogo (machete) and sliced Jioke's throat in sacrifice to our ancestors. That way, Jioke would not have died in vain.

Life has taught me since the demise of my beloved cow that in every family, in every relationship, and in every society, there is always a deviant, stubborn, and wild Jioke. At a very early age, I learned from Jioke's death that life pays us back what we put into life. Jioke put violence into life and life gave violence back to Jioke, which ended its blooming and active life.

Later, cow thieves visited our owoko one night, blew their magical uke, and sent us into a deep slumber. When we woke up in the morning, our adorable Ikpenyi had vanished with the thieves along with the rest of our cows. My grandfather's dream of creating a better and happier future for his offsprings had vanished in one dark night.

FRIENDS

My past has refused to lie down quietly and rest.

Nnaji uwhom (my friend) Nworie Nwankwo was my best childhood friend. He was an orphan child, but his wealthy father did not like him much. Obaji, his father's third wife, became Nworie's stepmother. Obaji discriminated against the orphan boy. Nobody quite cared for him. Early in the morning, this orphan boy would be forced by his father to herd the cows on an empty stomach. From sunup to sundown, Nworie trekked many miles in search of green pasture for his father's cows to graze. The irony was that a prince was doing the job of a servant, as prescribed by his own father.

On a few occasions, as I can remember, I begged my father to allow me to join his servants Nweke and Alo in grazing our own cows. If my father refused, I would remind him that my friend, Nworie, who was just one or two years older than me, was also a cowherd. Papa sometimes would allow me to go with the older boys from morning until evening when we would bring the cows back to their fenced barn (*owoko*) attached to my grandfather's hut.

Nnaji Uwhum's cows and my own were scheduled once in a month to fight each other. The purpose was part of our warrior training. We pitched the two cows against each other and shouted praise and instigated them to fight each other as we watched with anxiety praying for our own cow to win the fight. That was before Jioke was killed. Then, Ikpenyi became my favorite warrior, but its performance never ever compared with that of the rebel Jioke.

When our cows fought, my friend and I seriously became "enemies" to each other. For some days, I would not talk to him because his cows continued to win more fights after Jioke's death. Early in life, therefore, I felt the pain of defeat, and I swore never to lose any battle, any competition, or any struggle in life.

In Igbo culture, defeat carries a stigma. Early enough, I witnessed the shame that goes with defeat. It is not a good feeling to have. We are inferior to those who defeated us. As the vanquished person, one has no respect from the victor. Society looks at the defeated as a weak offspring and disgrace to one's ancestors, family, and society. Village social critics and song composers would sing negative songs about the weak and defeated citizens. Finally, after a while, Nnaji Uwhum and I would reconcile and become friends again. Early in life, I learned that time heals old wounds.

Later in life, I would learn that the dark moments or failures we encounter in life inspire us to aim for high heights. The light and darkness in our lives constitute stepping stones for a great era and happier future.

BULLY

Bullying is real, parents beware!

The colonial school was a hostile environment to the weaker village students. Nwonu Oroke was a bully, but our teachers did nothing to stop him. David, as he was later called after his baptism, was a terror to us. Every time I refused to show him my test answers while in class, he would ambush me on our way back from school and beat me up mercilessly. He was not my only bully. Mathias was even worse. For failure to share my lunch with him, he would beat me every day for five days nonstop. When angry, nobody dared to pull him off his victim because such a peacemaker would become his new enemy. I remember what my fearless father told me during my childhood—never make trouble with anybody, but if trouble comes knocking on my door, I must never run away from it. "Fight back," he said.

I prayed, "Chineke, please save me from the iron hands of the bullies." For two years, Nwonu Oroke David was one of my worst "enemies." He hated me because the teacher praised me in class and thought my class works were outstanding. Nwonu therefore would poke me in the back and warn me to secretly "pass on" the answers to arithmetic questions for him to copy. Sometimes I did, until the teacher caught us and flogged David and me twenty-four strokes of the cane.

On our way home that day, David waited for me at Onu Enyogwu pond area. As soon as I arrived there, David jumped up and down and brutally attacked me. I asked him, "What did I do wrong? What did I do to you?"

"You don't know what you did? You deliberately and clumsily passed on your answer paper which was why the teacher caught us. Just as you made the teacher flog me, that is how you will be paid back."

David's bullying continued for over two more years until my father took me to report the incidents to David's own father. David's father was a good man and a friend to my father. During the reconciliation, both David and I learned that we were related to each other and that David, who had lived and learned the art of wrestling at Afikpo, should rather use his martial arts skills to protect me, his weaker relative.

"Chineke," I prayed, "please save me from my bullies." Our class competed with his class in a soccer game that afternoon. I dribbled him left, right, and a hard shot. "It is a g-o-o-oal!" the crowd cheered. As the crowd cheered me up, Matthias Ejogu (*ejogu*, one who goes to fight) jumped and kicked me down from behind. "What is the matter with you?" he growled. "You're a fool and I will deal with you after school today. I will follow your way home and teach you a lesson. I will fight you for one week every day for trying to dribble me and make me look like a fool on the soccer field."

After school, Matthias followed me. I had never been so abused in my life. While David beat me up for about one hour, Matthias was notoriously dreaded for the duration of all his fights. He fought boys for hours, nonstop. The next day in school, the fight would continue until I had to kneel down to beg him, "Please let us become friends." Later in life, each time I ran into Matthias, I recalled his torture and mean spirit toward me. With time, especially since his father became the village outcast, I genuinely became Matthias's friend. We had seemingly forgotten the unpleasant past, but early enough I knew that past wounds might heal but the scars would remain as a reminder. My bullies permanently killed my interest in sports forever.

4

CATHOLIC SCHOOL

The seed of our present life hides in the past.

—Harold Klemp

IN THE COLONIAL Catholic primary school, I was taught to read and write. I learned about European war heroes and statesmen like Christopher Columbus the Great, George Washington the Great, Alexander the Great, Abraham Lincoln the Great, Napoleon Bonaparte the Great, Vasco da Gama the Great, and Mungo Park the Great, who "discovered" River Niger in Nigeria even though the river had existed since ancient times. Most of these European statesmen were called heroes because they killed many people in battle. Later, when Idi Amin, the Ugandan military dictator, killed so many people in his country and became notorious worldwide, I asked my teacher why we did not call Idi Amin "the great," like other European rulers who killed many people too. "Is it because he is an African?"

In primary school, I observed that I wasn't learning anything much about my own country. The history of my country was not important. I was banned from speaking my Igbo language and taught to speak and write only in the English language. I was severely punished by the labor prefects and colonial teachers each time I spoke "vernacular" (Igbo language) in class. English finally killed my ethnic Igbo language permanently. Now I have been totally dispossessed of my native tongue and tradition forever. And nothing is left to pass on to my children.

In secondary school, we were forced to use knives, forks, and spoons to eat, instead of our hands according to our own culture. In religion, we were taught to believe in Jesus Christ and to forget about Chineke, the Igbo Creation God. To the European clergymen in Igboland, everything Igbo was evil, everything African was evil. They forced us to believe that only the European spiritual path would lead us to their preconceived European heaven. For the Igbo people, there was nothing new to us about the Ten Commandments.

In the Igbo social teachings, we are taught that we must never kill, never steal, never violate another man's wife, never disrespect our mother and father, and above all to believe in one Great God called Chineke, Chi-ukwu, Okpuluwa, or Obasi. We were also taught to believe in our personal God called Chi which guides and protects us every minute, every day, anytime, anywhere. European Christianity is a great religion, but its dispossessing mission in Africa is not only dubious but criminal.

THE COLONIAL TEACHER

Most of our colonial teachers were committed and passionate about teaching European moral values, but some of them were bad moral examples. During my primary school days, I lived with three teachers—Donatus Oburah, Donatus Nwogu, and Fidelis Okolo. They were my mentors, and I owe them for my success today. While I was living with Mr. Okolo, something terrible happened to me. A young primary school teacher from Amuzu village was posted to teach in my village school, and he continually molested me for over one year. I became afraid of the night when he would crawl toward me. I could not report him to *Nnam ukwu*, my great father, Mr. Fidelis Okolo. I forgot to mention that I have two fathers, Unoke Ekirika, my biological father, and my great father, Fidelis Okolo.

Back to my story of molestation, I could not tell anybody about my ordeal because nobody would believe me. Rather, I would be severely punished for telling against the teacher. In those days, teachers were mini gods. Students dared not challenge them. I could not tell *Nwadam* or *Ogom* (as I fondly called Mama and Papa respectfully) because they would never believe that a man was attracted to a little boy. My parents believed girls were attracted to boys and men were not attracted to men or boys. Homosexuality is a taboo in our culture. Such a thing had never happened in the Ezza nation.

The victims of the colonial Nigerian residential school abuses ought to seek justice in order to heal and to deter future abuses.

My worst colonial school abuse was corporal punishment. If I failed one *mental arithmetic*, I was flogged twelve lashes of the whip. If I failed any homework in English, science, or history, I would be flogged. If I came to school late, I would be flogged. I will have closure, healing, and forget the past only when I receive an apology. Even now, I hold no hatred for the perpetrator, because to err is human and to forgive is divine. Not to forgive will hurt me more and hinder my progress in life. The Catholic church ought to apologize and take responsibility for the abuses of Igbo school children during the colonial period. My life is a series of turning moments.

COLONIAL SCHOOL

One day, the unthinkable happened. My best friend, Nworie Nwankwo aka Nnaji uwhum, was "arrested" and forced to attend the new Catholic primary school called St. Benedict's Ntsokara. Back then, it was like an awful thing to enroll in school.

When the new teachers visited *Ogom* Nwankwo Enyoku, he quickly handed over my friend Nworie to them for enrollment into the new school, which was considered alien and undesirable for our village children. I missed the company and friendship of "nnaji uwhum," who by now was in Infant I (kindergarten 1). The culture of insecurity pervaded the village community. People were afraid for their children. There was anger and danger in the air, as the pupils and teachers of the new school raided, arrested, and kidnapped school-age village youth to enroll in the school. The abduction became very necessary because no normal Ezza man with prudence would voluntarily enroll his children in a new culture like the one now threatening to destroy our own culture. In Ezza, children meant name-preservation, prestige, power, and family continuity. If a child was rooted out of his ancestral traditions and culture, then one's own father's home would one day become a forest.

At the time I was living with my grandmother, I felt protected. On Nkwo days, (Nnem Ochie) grandmother trekked long distances from our village to Nwakpi market in Ikwo. Such was the case one fateful day when she had hidden us perfectly well in my grandfather's *obaji* (yam barn). Inside *nkata oru ekwo* (large baskets), Otubo Echem, my cousin, Nworie Unoke, aka Abamenda, and I were covered up as if we were caged chickens. The reason was to hide us school-age children from being abducted and forced to go to school. The pupils and teachers of the new school had become a serious threat to the community's traditions. Christianity and colonial education were forced down the throat of our village community, which for many centuries had its own education and its own spiritual way of life.

Suddenly, the unthinkable happened. Without knowing it, we had betrayed ourselves when we innocently revealed where we used to hide to our friends. One boy shared this information with the teachers. The next day, as usual, we rushed to cover ourselves up in our large baskets. But alas, things had gone wrong! The invaders came straight to my grandfather's barn and kicked open the baskets hiding us. There we were, Otubo, Abamenda, and me. Little Nwobashi Nkpuma was also with us. As young warriors in training, it was as if we tied wings on our shoulders and fled into the Ntsokara forest. As we vanished into the bushes, the neatly dressed pupils who did not know the environment very well retreated. On their way back, they kidnapped Nwakpa Eguji, my teenage aunt who was already betrothed. How could my family, (led by my father as the ruling prince) pay back the dowry already received from my aunt's fiancé if she was forced to attend the new school?

That unforgettable day, my father summoned an emergency meeting. I remember all the people who were present. Sitting next to my no-nonsense father was my most powerful uncle, Mkpuma Ekirika. He was tall, stout, with a broad chest and highly charismatic. Uncle Mkpuma barely laughed, but when he did, he lit up the atmosphere wherever he was. In front of my grandfather's *Aliobu* (male shrine for family protection), my father addressed the family men. Chita Ekirika, my father's youngest brother and the most outspoken uncle, was present. Nweke Unoke and Alo Unoke, my father's blacksmith apprentices, there too. Ngwu Unoke and Nwawhor Orogwu, Uncle Mkpuma's own apprentices, were also present. My cousins Chita Nwekewa and Otubo-Echem were present while the family womenfolk kept their distance, but secretly listened to the discussion that ensued. As the family prince, my father, Unoke, asked the male children who sat on the ground, "Who will replace Nwakpa Eguji? You all know that your aunt Nwakpa is married and will soon leave to join her husband at the Okofia village. Which of you would volunteer to take her place in the new school?" *Kpri-ri-rigbi-din* (Absolute silence)! All of us kids were frozen in fear. Our silence broke the foundation of our family's culture of audacity, courage, and warrior spirit. Before Mgbom kindred went to any war, my family must give approval, since we are the custodians of the ancient war drums. Certain spiritual signals must manifest before we go to fight a just war; otherwise, we will not fight. Our cowardly silence as child warriors was disturbing to our father and uncles present.

After a long silence, I said, "I will go and take the place of Aunt Nwakpa so she can go to her husband." My inside was frozen with fear of the unknown journey I was creating for myself. I remembered that my grandfather was okpara (every first boy child in Ezza is a prince). My father Unoke was also an okpara and as my father's okpara (prince), I had to show courage in the face of any challenges.

My paternal grandmother, Anyigor Otubo, who I was living with, returned from the market, received the news, and mobilized our families' womenfolk to accompany her to the new school at Amaokpo where I was being enrolled to start school.

Upon arrival, she cursed out the pupils and their teachers. She did not see why the village elders and the *Kansuru* (councilor) should allow strangers to build an alien school in our community. Above all, my grandmother had earlier asked neighborhood pupils what the colonial teachers were teaching them in the new school. The village school children had confessed that one of the new songs was "zohanne-zohanna" (forget your mother, forget your father). My grandmother was outraged. She confronted the teachers, "So you abducted my grandchild in order to teach him zohanne, zohanna? So you want him to forget his own ancestors' culture? You want him to forget the things that hold us together, the things that protect us?" Grandmother lost the battle because it was my father's decision that I swap positions with Nwakpa, my married young aunt. Secondly, grandmother lost because I had already been registered to start Infant I (kindergarten) the next day.

EWA GOES TO COLONIAL SCHOOL

I remember my first day in school. When the village cock crowed to announce the new day, my mother got me ready for my most dreadful journey into a new alien culture. As Mr. Donatus Oburah called roll, we were taught to respond "Present, Sir" each time we heard our names. That we did. Early enough as I sat at the front row, I noticed the difference between Mr. Oburah and ourselves—shoes. He wore shoes. Shoes were strange to us. We were village lads who had never seen anybody wearing shoes in our community. Ogom, Nwadam, and my uncles never wore shoes. At first, Mr. Oburah appeared clownish with the "thing" around his feet. I thought such "thing" he tied around his legs would soon fall off his feet. I was wrong. Throughout the day, the shoes remained firm on his feet. So my earlier concept of clownishness gave way to curiosity.

Mother's only picture with me while Nwabueze stands

I knew from this first day in school that if I did my homework and read my books well, I would someday wear shoes like my first teacher, Mr. Donatus Oburah. My interest then was more on wearing shoes than on acquiring knowledge.

As a young Mgbom prince, I had no need for European education. I never lacked anything in life. I was secured, well fed, and happy. My destiny was assured: to marry many wives, continue our family warrior traditions, and to lead. However, in order to wear shoes like my teacher, instantly teaching became my first childhood dream. The value of teaching was not on my mind. I just wanted to teach in order to wear shoes.

On this remarkable journey to acquire a European education, my experiences would become that of *osondi owendi* (joy and sadness). On one hand, it was like I was forced to glory as a PhD and political scientist. On the other hand, I was terribly abused in the Catholic educational system. But quite recently, I summoned up courage and wrote a protest letter to the pope about the injustices I suffered within the Catholic residential school system.

5

HEAD

EARLIER, I HAD introduced my biological father, Chiukwu Ogbuinya Unoke Ekirika, and my second father, whom I call Nnam Ukwu, *my great father*. While my Infant I (kindergarten) teacher's shoes had become the compass that showed me the way to becoming a future teacher, my great father, Fidelis Okolo, aka "Head" (head master), as he was popularly called, was my greatest teacher and mentor.

Head was a legendary teacher, mentor, and sage. At Ezzama, Amuzu, Ntsokara, Amudo, Amana, and Ikwo, Head was many things to many people—community leader, teacher, medical doctor, healer, poor man's advocate, farmer, peacemaker, and educator. He loved life and enjoyed teaching. He was also a great artist and philanthropist. If I inspire my students today, it is only because I was taught by the Master, the Adept. Despite seeing Fide Okolo as a great disciplinarian, we, his children, would not have been as successful as we are today without his strict discipline. But, alas,

Onye ije, the great traveler, has made the final journey. As farmers, my two fathers and mothers sowed but could not wait to reap.

Ikechukwu Uchennegbunam Okolo, my great father's prince, is a mechanical engineer who has worked for major oil companies worldwide, including Nigeria, Oman, Pakistan, Canada, and Azerbaijan, while I teach in United States' colleges and universities just minimally stepping into the big shoes of our legendary great father.

Life is difficult without our parents. Our children, Aliuwa, Ekene, Jamike, and Dabende, will never know their wise grandparents. They will never know Anayo, Aloy, and Emeka who were starved to death by the military government of Nigeria. Without our lost ones, life is also difficult for Nma and Melody.

Mr. Romanus Nwogu, the gentle, soft-spoken teacher from Owerri, was posted by the Catholic Reverend Father at Sacred Heart, Onueke, Ezza to teach at St. Benedict's Primary School, Ntsokara. This was in 1957. The first month in his class, I knew this teacher liked me. He appointed me the class monitor in charge of the classroom. It was my duty to bring the teacher's basket, stool, and chalk, among other duties. He did not say it, but I knew he thought I was his smartest student. On many occasions, I heard him discuss my class performance with his colleagues. No surprise, Mr. Nwogu gave me a ride on his bicycle one day down to my home in order to see my parents.

At the end of the visit, my father asked me, "Nwoma Njoku (my warrior name), would you like to live with Onye-nkuzi?" *Onye-nkuzi* means "the teacher." For the second time, I had to show courage to my father. The first test of courage came when I was forced to go to school, and now I was being forced out of my parents' home which I loved so much. What about the security my mother and father and our home provided? What about my poor eating habits? I felt so much fear of the unknown. "Yes, Papa, I will like to live with my teacher." Since I had no personal property, I went back to school the next day and never returned.

When after one year Mr. Nwogu was transferred to teach at Ikwo, he packed my things and we left. But the newly transferred headmaster, Mr. Fidelis Okolo, would not issue me a transfer certificate. "Transferring Ewa will further depopulate St. Benedict's Primary where already the pupils here do not want to go to school." With this logic, my dream of a lasting apprenticeship with the loving and caring Mr. Nwogu abruptly came to an end. Mr. Nwogu fought back, but all in vain. Mr. Okolo had a superior power as headmaster. Early in life, I learned that when a weaker power clashes with a stronger power, the weak power succumbs. I learned also that what is justice most times is what the strong wants.

So, when recently a cospeaker (child soldier) from Sudan began his speech with, "Nothing in my rural village life had prepared me for the Sudanese crisis," I laughed. I laughed because in my case, I come from a warrior culture. From my childhood period, my family had prepared us not to run away from any fight that meets us in our home.

The new headmaster, called "Head," was the kindest and most humble teacher I had ever met. Within two weeks as headmaster of St. Benedict's Catholic primary school, Ntsokara, Mr. Fidelis Okolo had transformed the school, visited my parents, made friends with them, and took me to live with him in the school premises. The headmaster's large grass hut was massive and dwarfed the other long huts housing the teachers, one room each.

"Head" (my great father) was a bachelor. He made many male and female friends in every village he was posted. At Ntsokara, my father was his best friend. Head, who liked to cultivate his own farm, therefore, got my father to handle everything about land clearing and planting of his yams and cassava plants. Soon, Head brought in more poor children from Eke, his hometown, to live with us—Paulinus Anyanechi, Nwakaego Chigbo (Head's niece), and Emeka Okolo from Umuaniogwe, the famous blacksmith community in Eke village.

My Great Father Fidelis Okolo aka "Head" (Right)

During the beautiful, tropical hamattan nights, we would spread mats outside the grass house and lie down with my great father in our midst. I always lay next to him. He said my way of scratching his back was always the "sweetest." I delved into the contours of his back and gently scratched with both horizontal and vertical strokes. He would moan with satisfaction, "Oh! O yes! Scratch harder! O yes!"

All of us boys slept on two large mats on the floor while Nwakaego slept on a separate mat far from the boys. In the sleeping arrangement, Paulinus, Emeka, and I slept on the same mat with a newly employed young teacher from Amuzu village (name withheld).

Every night, the teacher made sure he slept next to me. It was a very terrible time. This teacher would molest me almost every night. I dared not report to anybody because nobody would believe me. He was a teacher and I was a pupil. The status gap was too wide for anybody to believe me. I will never forget the pain and humiliation I went through: I could not report my ordeal to anybody. I surrendered it all to God in prayers. My great father, the headmaster, would never believe my story. My biological parents and our village community had no idea about gay people, lesbians, or pedophiles. It just never existed in our society. Therefore, we had no name for it. However, the pedophile teacher was exceptionally kind to me and gave me money, clothes, and dried meat. The teacher's mother traded on dried bush meat at Eke Imoha.

Early in life, I developed the feeling that homosexual people are very generous people. But it is not the path Igbo people or I would recommend to my children. When he died after many years, I felt bad but relieved for his death, knowing that at least other children are saved from his molestation and abuse. Early enough, life had taught me that many parents have no idea that most times their children are sexually molested by their friends, uncles, teachers, and church leaders. Parents have very little idea about such abuses, while their children are intimidated and afraid to reveal their abusers. Child sexual abuse is a secret epidemic far worse in severity than other war crimes. As I stated earlier, on June 26, 2013, I wrote a letter to the pope on human rights abuses in the colonial Igbo school system. Life is a series of turning moments.

The next incident happened when I rode my great father's "Mobilette" motorbike.

"Who asked you to ride the mobillete in my absence?" he asked furiously.

"Nobody, sir," I replied.

"I will teach you a lesson you will never forget," said my father.

The beating that followed was like going to hell and coming back to life miraculously. I was battered and bruised from head to toe. When he was done, he threw my "portmanteau" box outside, rolled out the motorbike, and asked me to take it to my biological father to pay for it.

I had trekked about four miles rolling the bike (afraid to ride it again) until my great father caught up with me.

"Let's go back, you fool," he yelled.

And we did. For the second time I had been prevented from reporting my problems to my biological parents.

On the lighter side, many good things also happened at Ntsokara. Nzekwe and Maduche visited us a few times and extensive discussions followed. Next, my great father traveled home to Eke and Oha-imezi, where Nzekwe had identified a young girl for him to marry. For some strange reasons, it was not easy to find a suitable wife for my great father at his own Eke village. Either prospective wives thought our family was noted for making trouble or that we discovered certain character flaws in their own families.

Finally, Cecelia arrived at Ntsokara with her junior brother, Elochukwu, who would later become Desmond after baptism. "Madam," as we called her, though very young and beautiful, was quite humble, caring, and full of life. She was an expert story-teller who told amazing folklore tales about the animal kingdom. "Okwa ajugo, okwa ajugo ije akwukwo, anikirija okwa nwokwa ajugo ije akwukwo (Okwa, the stubborn bird has refused to go to school. Stubborn okwa has refused to go to school)." We would join her singing in unison.

Soon, the rest of the houseboys began to gossip about the preferential treatment "madam" gave to Elochukwu, her younger brother. What we found was that Elochukwu was an orphan child and Madam played the role of a surrogate mother to him. We did not reason that way. What concerned us was that madam went to Eke Imoha, bought six plastic plates of different colors, and shared them among the boys and Nwakaego, the only girl. When food was shared, Elochukwu's ration was much bigger than the rest. One day, Paulinus grabbed Elo's plastic plate and left his own plate for him. The punishment he received helped to silence our gossip. But another life-changing event would soon occur in our family. Head's first son, Ikechukwu Uchennegbunam, was born in November 1960. Early in the morning, Madam would breastfeed the baby, bathe, and rub powder and sometimes Vaseline on him.

Those were the happy times for us all. We loved the baby, who continued to get bigger and bigger every day. We concluded he was growing so fast because of *akamu* (pap) which was basically his main food after breastfeeding. Gifts of goat, yam, chicken, and fruit poured in from Ntsokara, Ezzama, and Amuzu. Briefly, after Ike's birth, Head was transferred to St. Paul's Primary School, Amudo.

I remember the day we left St. Benedict's School on transfer to St. Paul's Catholic School, Amudo. Riding on his *Rodge* bicycle, my great father took the lead while Madam with baby Ike tied to her back rode gently next to her husband while the rest of us trekked about ten miles to Amudo. I remember when Ike began to cry along the way. We all stopped at the Ntsokara end of the Ndende River. As we sat to rest, Madam breast-fed my kid brother who sucked and sucked until he dozed off to sleep. In a short time, we would be examining our new one-room home in the new school. I have always lived in grass huts and this was the first time I would sleep in a zinc house. But this time, since my great father was no longer a headmaster in the new school, about eight of us had to share one room. One thin curtain hung and separated us from our parents.

Head quickly befriended a neighborhood citizen of Amudo village who guided him on how to acquire farmlands for cultivation. By this time, I was in Standard 5 (elementary 5). When the December 1961 school year came to an end, I would know my first failure since I began school. Mr. Cajetan Onyemere was a tall, handsome, no-nonsense teacher, the headmaster who was replaced by Mr. Fidelis Okolo, "Head." This time, Mr. Onyemere was my teacher in Standard 5 class. At last I knew why I failed. The extensive farm work which began at noon about three times per week did not give me enough time to study. What I cannot remember is whether Paulinus, Nwakaego, and Elochukwu also failed. I was too angry to look backward. As I cried with my wooden school box on my head, I left for Ntsokara to tell Ogom (my father) and Nwadam (my mother) what had happened.

My biological parents consoled me and asked me to have hope in a better future. "It never rains forever," Papa advised me. In other words, there is time for failure and time for success in life. Failure does not last forever. Early enough, therefore, I learned that failure and success coexist in our lives. In life, there will always be either failure or success. When one comes, we wait for the next. I learned to fight back and to fight hard. I developed a deep hatred for failure and made up my mind I would never fail again. It occurred to me that people who study their lessons do not fail. The more one studies, the more successful one becomes. The less one studies, the less one will know. So, how can one study less and hope for success? It makes no sense. Since then, I have never failed in any academic test I have pursued. To me, therefore, failure is my greatest motivation to succeed in life. The dark moments of our lives are as important as the great moments in our lives. We learn great lessons from our unpleasant past.

ONE-DAY WAR: AMUDO

The year 1961 was an unforgettable one for me. In 1960, Amudo village (our new school) waged war against Ntsokara village. On that fateful Orie market day, people were selling and buying in the market. Suddenly, a riot broke out. One Amudo man got into a fight with another Ntsokara man. The fight spread throughout the market and beyond. I remember that two young men ran to inform my strong and energetic uncle, Mkpuma Ekirika, and other able-bodied Ntsokara men that war had erupted and Amudo people had forced all our villagers who lived across Ndende River to vacate their homes. The war began at twelve noon and by six that evening, the war was over. Amudo had won. Ntsokara lost a large span of territory from Ndende to the Orie market and up to the Onueke-Afikpo road.

Nobody knows the humiliation I suffered at St. Paul's Catholic school in 1961 at the hands of Amudo students who teased and reminded me that I was from their captive Ntsokara village. "All of you are now our slaves," they would tease me. From these experiences, I developed great and unforgettable friendship with the very students who tormented me. The bullying stopped when the highly respected Rexy Alo from Unwunwagu Idembia took me under his wings. Francis and Canice and Raphael (Aro-Amudo), the great soccer players of our primary school, became my best friends. Raphael, my worst bully, stopped harassing me.

AMANA

In those days, the resident reverend fathers had a way of transferring the teachers under their districts. There were too many transfers. Even as a child, I knew by listening to my great father that much of the teacher-transfers were punitive. Again, after only one year at Amudo, my father, Fidelis Okolo, was transferred to St. Peter's Primary School, Amana. To me, St. Peter's was better than St. Paul's Amudo purely on personal grounds.

First, I liked Mr. Tobias Chukwu, the Awgu-born disciplinarian and headmaster of the school.

Theresa Ewa and Bernard Ewa (sister and brother) were in my class, and I liked both of them. They were kind, friendly, and good company to keep, especially Theresa. Bernard was rather shy as a junior to his sister. But Polycarp Agada would become my best friend for many reasons. He was smart. He lived with the headmaster, Mr. Chukwu, and since all the teachers and headmaster lived together in the mission school, therefore, Polycarp and I did so many things together. We fetched water and firewood and did our homework together.

Mr. Chukwu had the best handwriting in the world, I thought. Since Polycarp lived with him for a long time, he too had become an expert in writing just as good as Mr. Chukwu. So, I had to befriend Polycarp in order to learn to write as good as Mr. Chukwu and himself. Both of them were so identical that it was difficult to distinguish between Mr. Chukwu's handwriting and Polycarp's own writing. So early enough, I knew it. I knew that if one finds any subject difficult to learn, one should befriend the best student in that subject. It is easier and less stressful to learn from a friend and classmate than from most teachers in class.

Directly opposite St. Peter's school was the home of Mr. Okolo's new friend. Mr. Okolo's tradition of making early friendships with close neighbors in his new society always pays off. At St. John's Amuzu, Our Lady of Fatima, Ezzama, St. Benedict's Ntsokara, St. Paul's Amudo, and St. Peter's Amana, my father cultivated life-changing friendship with men and women.

In Ezza culture, the wife of one's friend is automatically one's own "girl-friend" or is called "woman friend." Great Father had such women friends anywhere he was posted to teach. Such women and their husbands loved and remained loyal to this man whose charisma, humility, and excellent human relations are unequalled. So, Ezza men willingly shared their wives with Mr.

Okolo, without any reservation whatsoever. If the husbands misbehaved, their wives would threaten to report them to Mr. Okolo.

Fide Okolo was an extraordinarily gifted teacher. To the native Ezza and Ikwo people where he taught, he was also their personal physician. He owned a first aid box which contained iodine for fresh cuts, bandages, plasters, Vicks, APC, codeine, and other medications. If the villagers were sick, they would come to our residence at the teacher's quarters and get treatment from "doctor" Okolo. From small bites to a scorpion's sting, Mr. Okolo would disinfect the affected part before final treatment. Most times, he rode his old bicycle visiting homes and treating the sick. He never asked for any payments. It was all free. He was a teacher, an educator, a doctor, and also a "lawyer" who settled conflicts and disputes between husband and wife, village antagonisms, and students' crises. He was also a devoted Catholic and a great artist. In every school he was transferred to, his first duty was to change and transform the teacher's environment. He would spend week, after week drawing maps of the local area on the walls, maps of Nigeria, West Africa, Africa and the world. He would draw animals, trees, flowers, and label their parts. He was thorough and detailed. This was what many teachers would not know when they encountered him first. In those days, teachers were required to forward their "notes of lesson" not later than Sunday afternoon to the headmaster for grading. Mr. Okolo would read each teacher's teaching "plan" for the week. If approved, the teacher would use the plan to teach throughout the week. But if Head did not approve, he would simply write "seen" and this meant the teacher would rewrite the "notes of lesson" and resubmit it for approval. Mr. Okolo was a stickler for excellence and those of us who lived with him were gradually becoming little Okolos of excellence. With him, there was no room for mediocrity.

At last, Mr. Okolo, my father, was transferred again, this time back to St. John's primary school, Amuzu. I liked the location of St. John's. The Catholic primary school stood majestically between Oriuzor and Onueke on Abakaliki-Afikpo road. What made this location unique was because of its proximity to Sacred Heart, the best Catholic primary school in Ezza. It was very close to the Ezzikwo local government headquarters. St. John's was also close to Eke Ezza, formally known as Eke Imoha. This Ezza market was the largest slave market in West Africa. After slavery, it has become one of the best markets for buying horses, yam, cassava, palm oil, rice, and local works of arts. Lorries came from far and near as traders rushed to buy and sell their goods. Arguably, about two-thirds of West Africans were sold into slavery from Eke Imoha market. St. John's was just about a twenty-minute drive to the colonial provincial headquarters, Abakaliki, a little urban city where the British administrators lived and controlled the lives of the native people.

Canice Nwankwo was my best friend at St. John's. He owned a bicycle. I never knew that teenagers like us could own bicycles. Most mornings, Canice would give me a ride to Sacred Heart School where both of us were in Standard Six, the end grade in the primary school system. We were the seniors and the rest from Standard Five feared and respected us. Destiny was again at work as I reunited with Mr. Cajetan Onyemere, whose class I failed in Standard Four at St. Paul's Primary School, Amudo. This time, he was my Standard Six teacher. My residual knowledge of Shakespeare, I owe to this great Owerri teacher. Orpheus with his Flute Made Trees; The Merchant of Venice; The Quality of Mercy; Shylock and a Pound of Flesh. We enjoyed it all, memorized it all, and indeed became the young Shakespeares of our time.

Until today, William Ogbueghu, Sylvanus Ogbueghu, Canice Nwankwo, and I greet each other with the Shakespearean character "Orpheus."

At St. John's, I had the problem of mobility. Any day Canice did not pick me up, then I would trek a distance of about five miles to Sacred Heart. At first, I was happy to attend the most prestigious primary school in Ezza nation. But, with time, trekking ten miles every day to and from school began to take its toll. My father dared not give me his bicycle to ride to school.

THERESA OKOLO

One day, Theresa Okolo visited us from Ogoja. Theresa is the niece of my great father, Mr. Fidelis Okolo. After observing me trekking to school and back, she became so angry but kept it only between herself and me. When I returned, my great father sent me back to Onueke to buy him certain items from Eke market. Theresa asked her uncle to let me ride his bicycle to go on the errand. But her uncle hushed her down. As I trekked to Onueke, Theresa called out, "Camillus (my baptismal name)."

"Yes," I answered.

"Please wait for me."

"Odu nma," I affirmed.

"Why did your *Master* refuse to give you his bicycle?"

"His bicycle is very important to him, Theresa."

"No, Mr. Enwerem's boys ride his bicycle to Onueke. Don't you see them?"

"I think Nnam Ukwu is still punishing me for riding his motorcycle sometime without his permission," I answered.

"My great father was different." For Theresa, a more educated and the most beautiful girl I had ever known, to trek and suffer with me was an honor. I might never be able to pay her back. Recently, my brother, Ikechukwu Okolo gave me the sad news that "Theresa died."

Theresa taught me lessons on how to show love to the poor person. Although our love was not romantic, it was very genuine. Both of us could feel it. When she returned to Ugaga, Ogoja, she would write me my first "love" letter. I would treat Theresa's letters as the most important personal possession of my childhood life. When she told her siblings, Kate, Adolphus, John, and Vicky about me, she would make them have the impression that Uncle

Fide's native boy was a very "intelligent" and handsome boy. I never thought of myself that way really. Adolphus (or Adol, as we called him) had made an earlier visit to St. Benedict's Primary School, Ntsokara. Adol's visit to his uncle, Fide, was a memorable event in many ways.

First, Adol was just few years older than me. He was therefore my age-mate. And I became his closest friend during his visit. As a native boy, I led him to the swampy Onu Okpuru Nwofia pond where he collected frogs and toads for dissecting. It was strange for a youth like me to catch frogs and toads and worms in order to slice them into pieces to study their parts. Later, I would learn that the subject he was studying is called "Biology." It was not surprising to me that after a few years, Adol would travel to Italy and finally return as a medical doctor. Many times, providence shows us what we would become during our childhood. "The seed of the present life hides in the past."

Second, I remember Adol for the powerful stories he told. One was about Okafor, his childhood friend. As children they played together at Ogoja. While Adol's father, Bernard Okolo, was a church catechist and teacher, Okafor's dad was a carpenter. Most days Okafor would "build" a toy car by placing a plank on four balls. Okafor would sit in front and ask Adol to sit behind him.

"No shikwa ike (sit tight)," he would command Adol.

"Oo," Adol would respond, adjusting himself close to his friend while they sat astride the "plank" car.

"No shikwa ike, e move kwa m (Sit and hold me tight I am about to drive off)."

"Vurum, Vurum, vurrrrrum," Okafor would mimic the sound of a raving car to kick start the toy car. Later in life, Okafor became a professional driver, just as Adol's early life revealed he would become a medical doctor. I learned, indeed, that most times, our childhood interests help to foreshadow our future destinies.

The third important reason I remember Adol is his power to play tricks on us as a magician. This little guy knew too much.

He would gather us together and give us instructions. "All of you write one word you like and hide it from me as I leave you now." After a few minutes, we would call him to join us. We had written our secret "word," for example, "Emeka" (God has done well). The well-concealed word was written on a piece of paper, folded, and handed over to Adol. In our presence, he would throw the paper into his mouth and chew it. After a few minutes, Adol would spit out the blob of paper, open his mouth for us to see it was empty, and he would leave us with permission to consult with his "magic spirit." When he returned, he would ask, "Are you ready to hear the word you wrote down?" We would all echo back yes in unison. Adol would then say certain magical words like, "Come and see American wonder," "Come and see American wonder," "The more you look, the less you see."

"Are you ready for the magic word to be revealed?"

"Yes, we are."

"The word you wrote is *Emeka*," he would correctly reveal our secret word. Nobody would ever forget Adol and his magic shows. His American wonder abrakatabra magic shows created a fairy tale image of a great and happy America. From childhood, therefore, I began to dream and pray to visit the wonderland called the United States of America.

ADOL'S SHOES

The fourth reason I can't forget my friend, Dr. Adolphus Okolo, is this: at our age and throughout my life in the village, I had never seen anybody wearing shoes. As I said earlier, the first time I saw shoes was on my kindergarten teacher, Mr. Donatus Oburah. The first young person I saw wearing shoes was Adol. I remember his black, plastic shoes which he allowed me to try on at Ntsokara. The shoes fitted me so well. Then, I knew that if I could be as educated as Adol and my teachers, I could wear shoes one day like them. In my childhood eyes, I wanted to be like Adol, to wear shoes, to talk smart, and to teach in a primary school.

Fifth, Adol taught Vicky (his younger sister) and me how to dance cha cha cha. He was a great dancer and would command his female dance partner like a soccer coach guiding their steps to perform magical movements.

EKE TOWN IN UDI

I graduated with honors from Sacred Heart Primary School. The diploma is called "First School Learning Certificate," according to the British system. My great father promised to sponsor me if I passed my "entrance examination" into any Catholic secondary school. Nobody from my village had gone to secondary school. I was thrilled by the promise and plan for my future. However, for some reason the plan was never fulfilled. I could not understand it then. I passed the entrance examination to St. Adian's Secondary School, Unwuezeoka, but my great father told me he would not be able to sponsor me. Rather, he suggested that my other father should train me. My native parents did not have money to pay for my school fees. They were not salaried workers. They were rural people who had farm and food but without much cash at hand. I got the sad news in December of that year at Eke, my great father's hometown, where I was visiting for Christmas celebrations for the first time.

That Christmas was memorable. It was real love at first sight, as soon as Vicky and I saw each other. From that moment, we travelled to Ajali River together to swim, to wash our clothes, and more importantly to fetch water. Eke was one of the villages with little or no drinking water during the dry season. So people usually had owoko miri where large clay pots were buried in the ground filled with water as reserve for the dry season. In Eke, it was said that it is better as a guest to ask your host for food instead of water. During the few weeks we spent at Eke, Vicky and I knew that our lives were intricately interwoven. My second mother, Cecilia Okolo, was suspicious, but she had no evidence of any misbehavior.

One night, Mrs. Okolo, my lovely and caring mother, stepped into the large living room where we, the children, slept on floor mats. She noticed that I had no blanket or cover cloth to cover myself. The Christmas period in December is also the Hamattan season when the evenings become extremely cold. Mrs. Okolo went back to her bedroom, returned, and handed me a beautiful wrapper cloth to cover myself. I cannot forget this kind woman who helped to nurture me. My great father, either suspicious or out of intuition, came to the living room. When he saw his wife's wrapper covering me up, he shouted, "Who gave you that wrapper?"

"Madam gave it to me, sir," I replied.

"Come on, give me that wrapper. You have no idea how expensive it is. I wonder why she gave it to you to use as a cover cloth."

He ripped the cloth off my body and walked away with it. As he confronted his wife, I could hear the midnight commotion between my parents.

The next day, as Vicky and I returned from Ajali River, my great father summoned me and announced that he would not sponsor me to attend St. Adian's Secondary School. I was crushed. When the Ogoja team of the Okolo family decided to leave earlier after Christmas, Adol, Theresa, and, of course, Vicky insisted I must go to Ogoja with them to see "Papa Ogoja," as we called Mr. Bernard Okolo, their father.

We all mounted on top of the open lorry on a long trip to Ogoja. Adol took my new dormitory list and began to collect certain items for me, such as a bucket, table knives, spoons and forks, and some pocket money. Vicky gave me very extraordinary gifts including money, a handkerchief, and something I cannot name here. Whatever would keep constantly reminding me of Vicky would be fine. At Ugaga, Ogoja, we went to church together and visited Mary Knoll Secondary School, the most prestigious secondary school in the old Ogoja Province. The most remarkable memory, though, was the visit of an indigenous Ogoja storyteller simply called "Tory Boy" (story boy). Tory Boy had a unique way of telling stories. He was a social critic who used songs to draw attention to the critical social wrongs in the society.

"Make una listen because na mi dem dey call Tory Boy."
Our response would be, "Aya okoko?"
"Make una listen because I want to tell una tory."
"Aya okoko."

Tory Boy would proceed to sing the details of the injustices he wished the public to hear about. I have never seen anybody since then with such a natural gift for storytelling.

NEVER DEPEND ON PROMISES

I prayed for doors to open so I could become the first Ntsokara youth to attend a secondary school which we popularly called "college." But then, no villager would "squander" his assets by selling goats and cows in order to send a child to the new "obia leffie" culture called school (*obia leffie* means a negative alien culture that comes in the "noon" of people's lives). In other words, an unwelcome alien culture that comes to destroy the local people's own culture.

My alternative plan was to visit my indomitable uncle, Ewa Nwonu. To me, ogbom Ewa (my namesake) was the smartest Mgbom man. Due to his wealth and wisdom, the "Kansuru" (councilor) Orogwu Nweze appointed him as a "Tax Agent" in charge of Mgbom tax collection. The tax agents of the British colonial governments were dispersed to all our villages. Then, there were road blocks mounted to arrest people who had not paid their taxes. Ewa Nwonu, therefore, became an important man in our village. Our villagers were not poor. Rather, all their resources were in the form of farmlands, cows, goats, wives, children, seeds, and crops. They did not have much need for cash money at hand. Their community life was simple with only food, fruits, water, and shelter above their heads. They did not aspire to get rich. Their preoccupation was to live a virtuous, moral life and to build a just society. Therefore, corruption hardly existed then in our traditional society.

Such was the time. My uncle Ewa Nwonu promised that he would train me in "college" if I would enter a contract with him, which I did. My childhood best friend, Isaac Nworie Nwankwo, the orphan boy and I read the tax papers for my namesake Ewa, since he did not read or write. But he was very highly educated in Ezza culture and wisdom. Every day, we went to his home and identified people's tax cards after payment. Villagers could not attend to their businesses without having their tax payment receipts on themselves. Otherwise, they could be arrested for tax violations.

When it was time to begin classes at St. Adian's Secondary School, my uncle said he had two proposals for me. The first was that he could not sponsor me. The second was that he was ready to buy all my father's cows to enable him to send me to secondary school. However, the money I had saved from Vicky, Adol, and Theresa and the little tips from my uncle, along with my parents' contribution, would not even pay for my tuition or dormitory fees. I registered and asked for financial help from the college but was denied. I was given only four days to pay my school fees. I stayed only one day at St. Adian's and returned home. The excitement in the air fizzled away while my relative and friend, Alphonsus Nwankwo Chima, and my friend, Michael Nwaelili, continued to attend St Adian's. I could no longer keep my eyes on the prize. But deep, deep down in my stomach, I knew I had to fulfill my dream of obtaining a secondary school education. As the semester was getting to its end, I could not withstand the fact that soon, Alpho and Mike would return wearing their college khaki shorts and white shirts with St. Adian's logo on the left pocket. I considered how inferior I would look before my smarter and luckier friends. Just then, Nwivu Sunday Uwhoo returned from Onitsha township. The urban youth was quite different from the rural Ntsokara youth. Nwivu was handsome, outspoken, stylish, and looked more "civilized." I admired my friend who came to visit me as soon as he returned to our village.

"Nnaji uwhu (my friend), why not join me and let's go to live together in the city at once?" Nwiva asked.

"My father will not allow me; remember, I am his okpara (first boy, the prince)."

"I will convince 'Ogom' Unoke. He likes me. He will therefore trust that we will not spoil you at Onitsha township."

"Odu nma (okay)."

Nwivu held the discussion with Papa. As long as it lasted, I was frozen with fear of my father saying no to any idea of my going to live and work in the city. Finally, Nwivu walked back toward me with a smile. Papa consented, but with certain conditions. Number one, Ewa must not smoke and drink. Criterion number two, Ewa must return every Christmas period. Criterion number three, Ewa must write us letters frequently because his mother will not survive if she does not hear from him regularly. Nwivu took me to dad and both of us made a pledge before he gave us his final blessing and permission to travel to Onitsha township.

At Onitsha, the following day, Nwivu, whom I now call Sunday, introduced me to an hotelier who instantly employed me. After two days of clumsy performance, I knew I was not made for such a job. It was too physical—waking up at 2:00 a.m., cooking and pounding garri and cassava endlessly. After washing dishes without rest from sunup to sundown, I quit.

I began to crave joining my childhood friend, Isaac Nworie Nwankwo, who by then had also become my brother-in-law. My father had married his half-sister, Nworogwu Unoke, who became my father's third wife. Isaac and Peter, my protectors from bullying at St. Benedict's, were now living at Asaba.

The River Niger flowed serenely between the two Igbo towns of Onitsha and Asaba. Most sea travelers used the "ferry" which ran from one seaport to the other. Isaac was a petty trader who filled up medium-sized trays with cigarettes and kolanuts and hawked along the seashores of the River Niger. He also hawked his trade inside the Asaba urban area, especially ogbe Awusa. Peter Awoke was older than me but had the energy to lift heavy bags of garri on his shoulders all day long—onye mburu.

Sunday arranged immediately and took me to Asaba where I reunited with my other homeboys. Within two days, Peter and Isaac together contributed three pounds (six dollars) and Isaac took the money and went to Onitsha to buy cigarettes and kola-nuts for me to begin my petty hawking business. Then, six dollars was big money. In less than two weeks since I left our village, I had become my own boss, hawking cigarettes along the River Niger shores, down town and ogbe Awusa quarters.

6

LEGENDS

"Eboes" Walking on Water.

LIFE IS A paradox. Perhaps you have heard of the thirteen strange West African men who did the unthinkable. They cast themselves into the sea rather than live in slavery in the United States. This incident occurred about two hundred years ago. But it is sometimes regarded as the beginning of the US civil rights movement. While rejecting captivity and slavery, they came together. In chains and defiance, they plunged into the deep Savannah waters, chanting, "The water brought us here and water will take us back home."

Where is the *home* they're referring to? Who are these brave or stupid people? Are they fools or heroes? Is there any wisdom in their collective action to commit mass suicide?

On Saturday, August 31, 2002, a group of Igbo nationalists from Chicago and Canada converged at St. Simons, Georgia, to "pray for the souls" of the thirteen men who "gave their lives for freedom." In his own tribute, Emeagwali, another prominent Igbo son, writes on his website:

> On Igbo Day, I invoke the spirits of the [thirteen] heroic "Eboe" men, women, and children of Georgia's Sea Islands who jumped off a slave ship and drowned themselves to escape slavery." Sea Island folklore recalls how [thirteen] defiant and courageous "Eboe" slaves, shackled at their ankles and necks, chanted in unison, the eerie refrain: "The water brought us; the water will take us away," *invokes Emeagwali.* This "Eboe" slaves' narrative reminds us of the legendary Olaudah Equiano.

OLAUDAH EQUIANO

Olaudah Equiano, who was also known as Gustavus Vassa, became a famous African involved in the movement to abolish the slave trade. Enslaved as a teenage boy, he eventually bought back his freedom to become a prominent author, merchant, and explorer in South America, the Caribbean, the Arctic, the American colonies and the United Kingdom. His autobiography, *The Interesting Narrative of the Life of Olaudah Equiano*, depicts the horrors of slavery and influenced the enactment of the Slave Trade Act of 1807. Who is Olaudah and where in Africa was he born? There is a great debate concerning the birthplace of this legendary Igbo prince.

According to his own account, Olaudah Equiano was born in 1745 in the region inhabited by the Igbo people in what is now Nigeria. He lived with five brothers and a sister. He was the youngest son with one younger sister. At the age of eleven, he and his sister were kidnapped and taken to Europe as slaves. At this time, he endured the Middle Passage to the New World, where he was forced to work as a slave. There is a common political culture uniting the thirteen brave men, Olaudah, and Jaja of Opobo.

KING JAJA OF OPOBO

From the fifteenth century, Bonny, like most West African city-states, had become a wealthy, politically and strategically important kingdom. As an African slave, Jaja had worked himself up from slavery to freedom. Eventually, he became King Jaja of Opobo and protected his kingdom against the European seafaring merchants who craved to penetrate the Igbo hinterland in search of slaves and raw materials. Jaja was asked to sign a "treaty of protection" with the British empire if he surrendered the sovereignty of his Opobo kingdom. However, Jaja refused and was "lured into a meeting with the British consul aboard a warship, Jaja was arrested and sent to Accra, Ghana, where he was summarily tried and found guilty of 'treaty breaking' and 'blocking the highways of trade.'" At last, "he was deported to St. Vincent Island in West Indies and four years later, he died en route to Nigeria after he was permitted to return," according to Nigerians in America Forum website.

"Jaja's dogged insistence on African independence and effective resistance exposed British imperialism and made him the first victim of foreign territorial intrusion into West Africa. The fate of Jaja reverberated through the entire Niger Delta. Amazed at this turn of events, the other Delta chiefs quickly capitulated," according to the Black History Pages (BHP). The Black History Pages is an online catalog of black history websites on the Internet. King Jaja's downfall ensured victory for British supremacy and paved the way for the eventual imposition of the colonial system in this region by the end of the century.

The list of Igbo legends is too long to name here. However, we remember Dr. Nnamdi Azikiwe, first president and founding father of Nigeria's independence; Professor Chike Obi, first Nigerian mathematician; Professor Chinualumogu Achebe, author of *Things Fall Apart*; S. G. Ikoku; Dr. Michael Okpara; Dr. Akanu Ibiam; Hon. K. O. Mbadiwe; Hon. Jaja Nwachuku; Hon. Mbonu Ojike; Osita Osadebe; Celestine Ukwu; Dick Tiger; Onyaka Mgbada; Offia Nwali; and Paul Robeson.

There is something common to King Jaja of Opobo, Olaudah Equiano, Nwiboko Obodo, Igbo warriors, Igbo legends, and the thirteen Igbo men who preferred death by drowning to life in captivity. What is common to all of Igbo heroes is *Never Again*. All of them exemplify Igbo bravery, Igbo courage, and defiance in the cause of freedom. As one can see from the ancient history of the Igbo legends so far, our people have very strong values and virtues which sometimes are blessings and sometimes our nemesis. As I see it, the root causes of the Biafra–Nigeria war were partly because of unresolved colonial conditions, partisan politics, ethnic loyalty, religion, lack of transformational leadership, and Igbo arrogance.

One might not understand why the "Igbo Majors struck" or why we seceded from Nigeria or why we, *unwu Biafra*, the children of Biafra, marched to Government House, Enugu, to demand from our military leader, "Ojukwu nye anyi egbe, ka anyi ga zogbue ndi na amaghi Chineke, ndi na amaghi Chineke kere ha (Ojukwu, give us guns, so we can march over those unbelievers, those who do not know their God, their Creator)!"

Ndigbo believe they have an eternal covenant with *Chineke*, their creation god and commander-in-chief. As warriors for Chineke, therefore, their war must be for a just cause. Therefore, during the duration of the Biafra–Nigeria war, we, the child soldiers and adult Biafran military, did not abduct children as sex objects and slaves. People who have Chineke as their commander-in-chief could not kill fellow citizens created by Chineke. Nowadays, things have gotten out of kilter and people are killing innocent citizens all in the name of God. However, Igbo people are different and exceptional in many ways. Take for example the case of the Igbo child.

Igbo children are like baby lions.

In 1967, we, the children of Biafra, voluntarily joined our adult heroes (who had only 128 guns) to defend our homeland against the invading forces from Nigeria, Russia, and Britain. The battle lasted for nearly three years. But many Biafran nationalists today still believe that the clash between Igbo audacity and British imperialism remains an unfinished war.

An American journalist, Edward R. Murrow, indeed captured this brave and daring Igbo spirit when he wrote, "We will not walk in fear. We will not walk in fear, one of another. We are not descended from fearful men, not from men who feared to write, to speak, to associate and to defend causes which were for the moment unpopular. This is no time to keep silent."

There is indeed a joke that when Lord Lugard, the British colonial ruler, was handing over power to his successor, Lord McPherson, he advised him thus, "The ethnic Hausa-Fulani Muslims are gullible. Therefore, recruit them to form the bulk of the national army. Beware of the ethnic Yoruba. They are like two-faced swords and very unreliable. The ethnic Igbo are very difficult, stubborn and hard to convince. But, if you succeed in convincing one Igbo person to support your policy, then you have a reliable friend. Igbo and Yoruba like books. They want to be educated like Europeans. Therefore we established Yaba College and made them bend their heads reading books while we gave guns to the Hausa-Fulani." In a colonial Nigeria, therefore, the seed of disintegration had been sowed by the British colonial master by giving books to the Christian south and guns to the Muslim north.

Britain's fear of this exceptional Igbo brainpower was the unspoken secret behind Biafra's failure to assert its right to self-determination during five decades in Nigeria's captivity. Britain and Nigeria campaigned in Africa and worldwide against international *recognition* of our new country. Yet, having had both *de jure* and *de facto* recognitions from several nation-states, Biafra remains a sovereign state according to international law despite its present status as a captive state. The two countries can not erase the audacious Igbo democratic culture.

7

GOVERNMENT WITHOUT KINGS

The Igbo democratic model was direct, pure and better
than the European version of democracy before the
colonial interregnum.

Life is osondi owendi (a paradox).

WEST AFRICA IS the home of the original people of Africa. From
archaeology and science, we have learned that Africa is the old-
est continent and the original home of humanity. West Africans
claim they're the direct descendants of the original Africans.
According to the narrative, the Igbo nation is the home of the
original peoples of Africa. From over 2000 Bc, before the era of
Christianity, the Igbo ancient civilization had been in existence.
The ancient Ezza people (my clan) are reputed as the first society
to develop the metallurgical skills to smelt iron ore and forge iron
tools like hoes, knives, weapons of war, arrows, spears, and other
farming tools. Farming was the basic occupation of the ancient

Igbo people which offered both military and food security during normal times and in war. With their exceptional skills in iron smelting, the original Igbo people became West Africa's greatest warriors. My family is Avuravu, the descendants of the original African people.

With the power acquired from the use of military weapons, West Africans began to fight each other as their leaders desired to conquer other ethnic nations.

Another group of "Forest Kingdom people" also lived in West Africa. They are known as the Edo, Benin, and Yoruba empires.

While most West Africans lived in empires under their kings and queens, the Igbo nation did not have kings, queens, or empires. The Igbo village government was considered one of the most democratic in the world. Their democratic model was called "government without kings." In Igbo's "stubbornly democratic" government, everybody had a voice on community issues, including men, women, and children, old and young alike. Issues of common interest were debated openly by all. They still practice direct democracy today. The Igbos, therefore, had been living in a sovereign democratic nation over two thousand years before the advent of European colonial state experiment.

As a hardworking and warrior society, Igbos believed in what they called the "achievement" factor. In this philosophy, emphasis is placed on handwork and one's status in life, not on one's father's status. The Igbo person does not care whether one is the son of a king or a queen or president of a country. Rather, they would ask, "Who are you? And what have you achieved in life?"

The Igbo is not only a descendant of the original African people (avuravu), but he is also the providential custodian of the Iron Age endowment. Onye-Igbo (Igbo person) is a hardworking person and warrior. Their ultrademocratic culture makes them very stubborn, arrogant, cocky, and difficult to deal with. Despite their brash behavior, they are great innovators, businesslike and republican in political ideology.

IGBO-WORLD

The population of the Igboworld today is very important. Southeastern Nigeria is the homeland of over two hundred million Igbo people at home and worldwide. The people have spread throughout the world due to the transatlantic slave trade which scattered them throughout the universe—Bahamas, Haiti, Trinidad and Tobago, Washington, DC, Barbados, Detroit, Chicago, South Carolina, North Carolina, Cuba, Jamaica, Louisiana, Mississippi, Alabama, Georgia, Philadelphia, Maryland, New Orleans, Atlanta, Caribbean, Latin America, and Asia.

Biafra is one of the most important original ethnic nations in Africa. It occupies an area of about 29,000 square miles. But what it lost in size, it gained in density, economic potential-oil, hard work, highly educated class, aggressive business ethics and Igbo audacity.

Igbo-world includes all other ethnic nations that share certain cultural traits and proximity with the eastern region of Nigeria, some northern nations like Igala, Benue, Jos, Cameroon, Benin, Mamfe, Bamenda, Ondo, Ijaw, and many others. The distant northern region has had centuries of trade and commerce with Igbo people. A new political alliance based on this historical relationship is possible.

The areas of mutual interests include a shared future, a common humanitarian interest, peace, security, survival, and development. In the present geopolitical redistricting, most of the states are not viable enough to survive on their own alone. Greater participation and development will come only to those forward-looking states and societies that have the wisdom to form alliances in the twenty-first century.

And if the Nigerian federal union disintegrates due to current pressure from terrorists, the Igbo-world and other ethnic northern and eastern nations constitute a viable nation-state. I am in no way suggesting that Biafra cannot exist without its neighboring subnations. The world does not seem to understand that the Nigerian federation is in serious danger of falling apart sooner than expected.

8

AGHAUCHE

Life is osondi owendi (a paradox).

NIGERIA IS A *victor nation*. And most victor nations, historically, do not know how to deal with the injustices of the past. The country is also a postcolonial state and a political creature created by the British Empire. The creature, like its creator, neither knows how to reckon with its unpleasant past nor how to do justice so that society could heal and reconcile. The human rights community questions the legality of a *victor's justice* which enslaves and destroys human dignity, freedom, and security.

The primary goal of this narrative is to put Biafra on the conscience of the world and you, the reader. Our original Igbo ethnic homeland has fallen apart due to unresolved human rights violations. Yet Igbos are brave and courageous people despite the British colonial interruption.

From birth until independence, I was regarded as a "British protected citizen," even when I never asked or needed such protection. Effective October 1, 1960, I became a Nigerian. But Nigeria is a former British colony. On May 30, 1967, I regained my freedom and became a Biafran. Just as my personal identity rises and falls like a roller coaster, similarly, Nigeria and the *ethnic* nation of Biafra are destined for a tragic collision. During the conflict, it would seem more like divided we stand and united we fall. The religious divide between the Christian Igbo and Muslim Hausa-Fulani was too wide. The war eventually came and engulfed everybody.

Fifty years after the defeat of Biafra and forced reunion with Nigeria, national reconciliation remains elusive. Again, I have been forced with British guns and Russian-made guns to become a Nigerian. Therefore, I have a political identity crisis. But the only true identity I have is that I am a descendant of an audacious Igbo ancestry.

Dear God, Never Again is primarily a transitional justice true story of Biafra and my life as an Igbo teenage freedom fighter who survived to become a professor. In the fight to reclaim our God-given right to freedom, our overriding loyalty was to Biafra. From ancient times, the human society had been naturally grouped into ethnic nations. Such original ethnic nations had certain characteristics: a common past, common geographical area, common spiritual path, common language, and common ancestry. Therefore, the ethnic nation, born out of *ofu obi*—collective mind, common spirit, and common culture—is obviously a more legitimate sovereign nation than the artificially and colonially engineered nation-state.

It is not a question of which nation will maximize Igbo prosperity and minimize Igbo pain. Rather, Biafran nationalists still remember the blood covenant between their dead citizens and themselves. "We have truth on our side," the Biafrans claim. The Biafran national flag is a symbol of the ethnic people's pride, power, unity, military glory, and loyalty to the fatherland. Biafra is not alone. There are other forgotten ethnic nationalities like the Azeris, Kurds, Tamils, Native Americans, Palestinians, Scots, and Welsh who are still fighting for freedom today.

The Biafran nationalists assert their claim to Biafra as a natural right to their ancestral homeland, while the Nigerian federalists, on the contrary, claim that Biafra is theirs by the power of the sword. "Might is right."

In the twenty-first century, the idea that might *is* right might have been conceived in the astral plane and not in this physical world.

All that Biafrans ask for is justice, freedom, and dignity. Many Biafran nationalists insist that the audacious strategy of *aghauche* (intellectual power), not violence, would eventually lead to freedom.

Until justice comes, they argue, the union of the ethnic nations of Ibibio, Igbo, Ijaw, Ika, Ikom, Efik, and Ogoja will continue to seek freedom. Until freedom comes, the moral world will continue to question the ethical basis of a *victor's justice* which destroys a people's dignity and security.

9

FREEDOM

Freedom is never voluntarily given by the oppressor;
it must be demanded by the oppressed.

—Martin Luther King Jr.

Life is osondi owendi.

ON OCTOBER 1, 1960, an Igbo nationalist, Dr. Nnamdi Azikiwe, declared the independence of Nigeria. As a child, I had thought that our transition from colonial darkness to the dawn of freedom meant that Abakaliki, Ezza, Izzi, and Ikwo villagers had finally arrived at the *Promised Land*. We imagined that freedom would give us the right to protection, education, jobs, development, water, electricity, and life without taxation. Six years after independence, nothing much had changed for the long-dispossessed and long-politically excluded wawa Igbo subnations and the eastern region as a whole. The independence victory won by Igbo nationalists and others appeared to be slipping away. Nobody knew that our country was sliding away toward war. Soon we would hear the war cry in the air.

Is the looming war about the divide between eastern and northern Nigeria? Between the Christian Igbo and Hausa-Fulani Muslims? The determining causes of the civil war, or what the nationalists regard as the Biafra–Nigeria war, are in reality rooted in our unreconciled colonial history and prejudice. It seems there is a secret strategy to ensure that the postcolonial creature cannot be allowed to be greater than its creator.

The Biafran–Nigerian battle lasted between 1967 and 1970. Despite colonial prejudice against Biafra, there is also an invisible hand in Biafra's fight for justice and freedom. The political creature called Nigeria gained freedom from its creator, the British empire, in 1960. Seven years after, Eastern Nigeria seceded and became a recognized sovereign state known as the Republic of Biafra after thirty thousand Igbo Christians and other Easterners were killed by their Muslim neighbors—fellow citizens with whom they had shared life together. To the Biafrans, the British creature called Nigeria was a colonial mistake which lacked legitimacy since the country was not founded on the consent of the people.

Over three million Biafrans of all ages died in the war. Most of the children died from hunger-related diseases like *kwashiorkor*, anemia, and starvation. Although life continued without them, I can never see my kid brothers, Anayo Okolo, Aloy Okolo, and Emeka Okolo, again. Like us, my three siblings loved life and struggled to remain alive in order to fulfill their own destinies too. However, they were among the Biafran children deliberately starved to death by the military junta which ought to have protected them. Other Biafrans died on the war front fighting for freedom. Sometimes, deep, deep down inside, my inner self tells me that life is a fairy tale. What we don't see is more real than what we see.

However, for deliberately starving my three young brothers to death, I have no spiritual authority to cleanse Nigeria and the perpetrators of their blood guilt and karma—the mystical law of *cause and effect*. When we, the victims, tell the truth and the government carries out justice, then society will reconcile and heal. By telling the true story of our fight for freedom, I hope to awaken the world to recognize Biafra's right to self-determination and to do justice for past gross violations of human rights against Igbo people by Nigerian jihadists.

The Biafra–Nigeria conflict was Africa's first and most bloody Muslim genocide against an ethnic Christian people. And I was involved as a child soldier. But until now, nobody has told the Biafran child soldiers' story. Five decades after, Biafra lives on in my mind as an unfinished justice, unfinished freedom, and unfinished nation. Biafra has taught me that there is an invisible hand of destiny—*akalaka*—in our long struggle and long dreams for true freedom. Through the teachings of our Igbo ancestors and sages, we have come to understand that our land and our people need healing and reconciliation. There is, therefore, an urgent need to address the legacy of historical wrongdoings especially in this age of *inweronye* (long-marginalized citizens), awakening, and citizen power. For over five decades, the Nigerian government has not investigated past colonial and other historical crimes in which Chief Nwiboko, the committee of peacemakers, thirty thousand Igbo children, and my siblings were killed.

This memoir is not a story with a chronological timeline. Rather, this is a *transitional justice* memoir of a different child warrior in diplomatic and humanitarian soldiering. In particular, it is the story of how I rose from child soldiering to become a professor. My story spells out what life has taught me as a teenage freedom fighter, unit commander of BOFF, and as a civilian. My goal is to keep alive the memories and "turning moments" in my Igbo homeland's long fight for freedom. As a civilian boy who was abducted, tortured, and imprisoned by Nigerian soldiers, I have waited four decades for an apology from the government and the Vatican in order to heal, to reconcile, to forgive, and to forget the past.

It is believed that "truth telling" has the potent power of healing and reconciliation, because "truth" cannot be manipulated by authoritarian regimes and corrupt politicians. In our Igbo homeland, storytelling brings healing and catharsis. *Dear God, Never Again* also reveals the brave and unstoppable power of freedom and the resilience which *Igbo-Spirit* exemplifies. People who do not know Ndigbo very well take them for granted. But no matter how long it takes, freedom cannot be caged forever.

10

STREET HAWKER

Life is a series of turning moments.

THEREFORE, MY CHILDHOOD philosophy—"the harder the struggle, the sweeter the victory"—became my guiding star in a world of uncertainties.

As a teenage street hawker, my best customers were soldiers. Once in two months or so, a large contingent of troops moved from the eastern region into the midwestern region. Since they did not talk much with "idle civilians," we had no idea where their destination was. However, we were always interested in reserving certain favorite cigarettes they liked. For example, they loved to smoke Kent, Lucky Strike, or Marlboro cigarettes. Other soldiers loved to smoke SM, Three Rings, and Kool.

On this fateful day, the ferry bringing the soldiers arrived at the shore from Onitsha. They disembarked with heavy loads on their backs and hands and walked toward the seashore. We sold and sold many packets of cigarette as expected. Then civilian passengers began to climb out of the ferry. One Muslim man in his midthirties walked toward me and said he was capable of making me a talisman that would attract customers to flock around me always and that I would sell more cigarettes than any other youth hawker in Asaba. As a naive country boy, I jumped at the offer since it did not conflict with my father's moral laws. This mystical man spoke Igbo, which made me believe he was an Igbo conman parading as a Muslim medicine man.

On his command, we sat in a secluded empty shed where he began to lead me in a spiritual chant: Ije awele eeee! Ije awele eeee! He explained this mystical "word" to mean smooth sales and safe *journey* as the future customers would begin to surge toward me. To cut this long story short, this strange man made me follow him to ogbe Awusa, where he visited with a very young "harlot," as most Nigerians call prostitutes. Drinking and smoking my cigarette, the "ije awele" mystic man asked me to leave my large tray containing my three pounds hawking market and go back to the seashore to buy him Igbo kolanuts since mine were mostly "gworo," the Hausa-Muslim brand which Igbo people consider inferior and unspiritual. By the time I returned to the prostitutes' quarters, the man, his harlot, and my tray of cigarettes had disappeared without a trace. My life support had been cut. This type of bad luck never happened to Isaac or Peter who contributed money with which I began my trading. I wondered who would feed me and how I could survive with weak, clumsy hands and a smart head which nobody seemed to need in the urban area.

What is common to Peter, Isaac, and I was the fact that we were all primary school graduates. While most of my childhood primary school teachers were holders of the First School Leaving Certificate only, by now, it seemed like anybody with FSLC would no longer have a decent job. In the urban cities, no provisions had been made for the primary school graduate. The urban city was for those who were innovative and well-educated.

In my predicament, I was lucky to run into Richard Nworie Eze, a dear friend who also saved me during the years I was bullied at St. Benedict's Catholic Primary School.

After about two weeks, Richard, the motor boy with Amichi Brothers Limited Transport Company, took me to Lagos, the capital city of Nigeria. The other two friends and fellow hawkers, Isaac and Benedict, decided to join me to Lagos. To them, it was an opportunity of a lifetime. Throughout the night, the "gwongworo" (lorry) roared along on its way towards *Eko*, the federal capital city of Nigeria. Life is not a fairy tale, life is real.

11

IDDO MOTOR PARK

Life is a series of turning moments.

IN THE EARLY morning of the next day we arrived at the famous Iddo Motor Park. I saw a sea of Motor Park gangsters grabbing people's loads off their heads. It was chaotic!

Richard bought us breakfast of tea and bread and took us to Mr. Joseph and Mr. John. While John was from Ezza like us, his business partner was from Umuoji in Onitsha province. Both partners employed the three of us immediately.

Early in the morning, at about 4:00 a.m., we woke up at our Ikate, Surulere, residence and walked for about ten miles to the Ijora 7 Up Company where we lifted large blocks of ice covered with sacks. Each of us—Isaac, Benedict, and I—carried the frozen ice blocks on our bare heads and trek for another three miles to Iddo Motor Park where we would crush the block and spread the ice on bottled water.

After about a fifteen-minute breakfast, we loaded the cold water bottles about twelve in a wooden crate and began the day's hawking, and shouting, "Ice water re, ice water re, ice water re," throughout the day.

Our new bosses were kind to us, but the task of trekking almost twenty-six miles every day and carrying ice on our bare heads soon began to take their toll on us. The middle of our heads no longer had any hair. We looked ridiculous, with a wide hairless patch at the middle of our heads. Then I knew that job was not for me despite the great amount of money we made for Mr. John and Mr. "Ntua," as we later nicknamed Mr. Joseph. We were only paid one pound and ten shillings each month, an equivalent of six US dollars.

12

HOUSEBOY

Life is a series of turning moments.

At Iddo motor park, a light-skinned, female passenger gave me a hand signal to "come." I rushed to this charming lady, so light-skinned that she could pass for a Caucasian woman.

"Good morning, Madam."

"Good morning. I see you do not hawk Ginger Ale."

"No, Madam, but I can leave my ice water crate here and run and buy one for you from a nearby kiosk."

"Take this money and let me watch your crate."

"Yes, Madam." Within three minutes I was back.

"That was quick."

Strangely, the madam engaged me in a long discussion. Her questions were probing, personal, and engaging. At last, before her taxi took off to the University of Ibadan, she revealed who she was. "My name is Enoh Irukwu. I work with NBC, Ikoyi Lagos, but I live at Surulere. My husband and I have a little son, and I would like you to come and live with us as a houseboy so you can teach him how to speak good English. I have seen that you are a very smart boy, you speak very good English. Which school did you attend?"

"St. Benedict's Catholic Schools, Madam."

"Here is my address. But first go to the Federal Ministry of Labor and introduce yourself to the lady who will interview you."

She handed me a name and an address. After a long process, it was time for my last interview, this time with Madam's husband. It was an intimidating but brief encounter and indeed different from the kind and loving attitude of Madam. Joseph Ogbonnaya Irukwu was a London-trained lawyer and insurance executive.

"What is your name?"

"Sir, my name is Camillus Unoke."

"Whaaat? What a silly name is that? Don't you have another name? This one is a tongue twister."

"My confirmation name is Raymond, sir."

"That's better. From now on, we will call you Raymond, understand?"

"Yes, sir."

After this brief questioning from a very smart lawyer, I was employed. The position of houseboy became the first official job I got with my primary school diploma. My childhood buddies, Isaac and Benedict, began seriously searching for a houseboy job like mine. A houseboy job was more dignifying than that of a street hawker.

Every month, I was paid three pounds for doing domestic chores and taking care of Agu and later Ikechi, Chizor, Chioma, and Ola, the baby. Recall my botched childhood dream to obtain secondary school education. I did not realize my dream of enrolling in secondary school, but that dream was constantly kept alive in the Irukwu family. I saw firsthand what education could do. For example, Madam and Master (my bosses) met in London as students. Because of their high class education, we were able to live at 13 Adebola Street Surulere, opposite the National Stadium. Madam loved Volvos while Oga was a Mercedes-Benz man. Company drivers, John and Razaqi, drove him to work and anywhere he wished to go.

The West African Provincial Insurance Company paid monthly salaries to the cook, Abibu Kadiri, the gardeners, the drivers, and me. Our master, Barrister Irukwu, was the company's legal adviser. From this experience, I realized it was good to be educated because by then a college graduate in my country was entitled to have a cook, a driver, houseboy, a house girl, and a gardener.

Once, I overheard a conversation which revealed certain truths about my master's past. First, he was from Okoko Item in Eastern Nigeria. Second, his parents were poor and could not send him to secondary school, just like me. Young Joseph Irukwu, therefore, lived with relatives and, like me, he hawked oranges along the railway station in Northern Nigeria. That was when he learned to speak Hausa (Muslim) very fluently. One day, his uncle saw him hawking and took him back to Aba to sell books in his bookstore. In this bookstore, the young and handsome lad began to self educate himself. He taught himself until he passed his ordinary level (O level) examination which was equivalent to a high school or a GED diploma.

Furthermore, and more surprisingly, the young boy taught himself until he passed the advanced level examination with distinction. He then applied to universities and obtained both admission and scholarship to read Law in London.

After obtaining his LLB, he proceeded to read and obtain the highest professional diploma in insurance—Associate of the Chartered Insurance Institute, ACII. He became the highest insurance guru in the African continent, served as managing director for Unity Life and Fire Insurance after working for the West African Provincial Insurance Company as legal advisor. When his good friend, Eugene Okwor, became the Federal Insurance boss, we were not surprised when he was consulted to accept the position of establishing and heading the new federal government's first reinsurance company, called the Nigeria Reinsurance Company, fondly known as "NigeriaRe."

During the formative days of NigeriaRe, in our guest room downstairs, my master, Barrister Irukwu told Mr. Okwor that he would accept the offer to serve his country but with certain caveats. First, the federal government must give him the freedom to continue to travel abroad for all important insurance matters; second, the freedom to hire and fire; and third, the freedom to continue writing his books among other demands.

Early in life, I pledged to my *chi* (personal God) that "if Joseph Irukwu, the hawker boy like myself, could forget the pains of his childhood suffering and educate himself until he became the best insurance lawyer in Africa, I too could even surpass him." My great master's life taught me that my mind could not conceive any idea which my hands could not achieve. I was the only one who could stop my own *akalaka* (destiny) from manifesting itself. During his youth, I learned that Barrister Irukwu denied himself of having any relationship with any girl or woman because he kept his eyes on the prize—the future. From my childhood, therefore, I realized that education is our most powerful weapon to a happier and greater future. The future of our society depends on the education that our children receive to prepare them for a better life.

If my past mentors, like Romanus Nwogu, Donatus Oburah, Fidelis Okolo and Regina Etuk, motivated me to further my education, then Chief Joseph Jamike Ogbonnaya and Enoh Irukwu's home and history gave me a mentor and a model that fueled my unstoppable desire to succeed in life.

My dream of going to college and my improbable secret desire to marry Regina came to an abrupt end. How possible is it for a houseboy to marry his madam's younger sister from such a royal, well-educated, Etinang family? In my platonic love for Regina, she had warned me to go to school. "It seems you're satisfied just being a houseboy to my sister. But I see you differently. You're smart and I cannot marry you if you do not go to college like me. When I finish my university education in Canada, I will return and marry an educated, handsome Igbo man. If you do not go to school, my husband and I will splash mud water into your eyes as we cruise along Enugu streets in our sports car. So, promise me you'll go to college." I promised Regina that before I died, I would obtain a university degree. In those days, it was not easy to fund even a secondary education, much less a university education.

HOUSEBOYS GONE WILD

There was just one house between Irukwu's residence and Professor Njoku Obi's residence at Adebola Street, Surulere, Lagos. Mr. Whyte lived next to Professor Obi while Mrs. Williams, the kind Yoruba woman, lived opposite us. Almost every weekend, the houseboys in this neighborhood would close work at 7:00 p.m. and prepare to go to night clubs to dance to great juju and high-life music.

In two nights, we could attend Victor Uwaifo's Show at "Lawanson," Bobby Benson's Cabin Bamboo at Ikorodu Road, Fela Ransome Kuti's Kalakuta Republic, Sunny Ade and Ebenezer Obey and before 1:00 p.m., we were at Ikoyi, Lagos Island, Victoria Island, and Federal Palace Hotel. It was Miliki time! Owambe time! High life time! As Lagosian houseboys, we rocked!

Earlier, I had joined the Surulere Boys and Girls Club near the national stadium where we played guitar, drums, and games. There, I met Veronica Mechi, who I had a crush on. Later, Vero would become a big TV celebrity as Jegede Shokoya's feisty wife, Ovularia. Our friendship was sudden, fast, and ended abruptly. No doubt both of us will be thrilled to have a reunion in future. The period of the 1970s was a time of love, great highlife music, and beautiful night "clubbing." As young Lagosians, we were embroiled also in the conflicts and confusion erupting in the juju music world. The war of words between Ebenezer Obey and Sunny Ade generated so much anger and bad blood between the two greatest juju musicians and their fans. That was when Sunny Ade would release the popular song, "Of What Use Is the Bitter Kola?" The release of the chart-shattering album, *Board Members*, by Ebenezer Obey had propelled him on top of the juju music world, while Sunny lagged behind Obey.

As we took sides in the juju war of words, another musical war was developing as Fela Ransome Kuti clashed with the federal military dictatorship. The military invaded his "Kalakuta Republic," arguing that "you cannot have a Republic within another Republic." The attack left Fela, his over fifty wives, and his mother wounded. From injuries inflicted by soldiers during the invasion, Fela's mother died and he drove down to Dordon Barracks with a coffin supposedly bearing the remains of his mother and dropped it in front of the military barracks. "They killed my mama, my political mama, my spiritual mama," he sang in a new release that hit the top of the music charts.

We, the Lagos youth, were for Fela. He was the leader of our populist "civil rights revolution," for change and against social, economic and political injustice. Such was the time in Lagos when suddenly riots erupted in Western Region over an election dispute. As a youth, I did not understand the details of the crisis, but according to the news, it had to do with the western Nigeria political party known as Action Group (AG) whose leader was Chief Obafemi Awolowo. In Ibadan, Lagos, and other western cities, the AG was very dominant. Anyone who challenged it was indeed fishing in troubled waters.

13

COUP

Life is brutal.

JANUARY 15, 1966, is an unforgettable day in the history of my country. Early in the morning, the Nigerian Broadcasting Corporation radio announced that our first prime minister and the premier of Northern Nigeria had been killed in a military coup. Certain politicians from Western Region were also killed, but no politician from the Eastern Region was killed. Abibu Kadiri, our kind cook from Agbor, explained the meaning of "coup" to me.

In January 1966, I lived in my country's capital city, Lagos. I had served for two years as a houseboy to my "master," Barrister Irukwu, and "madam," Enoh. Barrister Irukwu's family and I lived at Adebola Street, Surulere, Lagos. As a naive houseboy from a rural village, I did not know much about politics.

As an Ezza youth with a Puritan-like upbringing, I knew that the killing of our Muslim leaders was wrong. When could the killing of our Muslim politicians ever be justified? They were Nigerian citizens and nobody had the right to kill fellow citizens. The soldiers who killed our political leaders had blood-guilt on their hands and should be prosecuted for human rights violations.

In July 1966, just as we feared, the Muslim soldiers carried out a very bloody revenge coup which wiped away nearly all of the Christian military officers and other ranks from the Igbo ethnic group and Eastern Region.

Earlier on May 24, 1966, Major General Thomas Aguiyi Ironsi (an Igbo) issued a decree proposing a unitary form of government for Nigeria. While the people of northern Nigeria protested against the idea of a unitary government, the emirs threatened to pull out of Nigeria rather than face any tribunal for the Muslim massacre of thousands of Eastern Nigerians on May 29, 1966, in the north.

On July 29, 1966, a few days before the tribunal to investigate the massacre, more killings of easterners resumed in Northern Nigeria. On the same day, Major General Johnson Thomas Umunnakwe Aguiyi-Ironsi was assassinated by a group of Northern Muslim army officers who revolted against his proposed unitary government.

Ironsi seized power during the first military coup in Nigeria and served as head of state of Nigeria from January 16, 1966, until he was overthrown on July 29, 1966.

On September 29, 1966, about thirty thousand easterners were murdered by Muslims in the North, West, and in Lagos, while most eastern soldiers were detained in Benin prisons and some killed.

Two major facts emerged from the above killings. First was the widespread nature of the killings, their locations, and dates of the massacre, May 29, July 29, and September 29, 1966. Second, the sequencing and continuous mass killings of Easterners in

Lagos, West, North and Midwest by both civilians and Muslim soldiers clearly indicate that Easterners were no longer regarded as citizens of Nigeria. Third, the massacre was well planned, premeditated, and executed by both the Muslim civilians and soldiers against Igbo Christians.

Again, I did not feel that revenge killing of innocent Igbo Christian citizens was the right thing to do. Or should revenge killing be encouraged and justified in our society today? As Abakaliki houseboys, we were known for our honesty. Killing is so wrong in my Ezza culture. That's what my father taught me—to stand up for truth no matter how bitter the truth was to swallow.

Then suddenly, in September 1966, Abibu and I heard from the NBC radio that thousands of Igbo and Eastern children, women, and men had been massacred in a carefully planned military-Muslim-mob action in Northern Nigeria. Overnight, age-long good Muslim neighbors had turned to murderers, slashing the throats of all non-Muslims in an unthinkable fire and fury.

The Igbo and Eastern soldiers had been accused of plotting the January 1966 coup that killed the prominent Muslim leaders. If so, was the July revenge coup that wiped away most of the Eastern Igbo officers not enough revenge killings? How then could the September killings of thirty thousand Igbo children and women by the Muslims be justified?

As you, the reader, might have heard, Igbo people are not descendants of a cowardly ancestry. As heirs to the ancient warrior culture of West Africa, we're born to fight. This explains the warrior culture and audacity of the Igbo slaves who fought back against historical injustices in America, Europe, Haiti, and Jamaica and in slave ships. As history shows, most slaves from Africa came from the Igbo ethnic nation. The Igbo nation [Biafra] is the land of brave and fearless warriors.

14

EZZA

He [the Biafran Citizen] must be brave and courageous: he must never allow himself to be attacked by others without fighting back to defend himself and his rights. He must be ready to tackle tasks which other people might regard as impossible. (The Ahiara Declaration)

Change requires Courage!
We dared to dream and fight for Biafra's freedom because:
We're Biafrans!
We're Igbo!
Igbo people do not like to be told what to do.

WHEN IT COMES to justice for Biafra, human rights abuses, kidnapping, and terrorism, we will not walk in fear. Like Edward Murrow's poetic verse cited earlier. Igboland is a warrior nation. We do not walk in fear of bad politicians or terrorists. We're among the most endowed warrior nations in Africa. We have rich soil, a good climate, and abundant natural and human resources.

Nevertheless, our ethnic home is also one of the most forgotten, most exploited, and most hated in the world. However, Igbo people are ironically among the most respected within the continent. As descendants of legendary warriors of Africa, we were trained from childhood to become the eagles and leopards and lions of war.

What the colonial British Empire, which hanged sixty Abakaliki peacemakers, did not know; what the Muslim Jihadists, who have continued to kill Igbo people in northern Nigeria, did not know; what the Nigerian government did not know; and what the world did not know was the fierce audacity and warrior culture of Ndigbo (Igbo people). The Igbo is born to fight. We fight just wars and win most times because we believe in the natural law of karma—cause and effect.

In ancient times, the Igbo nation was a militarized society. There was so much chaos and so many unprovoked attacks on weaker clans and villages. While certain Igbo villages fought in self defense, others became mercenaries who fought for martial glory, honor, and recognition. One example is the Ohafia society in which the culture compelled the youth to look for wars to fight despite the cost and the danger involved. From ancient times, it became customary to organize the Igbo society in age groups, similar to military platoons and military regiments of today.

From early teenage years, the youth were sent to the war zone under the command of their fathers. "Those boys in the age group who first cut-off [human] heads and brought them home were called *ogbu sue* meaning first to kill. This gave the boy authority over his age mates," narrates A. O. Arua, a notable historian and leading scholar on Ohafia warrior culture. Those who could not kill and take the head home were considered as *ujo*, or cowards. No Ohafia youth would like to be called ujo because of the political problems associated with such cowardly status. First, ujo loses his right to marry a beautiful girl in the village. Second, both he and his wife would lose their natural rights to participate in certain cultures. Ohafia-Igbo-warrior fathers preferred to lose their boys in war than have cowards and weaklings as sons.

The most legendary Igbo warrior societies were: Abakaliki, Abiriba, Afikpo, Aro, Igbere, Ikwo, Izzi, Item, Ohafia, and Ezza subnations.

In Abakaliki folklore narratives, Ezza people were paradoxically loved, feared, and hated. Their *power politics* ideology promotes economic justice and spiritual freedom. But Ezza warriors do not go to war unless it is a *just war*. The Ezza's power to fight is limited unless they are attacked or hired as mercenaries to fight other weaker societies' just wars. Ezza is my ethnic subnation in Igboland. We are audacious warriors for freedom.

Unlike Ohafia warriors who fought for martial glory, Ezza warriors fought in defense of *kamenu le nhamuha* (natural justice and honesty). Ezza nation is a Puritan-like society which strives continuously to build and sustain *uwaoma*—a fair, just, and great society. While nation-states' priority is their security, economic, and ideological interests, the ethnic Ezza nation's primary interest is the quest for a just and virtuous society where evil people and injustice are not allowed to exist.

From early childhood, therefore, we were trained in ethics, wrestling, hard work, and storytelling in preparation for war.

Our war weapons were made of *opia* (wooden knives), spears, arrows, and stones. Others include *omu, uke, opu-ogu,* and *war drums*. Later, the Europeans introduced guns to our people. War period was a time of total abstinence. For us, it was a period of purification. During Ezza war period, only virgins could cook for the warriors. Sacrifices were made to Chineke and our ancestors. What follows is an assurance of safety, victory, and protection because of the renewed covenant between the warriors and Chineke, the Creation God.

The most legendary warrior in Ezza oral narrative is Akputa Nwa Unoke. The Unokes of Ezza are considered his descendants including my own father, *Ogbuinya* Chi-ukwu Unoke Ekirika. Obviously, in Mgbom wars, the Unwu-Chita family has the sacred duty of leading our village into war, which is a daunting task. There are so many rituals to perform before we roll out the war drums. In Ezza oral narratives, Ntsokara village (my village) is one of the major frontline villages that lead and fight most of the Ezza wars in the eastern zone. Other frontline villagers include Amagu, Amaezekwe, Amana, and Ameka. These villages have fought wars with their Ikwo neighbors in the past, but now there is great harmony among them since indeed the Ikwo, Izzi, and Ezza peoples are descendants of a common ancestry. It is only politicians who do sometimes attempt to sow the seeds of division among the three brotherly clans.

In contrast, while the Ezza warrior was interested in a just war, the Aros fought for political and economic reasons while the Ohafia warriors fought for honor and glory. Among the Igbo ethnic warrior cultures, certain villages and clans which have blood-link ties usually enter into unwritten but binding treaties of nonaggression between them. If the Ezza warriors were interested in expansion, as my fellow Izzikworo kinsman Njoku Afoke suggested in his thesis, "Ezza in an Age of Expansion," then the Ezza people would have dominated the entire Igboland and also the Cross River Area. In view of the distorted war history of Ezza people, it is imperative to state that Ezza people are ideologically hotheaded libertarians, Republicans, and, at the same time, they are Democrats too—a very complex society.

Because of their ultrademocratic culture, Ezza people do not want to rule anybody or any other society. Similarly, they do not want to be ruled by any other society or foreigners. Ezza abhors political subordination. As an Ezza, I feel sometimes that my people lack the cardinal concept of multiculturalism, diversity politics, and compromise. The Ezza politician believes in Kamenu and *nhamuha*, or karma. Any compromise that deviates from truth telling and natural justice will likely be rejected by him. I am not naïve; I know things have changed. As the Igbo people say, "When the goat that does not eat cassava-leaves befriends the one that eats, then, it could develop a similar habit." Many Igbo politicians have long abandoned our ancestral path to truth telling, honesty, and a virtuous life.

EZZA WAR STRATEGY

As an Ezza prince and warrior, I am limited by Ezekuna war rules to disclosing only certain ancient war strategies. However, first, we usually carried out raids before the cock crowed at dawn. Furthermore, surprise was an essential strategy in Ezza warfare. Third, *omu* was tied around the chosen wrist as identity during night raids. Fourth, in battle, we would bite and hold *omu* leaves with clenched teeth until the fight was over.

Because of my family's leading role in village warfare, my grandfather is said to have been buried along with a human skull preserved from the days of our ancestors. Only Ezza heroes were buried that way. Grandpa, *Ogom* Ekirika Chita Effia, was respected for his legendary oratory, wealth, wisdom, and fighting skills. His traditional *Ogbo Amaenyi* (Age Group of the Generals) military rank is a symbol of his brave and courageous victories in battle. The next military rank is that of *Ogbo Ugo*, the golden eagle age group which is equivalent to brigadier rank in Western classification. The third rank is Ogbo Baragu, the fearful warrior majors. The fourth rank is the Ogbo Iruali, or the child soldiers. Our military and political motto was "Seek ye first the just and virtuous society and everything else would follow." Before my father died, he had the rank of Ogbo Ugo. Ezza warriors are feared and respected even today.

In a just war, the Ezza warrior becomes as ferocious as a lion and as fast as lightning. My people are political realists—people who believe in power politics or use of force. My people were feared and, as such, agriculture, trade, and interaction with the wider world progressed. Like the Igbere, Abiriba, Edda, Abam and Ohafia, and Ezza people, our society's highest honor was

bestowed on the heroic warrior. What is common to Igbo subna-
tionalities named above is their military or martial arts traditions
and techniques. They sometimes fought for other villages and
societies. Another common element is the Aro question.

The Arochukwu Igbo have a paradoxical status in Igbo war
narrative. First, they are loved for their unsurpassed and aggressive
business sense and coastline trade with early European traders.
They were first to be educated and first to understand and speak
English. However, they were also the middlemen responsible for
most of the Igbo citizens sold into slavery. Until today, Ezza people do not intermarry with the Aro-Igbo, maybe because as I said
earlier, we are Puritan-like. Ezzas believe that Aro people have
not been cleansed of their blood guilt associated with slavery.

However, the Aros were great travelers and traders and a
very cunning set of people who deceived so many Ezza people,
including my unsuspecting father whom Inyoma took to the
Arochukwu *Long Juju* and swindled many times. If Papa comes
back to life, he would almost disown me if I ever ventured to tell
him that the *Long Juju* known as *Ibina Ukpabi* was a fraud.

In those days of slavery, the Aro invented a miraculous shrine
where all human problems were said to be solved through the
spiritual powers of the oracle known as *Ibina Ukpabi*. Most times,
people who went to resolve their life issues were secretly handcuffed and sold into slavery to the Europeans and Americans
at the seaports. Such people never returned again. They were
"killed" by the oracle, the tricksters would falsely explain. My
naïve father miraculously escaped becoming a captive slave when
his Aro "friend" Inyoma led him to *Ibina Ukpabi* oracle where
they extorted cows, goats, chickens, yams, and cash from him.

If Igbo people are hated today, it is partly because of this
Aro people's historical trick and role in the slave trade. The
Aro Underground Slave Network was responsible for the massive Atlantic slave trade in which Igbo people became the largest victims.

15

AFRICA'S LARGEST SLAVE MARKET

BECAUSE OF THE militarized nature of my homeland, it is believed that Igbo people constituted the largest number of slaves sold during the transatlantic slave trade. The then-infamous Aro citizens constantly visited Igbere, Abiriba, Item, Ohafia, Bende, Afikpo, Akpoha, Uburu, Uzuakoli, Opobo, Eda, Ohuhu, Azumini, and Eke Imoha to trade and buy slaves. Most of these warring subnations did not have sufficient variety of crops to feed their people. Ezza, Izzi, and Ikwo societies became very important strategic zones for a food supply and the slave trade.

The most important slave market was Eke Ezza, formerly called Eke Imoha. It was the largest slave market in West Africa. More than three-quarters of the slaves from West Africa were sold and bought at Eke, my ancestral homeland. Ezza people traded externally with the Aros in uffie, odo, cotton, palm oil, salt, cows, pepper, and slaves. According to U. O. A. Esse, the Aro people used to pass through Igbere when travelling to Afikpo, Uburu, Ezza, and Akpoha. Because of the large food production, strategic location, and security which Ezza warriors provided the traders, the largest slave market in Africa emerged.

What many people don't know is that most original black people in the United States, especially in Virginia, Alabama, North and South Carolina, New Orleans, and in Brazil, Caribbean, Cuba, Jamaica, Haiti, and Bahamas are from the Igbo ethnic nation, especially Ezza. Sometimes, I wonder how the internet experts are capable of tracing West African ancestry of the massive population of our people who were kidnapped into slavery without revealing the Igbo factor.

I have given a detailed account of the warrior culture of Ndigbo for certain obvious reasons. First, to establish that most of the slave rebellions in the Caribbean, United States, Jamaica, Haiti, and on slave ships were organized by stubborn Igbo slaves whose culture did not tolerate any form of injustice.

Second, I wish to clarify that Igbo slaves were not "suicidal," as American history portrays them. Rather, the enslaved Igbos were militarily trained to fight against all forms of injustice and oppression.

Third, about two-thirds of the transatlantic slave trade captives were native Igbos from Abakaliki, especially the Ezza, Ikwo, and Chief Nwiboko Obodo's Izzi clan. Why? Our society was a Puritan-like society that constantly purged itself of evil men, criminals, rouges, witches, and bad people. Our ancestors fought various wars and captured slaves who fed the infamous trade through the "underground railroad" created by the not-so-liked Aro people who served as middlemen between the slave traders and the indigenous people.

The fourth reason is to remind the United Nations, United States, Britain, Muslims, Nigeria, and the human rights community that Igbo people's attempt to come to terms with their past has failed because the world has forgotten them and their cause.

Fifth, the continuous killing of Igbo Christians by Muslims in Nigeria has revived the struggle over Igbo national identity as citizens of Biafra. If the above countries and peacemakers fail to follow the current global trend in seeking redress for the Igbo nation, then the world must be prepared to face another blood-bath when the Igboworld warriors decide to launch a revenge war against the jihadists.

Sixth, the cocky, smart, and stubborn black persons in America, Caribbean, or Latin America are likely to be descendants of the conservative, intelligent, ultrademocratic, but brash and no-nonsense Igbo sages and warriors from West Africa.

Seventh, Western and Niger Igbos are somehow different in military culture. There were a handful of kings within the western and Niger Igbo societies, while in the rest of Igboland, there were basically no such kings. Most Igbos from the western zone trace their origins to Benin and the Yoruba kingdoms which further unites the Igbo with Benin and Yoruba ethnic nations culturally, geographically, and politically. This common ancestry, when harnessed, could foster a new political power bloc in the strategic agenda for a greater and more peaceful federation, if Nigeria still seeks to remain one nation.

16

ONWUAMAIBE

Dear God, Never Again.

Nigeria today is a political fiction. It was never intended to be a state or an amalgam of 250 different ethnic nations. Nigeria is a colonial mistake. How could our Muslim neighbors kill and kidnap innocent children and pregnant women? Time after time, those who had the power to stop genocide did not. One day, we, the children, stood up to bear witness as the world turned and looked away.

Sometimes, we do not choose the battles we fight. Sometimes, the battles of life just come to us. Then we would stand up even as children to bear arms and bow down to the call of our fatherland. That moment came when we saw a strange looking Igbo man on national television. Like me and many other Igbos, he too returned, but he returned without his head. His head had been chopped off by northern Muslims only because he was an Igbo person. The headless body of Onwuamaibe Anyaegbu became the single most brutal but uniting call for collective action from Ndigbo when we said, "Mba, ozo ama emezi anyi (Never Again)." It suddenly dawned on us that even as children, there are times when we had to use force in order to stop bad people from committing evil. As Igbo say, "It is the duty of the cock to crow and usher a new day at dawn, but the mother hen also knows the dawning of a new day." Even as kids, we knew we had to do something to stop bloodshed in Eastern Region. We took it to Chineke in prayers: "Dear God, Never Again."

Another displaced Igbo woman, tired and dazed, arrived back in her village after traveling for five days with only a bowl in her lap. When she opened the bowl, it contained the head of her only child, severed off by Muslims before her eyes. We, who believe in freedom, cannot rest until we obtain justice for Onwuamaibe and the Biafran children who were brutally murdered by their fellow citizens. Life is a series of moments.

When we talk of Biafra's freedom or self determination, it is irrelevant to think of comfort, economics, or wealth. As Biafran nationalists who fought the war, we owe it to our dead citizens to seek justice against perpetrators and human rights violations of our people. Our consideration is based on the national and human interest of the Biafran people, dead or alive, and not only on the viability of the Biafran state. On the lighter side, Biafra, with its enormous human and natural resources, is a viable and vibrant state. There is a limit to what can be done and what cannot be done to a people. We're not fearful people.

Chukwuma Nzeogwu, an Ika-Igbo military major, committed an atrocious crime when he murdered our Muslim leaders, Abubakar Tafawa Balewa (prime minister) and Ahmadu Bello, (premier of Northern Region). The Muslim soldiers who subsequently assassinated Gen. Aguiyi Ironsi and Igbo officers in retaliation also have blood guilt on their heads and hands. In September 1966, an angry Muslim mob along with Nigerian

Muslim soldiers in northern Nigeria combined to massacre Igbo citizens who were residents in their communities including Onwuamaibe Anyaegbu and the Igbo baby whose head was returned to us. According to Wole Soyinka, "The man dies in him who keeps silent in the face of tyranny." The human spirit dies in those who keep silent in the face of evil and tyranny.

We, the children of Biafra, did not fight to avenge the death of our fellow Biafrans. Rather, we fought and died for the right to be free. That right is a humanitarian right, and we have not stopped fighting for it. What we dread is bloodshed. We saw blood in Biafra and Nigeria. This is why some of us have embarked on *agha-uche* and diplomatic soldiering in the cause of our brothers and sisters and uncles and parents and children who were killed because they were Igbo.

Almost every month in Nigeria today, our people are continuously murdered by the same Muslims who the British, Russians, and Egyptians armed to carry out the genocide that killed thirty thousand Igbos and fellow Easterners in 1966. We were not surprised to see the Russian use-of-force strategy repeated recently against Ukraine in the Crimean conflict. Similar Russian guns were used to silence the Biafran dream for freedom between 1967 and 1970. Ask the Biafran and he will tell you why Egypt is experiencing the freedom awakening uprising.

This culture of Islamic jihad against Igbo Christians has taken a new dimension—attacking fellow Muslims. Recently, terrorists abducted over 230 secondary school girls from Chibok in Borno State. The world was jolted into swift action. Despite my past ordeal in the hands of the jihadists as an Igbo, I joined the global campaign to "Bring Back Our Girls." Like Biafrans and Igbo people, the kidnapped school girls and the subsequent victims deserve freedom and justice too. One of those teenage girls could have been my own daughter or niece.

17

BRING BACK OUR GIRLS

Dear God, Never Again.

Press Release: The Director of the *KCKCC Henry Louis Center for Global Transitional Justice*, Professor Ewa Unoke has appealed to the President and the U.S. Congress to save the lives of the recently kidnapped school girls in northern Nigeria.

On the night of April 14, 2014, about 230 girls were abducted from their boarding school in Chibok, Borno State, by a group of Islamist militants. The name of their group means "Western education is a sin." According to Prof. Unoke, "This is not only a parent's nightmare but a crime against humanity and peace: that your child goes to school and never returns home."

"If the world is united in the search for the Malaysian missing plane tragedy in which 239 passengers are feared dead, the United States and the global community should also assist the Nigerian government in bringing back the innocent school girls who have become victims of adult abuse," argues Dr. Unoke. For over one year, the northern Nigerian States of Adamawa, Borno and Yobe have remained under siege because of the relentless atrocities blamed on the jihadists. The group has continued to bomb buses, churches, markets, mosques, schools, bus stops, and kidnap innocent women and children.

Amnesty International estimates that over 3,000 people have been killed by this militant group including foreign residents and United Nations' workers. Consequently, while the Nigerian military is engaged in a lifetime battle to defeat the jihadists, certain Human Rights organizations and TV journalists accuse the Nigerian military of indiscriminate killing of citizens. We, at the Henry Center believe that no visionary government will fold its hands while innocent children and their mothers are abducted, abused and sold as sex objects and slaves.

Islamic fundamentalism, over the years, has become more brazen in its attacks on innocent citizens. And, the Nigerian people have been living in unprecedented fear since the girls were kidnapped. The Nigerian brand is opposed to the education of women because western education clashes with Sharia Law. Under Sharia Law, the role of women is at home; to take care of children and their husbands. This is why the insurgent group targets students, women and academic institutions. According to the founder, Mohammed Yusuf, the objective of their movement is to establish an Islamic Nigerian State with Sharia Law as national Constitution. Since Yusuf was killed in 2009, his group has become more ruthless in retaliation and in its fight for self-determination.

The Jihadists' horrific act affects the U.S. national interest: security interest, economic interest, and ideological interest since Boko-Haram is linked to Al-Qaeda, the terrorist group involved in the plane hijacking and attack on the U.S. on September 11, 2001.

According to Dr. Unoke, the blame on President Goodluck Jonathan is unwarranted because terrorism is a global challenge and no single nation is capable of dealing with this scourge alone. "When it comes to crimes against humanity and peace, the world must shift emphasis from *national interest* to *humanitarian interest* such that an attack on one nation is an attack on all nations. Professor Henry M. Louis whom our Center is named after, was a man of peace and an advocate for peaceful coexistence and multicultural harmony. Dr. Louis would not have kept silent in the face of the current Human Rights abuses of innocent African children. If the moral world wants to fight terrorism, there must exist a collective political will, power, and commitment to fight and defeat the perpetrators. There are no half measures and half strategies capable of eradicating terrorism except a persistent and total war.

This press release to bring back our girls was published in major US newspapers on May 6, 2014. On May 7, 2014, I sent out an e-mail seeking supporters to join my campaign to appeal to the US Congress and the president to help to free the abducted girls who hailed from the same Muslim region as the jihadists. The abducted girls are not Igbo, but they are as precious to me as the thirty thousand Biafran children and their parents who were similarly abducted and killed by Muslim fundamentalists in 1966. About thirty faculty and staff of the Kansas City Kansas Community College supported my campaign to free the Nigerian girls.

On May 07, 2014, the KMBC television crew interviewed me on my recent campaign to "Bring Back Our Girls."

The news release

A Kansas City Kansas Community College professor is asking President Barack Obama and the U.S. Congress to "bring our girls back."

Ewa Unoke was a former child soldier in Nigeria and said Americans don't hear nearly enough about the terrible things happening in his home country. He said he's particularly passionate about the girls who were taken because he was abducted as a child himself.

He said he woke up one morning [during his teenage years], and all the Christians living in northern Nigeria were being slaughtered by Muslim militants.

"Within two days, 30,000 Igbo Christians had been murdered, massacred," Unoke said.

He said the militants want an Islamic state and don't like western democracies. He said their tactics are horrific.

"They cut off people's heads. They killed pregnant women. They chopped off the heads of kids and sent headless bodies down to the Eastern region," he said. "For over 40 years, this idea of killing, killing, killing in the north has never stopped."

He said that unlike the many of the girls who were recently kidnapped, he was able to escape. He said someone needs to stand up to the people who have taken responsibility for the kidnappings.

"The world has to come together to set an example with this [terrorist group]" he said. "Just yesterday, they abducted another eight teenage girls, so it's not going to stop. There has to be an example."

It is believed that this group has done far worse things, but this might be the situation where the world steps in and makes the terrorists stop.

He has appealed to Congress and the White House to use all technology and resources to help the girls. He said he'd also like to see the world put up a united front against terrorism.

"No one country can fight terrorism," he said. "The world should shift from national interest and make a paradigm shift to humanitarian interest."

He said he hopes the world will keep its eyes on Nigeria and want to help, like it did with the missing Malaysian Airlines jet.

Unoke is asking everyone to contact their Congressional representatives and local leaders to let them know how important it is to bring those girls back.

On May 2, 2014, in Abuja a car bomb at a bus station on the outskirts of Nigeria's capital killed at least 16 people just weeks after a deadly attack hit the same spot.

On April 14, 2014, Reuters News Agency had reported an early morning bomb attack which killed at least 71 people at a Nigerian bus station on the outskirts of the capital city Abuja.

18

LETTER TO POPE

Professor Ewa Unoke's Letter to the Pope on human rights abuses at the Igbo Residential Schools established and run by the Colonial Catholic Church in Nigeria, between 1914 and1959.

June 24, 2013

Most Holy Father,

Re: Killing the African in the Child

Let people speak truth; let the churches do justice; then, society will heal and reconcile.

On March 13, 2013, when white smoke appeared from the Sistine Chapel chimney indicating that you had been chosen by God to lead the Universal Catholic Church, the human spirit rejoiced. Your new role as Pope brings hope to the long-abused African societies; especially the ethnic Igbo Christians in Nigeria now targeted and killed by Moslem jihadists.

Most Holy Father, I am from the Ezza clan of the Igbo ethnic nation in Ebonyi State, but now reside in the United States. I write to you as an abused human rights victim of the church and as a member of the Kansas State Advisory Committee, U.S. Civil Rights Commission. The Catholic Church has made great contributions to the education, healthcare and welfare of the African people. Among the earliest Europeans who arrived in Igboland were Catholic priests, sisters, and nuns such as Mary Slessor of Calabar, the pioneer missionary who convinced our people to accept twins as normal children of God, and not as a curse or evil.

Our ancestors showed the newcomers great hospitality by providing them with shelter, food, land and protection. In return, the Catholic clergy soon established churches, schools and hospitals all over Igboland in both rural and urban areas. By the early 1940s and 1950s, the Catholic Church had established schools in all the twenty four villages within the Ezza clan:

Abaomege, Amagu, Amana, Amuzu, Amaudo, Ameka, Amaezekwe, Echara, Ezzama, Eka, Effium, Idembia, Ogboji, Okpoto, Okofia, Oriuzo, Imoha, Inyere, Umuogharu, Umuezoka, Ukaghu, Umuezeokohu, Umunwagu and Ntsokara.

The Igbo names of the above primary schools were considered "pagan" and replaced with such names as: St Benedict's, St. John's, St. Paul's, St. Patrick's, St. Francis, Sacred Heart, St. Martin's, St. Peter's and more.

Inside these schools, we were forced to renounce our original Igbo names given to us by our parents. Most Africans today still bear testimony to this injustice as our first names are European like John, Michael, Patrick, Raymond, Camillus, while the only native identity left with us is our African surnames such as Achebe, Azikiwe, Ojukwu, Mgbada, Unoke and Mbadiwe. In 1957, I was "kidnapped" and enrolled at St. Benedict's primary school.

After passing several catechism tests, we were sent to Sacred Heart central parish for a two-week forced labor. It was called "retreat." Many of us were brutally assaulted and terrorized by "Mr. Ogbunku," the catechist that everybody dreaded. The explanation was that hard labor was a necessary penance in order for Jesus Christ to forgive us our "original" sins, without which we could not be baptized.

From sunrise to sunset, we cut grass, fetched wood, and tilled the land endlessly without water, food or shelter for two weeks.

During baptism, we were ordered to get new names from the list of saints of the church. We could no longer bear our Igbo names. "All Igbo names were pagan names." Again, in 1957, the Head-Master, Mr. Cajetan Onyemere chose "Camillus" as my baptismal name. St. Camillus' birthday is July 18 (verifiable) and this date was imposed on me as my birthday till today. Later, I was given a second name, "Raymond," as my Confirmation name.

During my childhood, therefore, I had no right to a name. We were taught to reject Igbo native doctrines as "pagan" culture. At school, we were severely beaten for speaking Igbo language which the teachers regarded as "vernacular." Our customs, ways of life, festivals and memorials were tagged "pagan" and "devilish." We were beaten for being late, for failure to recite multiplication tables correctly, for over-grown hair, for over-grown nails, for everything non-European; we were abused and punished with hard labor. Most Holy Father, we attended primary schools and colleges where we were taught that everything Igbo was evil: our language, our culture, our carnivals, our names, our family, our society, our ancestors, our friends and our shrines. We were caged birds in the brainwashing and assimilation processes of killing the Igbo in the Igbo child.

My grandmother fought back in 1955 when I was abducted and forced to attend St. Benedict's Catholic Primary School. She accused the colonial church of teaching the native Igbo kids an alien culture of zohanne-zohanna—"Forget your mother. Forget your father." Today, as an American resident, I realize that I have been miseducated to abandon and "forget" my indigenous Ezza society which needs me more than the United States needs me.

Holy Father, as an abused person seeking justice, I write you today because of the failure, for over 45 years, by the British and Catholic authorities to address the rampant injustices of human-rights abuses in the African residential school system.

Most Holy Father, I write you because I was abused for two years by a Catholic pedophile teacher, Mr... (Name withheld). This teacher took away my dignity and stole my childhood. Mr..., whose son is now my village priest, has left a permanent scar on my mind and soul. This priest will be lynched in my village, today, if I reveal his father's abuses.

Holy Father, I am contemplating a legal action because these decades of abuses have left damaging emotional pain, fear, anxiety and a permanent feeling of worthlessness. I am diagnosed with asthma, high cholesterol, high blood pressure, nervousness, COPD and blocked left ear, most of which are attributable to the abuses in my past. My hands and mouth tremble and shake now when I lecture. I can no longer accept public speaking engagements due to this condition which is linked to my traumatic past. My body bears the pain of my unhealed past.

The legacy of corporal punishment and sexual abuse still continues in African schools today. My goal now is to educate and to stop the sexual predators in African schools.

The British colonial government and the Catholic Church forcibly removed indigenous Igbo children from their families and compelled them to live in school dormitories under the control of priests and teachers. Here, we were instructed to eat with knife, fork, and spoon instead of our hands, which is our way of life.

We had no school nurses, no emergency workers, and as such, many students died.

Like the Australian and Canadian examples, "The Catholic Church entities thus became part of a tragic plan of assimilation that was not only doomed to fail but destined to leave a disastrous legacy in its wake. Many children died in these schools, alone, confused and bereft. Countless others were physically, emotionally and sexually abused. The fabric of family life for thousands of our people, young and old was shattered."

We have suffered unspeakable pain in our minds and bodies. So much has been lost and we have not healed. About 97% of the Igbo youth from the twenty four villages within the Ezza clan, named earlier, have no college degrees. Most of them are primary school dropouts. About 83% of the street hawkers in major urban cities today are from Ezza, my Igbo-sub nation. In Ntsokara village of over 120,000, I am the only PhD graduate since 1954.

The Catholic residential school system in Africa had good intentions, but its mission and effects on the African people were not only cruel but criminal. Consequently, I want to launch a transitional justice campaign on this issue.

Yet, we honor the good works of the many Irish reverend Fathers, Holy Ghost Fathers and the teachers who worked tirelessly to give us a bright future through education. It is the legacy of these great men and women that we wish to pass on to a new generation.

Most Holy Father, I am still a Catholic. But the Catholic faith has been terribly damaged in Africa, especially, in Igboland. In my village, we had only two Catholic Churches in the 1950s through the 1980s. But, now, there are over 30 different church denominations. People have lost hope due to child predators like Mr. (name withheld) who took away my childhood innocence.

Most Holy Father today is a new day. I have tried not to contribute to further damaging the reputation of the Church through litigation. However, five decades is enough. If I do not hear from the Vatican soon, the next mail on this issue will come from my lawyers.

The Catholic Residential School System has damaged our lives. There are the following needs:

1. to apologize, and

2. to compensate.

With your modest compensation, we will begin the following year:

1. to establish a Pax-Africana community college at Ntsokara village,

2. to empower the street-hawkers, poor rural kids, and adult-learners, and

3. to establish an African Healing Foundation (AHF).

As the first doctor-victim of sexual abuse and corporal punishment in the Ezza subnation of Igboland, my life proves that poor children and surviving elders of the Catholic residential school system can be re-educated and re-integrated into society as useful citizens. Most Holy Father, when victims speak truth and the church does justice, then society will heal and reconcile.

Ndewo, thank you.

Ewa Unoke PhD
Associate Professor of Political Science and Transitional Justice Studies

19

A DICTIONARY OF POLITICS

I have a political problem.

ON MARCH 24, 1977, I walked into the CMS bookshop in Lagos and bought the most important book in my youthful life, *A Dictionary of Politics*. I signed and dated it March 24, 1977, in remembrance of my first salary as an insurance clerk in the claims department of the Unity Life and Fire Insurance Company. Why is this book on politics so important to me? "Because, it contains the details of the Biafra–Nigeria war in which I was involved, as a child soldier."

Seven years after the war, I had not healed. I was seeking answers to certain persistent questions about government and politics. My father was the governor of our family. However, I could never forget how my powerful father was humiliated, handcuffed, tortured, and jailed by the British colonial administration at Abakaliki for not paying his taxes on time. Early in life, I learned that we lived in a world where one has to be strong in order to survive. Now, as a former teenage soldier with the Biafran Organization of Freedom Fighters, why did Nigerian soldiers call me a "rebel" during the war? Didn't I have the right to fight for my freedom? In a war we did not start, was it morally wrong to defend our own lives?

Does the child not have the right to revolt against rampant injustice and wrongdoing? Do citizens still have the right to life, freedom, justice, and human rights?

Even as a teenager without much knowledge of politics, it seemed to me that my government had the power to punish criminal behavior. Did the Nigerian government not have the power (like my Ntsokara, Ezza village warriors) to protect its citizens, to maintain law and order, and to guarantee peace and security? We did not have a police or an army in my village, but everybody carried the laws of the land etched in his or her mind. Right or wrong, we did not allow evil men and women to mix and mingle with honest and virtuous citizens. We were Ezza people and Ezza citizens were Puritan-like. We purged society of bad people, even today. It was my hope then that A *Dictionary of Politics* would help me in my search for answers to life's most persistent political questions.

ESCAPE FROM NIGERIA TO BIAFRA

In September 1966, Igbo men, women, and children arrived with arms and legs broken, hands hacked off, mouths split open. Pregnant women were cut open and the unborn children killed. The total causalities are unknown. The number of injured who had arrived in the East ran into thousands of Easterners. After a fortnight, the scene in the Eastern Region continues to be reminiscent of the surge of exiles into Israel after the end of the last war. The parallel is not fanciful.

Throughout Lagos, dead bodies littered Ikorodu Road, Alhaji Masha, Western Avenue, and all over. Easterners were being lynched and burnt alive and their property looted. "Alas, a snake has bitten me," I moaned silently in fear. I was no longer safe. No Igbo indigene was safe anywhere else in Nigeria except in the Eastern Region, our ancestral homeland. But on the way to the East, one had to drive hundreds of miles through enemy territory. Cars and vehicles were stopped and Igbos filtered out and killed. It was under such an anarchic state that my master, Joseph Ogbonnaya Irukwu, fled back to the East with his family. I was left behind to take care of the house and property. I did not think I was left behind because I was less important. I sincerely believe I was left in order to protect our Adebola Street residence and our property, such as cars, furniture, building, and ground.

When the situation really fell apart, I loaded almost all my master's property into two Aba-destined lorries and convinced the drivers they would be paid in the East by my master and madam who had already left. I traveled subsequently in a different car driven by Dr. Eugene Mgbojikwe's fiancé, who ironically was Yoruba from Western Nigeria. While the Igbo people were being massacred in the North and West, nobody molested the young, beautiful fiancé of Dr. Eugene Mgbojikwe in the East. We made few stops to refuel and to buy food along the long drive to freedom. The only thing I left behind from my master's property was one small wooden mutter for pounding yam. I gave it to my kind friend, Mrs. Williams, who lived opposite us. Mrs. Williams had hidden me in her home despite the fact that she was from the Yoruba ethnic nation while I was from the Igbo nation.

Several times, strange looking youth and men stomped into our residence to demand that I tell them about my master's whereabouts. They threatened to kill me if I did not tell them where Madam and Oga were hiding. Then I knew the bloodthirsty mob could come for me at night when it was so easier to kidnap, kill, and escape without penalty. The few fellow Igbo people who remained in Lagos spoke either Hausa or Yoruba fluently, so they disguised themselves in Yoruba traditional clothes.

By the second week of the conflict, over 1,800,000 victims had returned to the Eastern Region. Like the past killings of Igbo people in 1945, 1953, and 1959, the May and September 1966 killings were ignored by the Muslim-led military government, just like the former civilian government of the murdered prime minister did. Why did both the civilian and military Muslim regimes ignore the issues of healing, reconciliation, justice, and reparation for the Eastern victims? Nigeria, since then, has continued to fall apart due to anarchy and prebendal politics.

20

SELF-DETERMINATION

BIAFRA WAS NOT the first ethnic nation to dream of breaking away from Nigeria. The idea of seceding has been brewing for over five decades in Nigeria. In 1953, Awolowo had threatened that the West would secede if Lagos was declared the capital of Nigeria. To every Easterner in 1966, Nigeria had become an anarchic state. The government could no longer maintain order or protect Igbo citizens and fellow Eastern Nigerians. Secession was brewing in the air.

Earlier, the northern House of Assembly had campaigned to divide the country into "North for Northerners and East for Easterners." By April of 1967, the irreconcilable disagreement between Colonel Yakubu Gowon and Colonel Odumegwu Ojukwu, the military governor of Eastern Region, had deteriorated. Gowon refused to protect Eastern citizens against the combined attack and dispossession of the Igbo people by the military and the Muslim civilian mob in the North, West, and in Lagos. Gowon also refused to pay all Eastern federal workers who had fled to the east for security reasons.

Ojukwu consequently froze all federal assets in the East. Earlier, Gowon assured the nation that the massacre of Eastern soldiers and civilians would stop. He also promised to set up an inquiry into the murder of General Aguiyi Ironsi, the former military head of state from the East. On both issues, Gowon never kept his promises. The massive influx of displaced Easterners who returned from all over Nigeria had become a huge demographic problem. Such victims needed food, healthcare, and shelter. But the federal military government refused to take care of its own suffering citizens.

Again, Ojukwu found it difficult to recognize Gowon as the legitimate ruler since there were at least six other senior officers who were higher in rank than Gowon. The military counter-coup in May 1966 led by northern officers was a revenge coup. Therefore, the northern officers could no longer respect the military tradition of leading according to seniority. With over 1,800,000 "refuges," as we called the displaced citizens, time was running out for "One Nigeria."

RIGHT TO SELF-DETERMINATION

In the early hours of May 30, 1967, diplomats and journalists converged at the Enugu State House for a historical declaration:

> Fellow countrymen and women, you the people of Eastern Nigeria: conscious of the supreme authority of Almighty God over Mankind, of your duty to yourselves and posterity; Aware that you can no longer be protected in your lives and in your property by any government based outside Eastern Nigeria; Believing that you are born free and have certain inalienable rights which can best be preserved by yourselves; Unwilling to be unfree partners in any association of a political or economic nature; Rejecting the authority of any person or persons other than the military government of Eastern Nigeria to make any imposition of whatever kind of nature upon you; Determined to dissolve all political and other ties between you and the former Federal Republic of Nigeria; Prepared to enter such association, treaty or alliance with any sovereign state within the former Federal Republic of Nigeria and elsewhere on such terms and conditions as best to subserve your common good; mandated me to proclaim on your behalf and in your name, that Eastern Nigeria be a sovereign independent Republic.
>
> Now Therefore I, Lieutenant-Colonel Chukwuemeka Odumegwu Ojukwu, Military Governor Of Eastern Nigeria, By Virtue Of The Authority, And Pursuant To

The Principles Recited Above, Do Hereby Solemnly Proclaim That The Territory And Region Known As And Called Eastern Nigeria, Together With Her Continental Shelf And Territorial Waters Shall Henceforth Be An Independent Sovereign State Of The Name And Title Of "The Republic Of Biafra.

With these few words carefully crafted by Ojukwu, Biafra, the youngest nation-state in Africa, was established in both fact and law.

By this time, it had become clear that all easterners left in Nigeria were seriously endangered. One week after the Declaration of Independence, I began my journey back home to the east, now known as the Republic of Biafra. As I said earlier, I travelled with Dr. Mgbojikwe's fiancé who did the driving. A little bit of order had been restored, or rather, Nigeria went into a political coma at the news that the easterners did not wish to be called Nigerians anymore. So, the road from Lagos, through Benin City and Asaba to the east was relatively safe, except for a few intimidating incidents at the hands of the soldiers who had mounted road blocks to fish out Christian Igbo people.

At the Asaba end of the River Niger bridge, we were searched, questioned, and allowed to continue our journey, which is now less than five miles into the preverbal "promised land"— Aligbo (Eastern Region or Biafra, as it is called now). We drove across the majestic *Niger Bridge* into Onitsha, the gateway city to the new Republic of Biafra. I will never be able to capture in words the feeling of safety that engulfed us as soon as we set our feet on the soil of our motherland. Then I discovered that there is a secret, spiritual bond between the citizen and his native homeland. This bond is bigger than the love we have in interpersonal relationships. It is this patriotic spirit which fires citizens up to lay their lives down for their beloved country.

However, Biafran soldiers stopped and searched our car and loads relentlessly. I thought it was over, but we would be held back for up to two hours answering questions from the Biafran artillery soldiers. They did not like the idea that we did not heed the earlier calls by the military governor that all easterners should return immediately to the east. The soldiers suspected all Igbo people who were returning late to the east.

"You could be Gowon informants just retuning to gather strategic information for the Nigerian military junta," one soldier accused us. The fanciful cigarette lighter which my friend Kenneth from Freetown, Sierra Leone, gave me was confiscated after accusing me of bringing in a rifle to kill Biafran citizens. The situation was not only humiliating but paradoxical. I had survived the Lagos lynching of Igbo people and the road killings and safely arrived at my fatherland, only to be accused of being a *sabo* (saboteur).

"Why are you returning late?"

"I am a houseboy. My Oga left me behind to secure his house and property."

"Where is your Oga now?"

"At Aba, his hometown."

"Where are you from?"

"I am from Abakaliki Province."

"What part of Abakaliki?"

"Ezza."

"Wait a minute; I think there is a soldier here from Abakaliki," he said.

"Can you speak Ezza dialect?" my new interrogator asked me.

"Yes, sir, I can."

My heart palpitated as I heard my dialect well-spoken by this soldier whom I never suspected to come from my own remote part of the Igbo nation.

"Ebu onye awe le Ezza (What part of Ezza are you from)?"

"M bu onye Ntsokara (I am from Ntsokara)."

"I jeru skool le awe (What school did you attend)?"

"Mu guru Standard Six le Sacred Heart, Onueke, Ezza (I graduated from Sacred Heart Primary School, Onueke, Ezza)." The tense atmosphere changed automatically and all of the soldiers began to sincerely welcome us. "Welcome back home, our sister and brother." One can never know the true value of freedom until one loses one's own. This incident taught me that my ethnic Igbo language is a great protective identity in times of danger.

Finally, I reunited with Madam Enoh Irukwu at the Owerri Catering Guest House.

CONFLICT
LEAVE THE SLEEPING LION ALONE

At the government guest house, Mrs. Irukwu's mother and the neighbors began to celebrate me as a hero. I had brought back all our property from Lagos except for the wooden mortar which I gave to Mrs. Williams, our kind neighbor on Adebola Street in Lagos. Many of the rich people at the guest house had past experiences with Abakaliki houseboys and their honesty. During those years, the highest job an Abakaliki youth could get was as a servant to the urban business people and other more educated Igbo classes. Until today, the gap still exists. Ebonyi state and Abakaliki have the highest number of street hawkers and unemployment in Nigeria, forty years after my own street hawking ended.

At last, we settled down at Over Rail, Aba Ngwa, where "Oga" Irukwu had rented a three-bedroom apartment with one room at the boy's quarters where I lived and served the Irukwu family.

"Madam" was beautiful and above all very intelligent. As a Nigerian woman educated in London, she was the first in many things—first Eastern Nigerian prominent female broadcaster, NBC Director of Women's Affairs, and the list goes on. A great conversationalist, she spoke softly in front of her husband whom she adored. She gave her husband so much space to live his life.

For over three years, I lived with the Irukwu family, I never heard the spouses quarrel. If they did, it was in their bedroom. My master was not a bad person. It was only that he associated only with his fellow elite group: Dr. Eugene Mgbojikwe, the medical doctor; Chukwuma Azikiwe, son of Nigeria's first president; Eugene Okwor, Insurance Commissioner; former Biafran Brigadier Alex Madiebo, Major General Danjuma, Professor Agu Ogan, Dr. Ifegwueke, and top insurance executives from other West African countries. There was no personal relationship between Joe Irukwu and myself except that I was his houseboy. There was no trouble unless I slacked in my responsibilities: polishing his shoes, ironing his clothes, sweeping, caring for his kids, and serving breakfast, lunch and dinner. Then I would get a piece of his lawyerly rage.

"Where is this bloody fool called Raymond?"

"Sir."

"Come here, you fool. Why did you leave this stain on my shirt?"

"I am sorry, sir."

"Sorry for yourself. Come on, clean it and wash it again."

"Yes, sir."

I noticed also that Mr. Irukwu was not close to his children. He loved them but showed little emotions toward them. He hardly had time to play with his kids as his wife. My master worked too hard.

One day, Mrs. Enoh Irukwu and I had gone to do the usual Christmas shopping for the kids along Broad Street in Lagos. That's where the big shopping centers were located: R.T. Briscoe, UTC, UAC, Kingsway, K.C. Chellarams, Speedy Creation, and "Esquire for men." When we ran out of money, we headed to master's office located at 9 Nnamdi Azikiwe Street, Lagos Island. Madam refused to step out of the car. Rather, she gave me a note to run upstairs and give to her husband.

MADAM AND ME

I returned almost immediately with a large envelope filled with money. We continued our shopping spree. Madam and I were very close.

"Madam, why did you refuse to visit Oga's office? I am sure he would have been happy to see you. I have never seen you enter his office. Why?"

"Raymond, your Oga and I schooled in London. Both of us have different backgrounds. He suffered and worked hard in order to become successful in life. He denied himself many things in his early childhood years in order to build a better future for his family. Therefore, I do my best to give him his space and to respect his freedom. I do not want to go to his office uninvited, so as not to embarrass him. He has worked hard all his life and should do whatever makes him happy."

This is the sort of rare wisdom and intelligence my Madam had. I am not sure that many American or African women of these days have such a superb sense of dignity. Rather, today, most women and their spouses think they own each other. Having lived and having seen a couple who quarreled only in the con-fines of their bedroom and who respected each other's freedom of association, I do not think I will ever become a "good" husband to Melody. As the saying goes, "You cannot miss what you're not used to." But for those of us who have witnessed such freedom, it is difficult to keep us caged. Marriage, from a Western viewpoint, has become like a prison sentence where husband and wife own each other like properties.

Back to our residence at Aba-Ngwa located at Umunna Street, across "Over Rail," life went on as normal, yet there was so much tension in the air since Biafra's declaration of independ-ence. Before the war broke out between Nigeria and Biafra, my father had consulted his oracles and had foreseen danger. He sent his brother, Abamenda John Unoke, to come to Aba and bring me home. Despite my education and urban life experiences, my father's word was a command. He carried too much charisma. Everybody feared and respected him. I understand that my grandfather was even more charismatic than Ogom.

Madam did not like the idea of allowing me to go back to my home at Abakaliki. I was her reliable confidant, but she did not hesitate to give me two weeks leave to visit my parents whom I had not seen since I survived the Lagos lynching and genocide. It is only an Abakaliki houseboy who would remain so humble not to go home after surviving the bloodbath in the north and Lagos.

"OGOM" WANTS ME HOME

My father, whom I call the pet name Ogom, wanted me home. "Bob" my uncle and I left Aba for Abakaliki and finally home at Mgbom, Ntsokara, my village. Since there was no public transportation between my village and Onueke, Ezza, we had to walk about ten miles to get home. Such was the time.

Joy! Joy! Joy! Mama danced and danced and danced, chanting and praising Chineke for her son's safe return and my father chanted the long list of my warrior-names:

"Nwoma Njoku."

"Ebem daru legu nwawhor."

"Nwogamba vuru nku."

"Uriom."

"Onyeije enwe iro."

"Agu Idemba."

These are the heroic battle names given to the warrior sage whom I am named after, Ewa-oru. They are the badges of honor awarded to him in each war he fought and won (Njoku's brave son; the lightning that struck the enemies in the wilderness; the public ambassador who enters other people's society carrying his own firewood; the traveler ought not to have enemies; and "the roaring lion"). As my father and his three wives chanted my warrior names, my head began to swell up in appreciation. From the day I courageously volunteered to go to school in replacement of my married aunt, Nwakpa Eguji, my family people have always thought I am the family's youngest hero with a very big future.

In our home, there were six huts mushrooming around the central grass hut which was the abode of my father. Every Ezza home had such a central hut for the man of the home where he is the first to see whoever was coming into the home. The location of this hut is not only for security reasons but more importantly, my father's "Ishinka" shrine, which Inyoma helped him obtain from the Arochukwu Long Juju, is also housed in the man's *nwulo*. From the nwulo hut, my father could also see and communicate with his Aliobu, the temple of his personal chi (God.)

It was so peaceful to reunite with my family and the land in which my umbilical cord was buried. In the morning of the first night at home, the village roosters began to crow and to announce the dawn of a new day for me, for Biafra, and Nigeria. As I lay there, a flurry of thoughts flashed through my mind. I remembered the day I was permitted to leave home with Sunday Nwivu Uwhoo. I remembered when "Hero" came to Asaba and made me smoke my first and last "wewe," as they called marijuana. I had gone crazy. I stripped off my clothes and ran into the streets. I remembered the "Ijeawele" impostor who destroyed my means of existence at Asaba. However, above all, I remembered those children, old men, and women who were slaughtered in cold blood by the northern army officers and the Muslim mob. It is not like Ndigbo wanted to voluntarily pull out of Nigeria, not at all. Ndigbo were forced out of the federation. I thought of the NCNC, Zik, and the Igbo nation, the trio of which constitute the founding pillars of the modern Nigerian state.

Ndigbo, especially Nnamdi Azikiwe and the National Council of Nigeria and Cameroon (NCNC), were the foremost nationalist actors and proponents of the concept of an "independent Nigeria." I remember that as an ethnic nation, we had been undemocratically forced to renounce our original ethnic sovereignty and to assume a new identity as Nigerians. To the Biafran nationalists, Nigeria was a British imposition. Once again, we were forced out of Nigeria, and we, therefore, recreated our original identity for ourselves as Biafrans. Early enough, I came to understand that in life, no condition is permanent.

Meanwhile, the Nigerian military ruler promoted himself to major general and began to warm up for war. He would not tolerate secession. However, there seemed to be a cool-off period when Ojukwu and Gowon accepted to hold a peace meeting at Aburi in Ghana. When the news of a possible peace accord came from Radio Biafra, we went ballistic with joy. After a few days' deliberation in Ghana, the Biafran leader returned. At the Enugu Airport, Biafran citizens, young and old, lined up the Emene-Abakaliki Road to welcome the hero of our revolution. Virtually all of us wore white T-shirts with the inscription, "ON ABURI WE STAND," meaning that we supported our military leader's position during the Aburi accord. I did not know the details of the meeting between the two leaders, but I heard that Ojukwu wanted a newly structured Nigerian federation in which the central government gave more autonomy or power to the regions. When Gowon returned to Lagos and briefed his military-civilian cabinet, they persuaded him never to accept Ojukwu's plan for peace. "A strong federal government is necessary to be able to control the regions," they reasoned.

In Biafra, it was rumored that Ojukwu, an Oxford University graduate of history, had used "big words" which Gowon, with only a secondary school education, could not understand during the Aburi meeting, which eventually collapsed. Between Ojukwu and Gowon, education clashed with ignorance. And Africa's first and biggest bloodbath was about to spill over like a volcanic eruption.

TO KEEP NIGERIA ONE

On July 6, 1967, with the slogan "To Keep Nigeria One is a task that must be done," Nigeria launched an attack on the young

Republic of Biafra. Nigeria and Africa did not want the continent "balkanized" or split into smaller nation-states. If this argument is genuine, why did Ireland secede from Britain? Why did the United States secede from Britain? Why did European countries balkanize Africa in 1884?

When the war began, the global community had neither a firm understanding of Igbo audacity nor the genocide and other injustices that triggered the revolution which gave birth to Biafra. This is why one of the primary goals of this memoir is to recreate the past in order to remind the moral world about the Igbo people and the unfinished state of Biafra.

21

WAR

On July 6, 1967, Nigerian artillery began to bomb our hometown of Ogoja, a border town within Biafra. Never in African history has there been such a paradox between two military fighting forces. While the Nigerian side fought with eighty-five thousand armed soldiers with the most modern weapons of war, the young Biafran side was only a mass collection of youth, students, and civilians who volunteered for the defense of their fatherland. For thirty months, Biafran "gallant" soldiers courageously battled the better-equipped Nigerian army. Because the bulk of the Biafran military was composed of students and young people, Nigerian military leaders called them "an army of pen-pushers" which would soon be run over in a matter of days.

As the war progressed, Radio Biafra continued nonstop to report on the state of the war fronts at Gakem and Ogoja. In a few weeks, Nigerian soldiers strategically opened another warfront at Nsukka, close to one of the nation's most prestigious universities—University of Nigeria, Nsukka (an Ivy League-like college, as Americans would call their most prestigious college).

At the Onitsha sector of the war, Radio Biafra broadcast the invasion and overtaking of the Midwestern region by the "brave and courageous Biafran soldiers." Major Victor Banjo's gallantry news was received with joy by Biafrans. At last we were taking the war back to the aggressor, since Banjo and his men by now had advanced to Ore town. The ancient city of Benin was already liberated by the brave and courageous Biafran military machine.

Radio Biafra began to give conflicting and disturbing news. On the Nigerian side, the Nigerian Broadcasting Corporation, NBC news, contradicted Radio Biafra. Rapidly, Enugu, the Biafran capital city, was captured by Nigerian soldiers. The over six-million-pound Niger Bridge was blown up on October 6, 1967, to prevent the advancing enemy soldiers from capturing Onitsha.

By then, Onitsha, the gateway city to the east, had been captured by the federal troops. Ogoja and Abakaliki, my hometowns, had also fallen into federal hands.

In April 1968, a massive retreat of the Biafran army, rangers, and commandos began. As kids, we lined up the Ntsokara highway as the hungry and deflated Biafran warriors trekked over twenty miles through the bushes and moved toward Abaomege, Afikpo, and Amasiri towns. They walked silently carrying their guns, sticks, knives, and sacks on their backs and whispered to us that Abakaliki, our only urban city and former provincial headquarters under colonial British rule, had been captured by *Ndi Awusa* (Muslim Hausa soldiers).

In less than two weeks, Nigerian military tanks, artillery, and guns began to bark along the Abakaliki-Onueke-Afikpo road. Soon, Akpoha Bridge was bombed and destroyed. Ezza, Ikwo, Izzi, Ohaozara, Ukawu, and Abaomege were now under federal control. It was so painful to know that we had ceased to be Biafrans through the use of force and military conquest. But in our hearts, bodies, and spirit, we were still Biafrans. Guns cannot erase a people's true identity, true patriotism, and nationalist flame.

By this time, Radio Biafra and Oko Oko Ndem, the great war orator and radio commentator, began to describe an unthinkable brutality which Colonel Benjamin Adekunle had plunged the people of Port Harcourt. "Black Scorpion," as he was called, murdered and murdered and murdered civilians with impunity, we heard.

On the Biafran side, this time, soldiers were not only worried about their diminishing strength but also feared, and in fact dreaded, one Colonel Steiner (a mercenary military commander) and one Colonel Achuzia, whom they claimed shot and killed any Biafran soldier running away from the war front. However, what kept the soldiers' morale high was the respect and trust they had on the Biafran military governor Chukwuemeka Odumegwu Ojukwu, the will of the people and the fear of a worse genocide which would follow Biafra's defeat.

22

DEAR GOD, NEVER AGAIN!

The world remembers:

- Five million Jewish Holocaust victims
- Eight hundred thousand Rwandans massacred in Hutu-Tutsi Genocide
- Forty-eight years of apartheid in South Africa

But the world has forgotten:

- Thirty thousand Igbo Christians massacred in Nigeria by Muslims in September 1966
- Two million Biafran victims of the policy that "starvation is a legitimate weapon of war"
- The killing of Anayo, Aloy, and Emeka (my kid brothers) by a food sanction
- Biafra is still a recognized sovereign nation-state

TRANSITIONAL JUSTICE

THROUGHOUT THE POLITICAL history of the world, bad people and tyrants have been in existence oppressing their people and violating their rights to dignity, justice, and freedom. After the rule of such evil leaders, society tries to rebuild and to recover from the injustices of the past. This idea of dealing with the unpleasant past is the major concern of what political scientists call *transitional justice*. For example, in the aftermath of the Biafra–Nigeria war, how did the subsequent civilian and military governments of Nigeria deal with the past human rights abuses which the January 1966 coup plotters were involved in? How did the transitional governments deal with the issue of justice for the individual victims, for the Muslim society whose prominent politicians were killed?

Like the Nuremberg Trials, transitional justice seeks to address critical postconflict issues such as democratic renewal and consolidation, national recovery and reconstruction, rehabilitation, reconciliation, and restorative justice, truth telling, pardon, and punishment, deterrence and catharsis, memory, reparation, children and youth justice, and institutional reform. Did the victor nation use any of these transitional justice themes to address the crimes committed against humanity and peace during and after the war? No!

BACK TO THE WAR STORY

Frustrated that the now-shrunken Biafran territory had a serious food crisis, some teenagers and young men began to trade on food, especially salt, sugar, bread, and dried fish. The federal military government's sanction against our new country had been fatal. We, the Ezza teenagers, called ourselves *Umuazu* (the fish guys) began to trade on these scarce commodities. The disease caused by starvation was called *kwashiorkor*. This terrible hunger sickness was killing more children in a day than the casualties of the war combined for over three months. We, the "conquered" Biafrans living outside Biafra-controlled areas, had to do something. Biafrans living in "Nigerian-conquered territories," therefore, established secret "underground markets" between the Biafran side and the Nigerian captured areas in order to sell salt and other essential commodities to our starving people within Biafra.

At Ameka, an ancient salt pond, was reactivated. Ezza youth milled out to "fetch and boil salt water." Without any knowledge of chemistry, every youth, woman, or girl involved knew the process very well: *Kuta unu* (fetch the salt) and boil it until it began to evaporate. After a few hours, the crystal salt dust emerged. We would then mold it into a conical shape and it was ready for sale. Most times Umuazu bought large quantities of the Enyigba salt and secretly crossed over to sell it on the Biafran side at Azuebonyi River.

By then, the federal troops lined along major highways and were in charge of urban areas, but we, the civilians, lived in our villages and tried our best to avoid them. Such was the routine when we traveled in a group that fateful morning. Earlier, Ogom had a bad dream and warned me to stay home that day.

"How can I stay home in war time when all my friends are out there fighting to protect us?" As civilians, virtually every sound-minded Biafran was contributing toward the war in various ways. Ours was a populist revolution for survival.

After selling our salt, we bought electronics, Philips and Sony radio sets, bicycles, gramophones, and began our journey back home on the Nigerian side. We crossed Ebonyi River successfully with our goods and rode our bicycles in a single file along the narrow path we used. For security's sake, we rode in groups of two or three and allowed a distance of half a mile between the groups.

At St. Paul's Catholic School, my former primary school where I had failed in Standard 4, danger lurked around us. In the lone building located south of the school, a group of about one dozen

Nigerian soldiers lay in ambush. How they got information about us we still do not know today. However, no Amudo village lad was a member of Umuazu, our group. Second, was Amudo still hostile to us because of the 1961 "one-day war" between them and Ntsokara, my village? Since we were *Ahia Attack* traders (war traders), why and how did we become a threat to the federal troops? We carried no weapons. We wore no uniforms and carried nothing military on our bodies. Not suspecting any harm, we were shocked when a group of uniformed soldiers jumped out of the classrooms, guns cocked and pointed at us and yelled, "Lie down on the ground, nyamiri Ojukwu soldier." The torture began. I had never, ever experienced such pain, such fear, such humiliation. Our bicycles and electronic property were loaded along with us and driven to their zonal headquarters at Abaomege.

In the second wave of torture, the soldiers asked us to disclose the locations of the Biafran army. We did not know, and so they went inside their makeshift offices, broke empty Guinness beer bottles and used the jagged-edges of the bottles to slash our hands and legs into a bloody mess. The pain was unbearable. Today, I bear the pain and the scars of this injustice.

Thirdly, the soldiers marched toward us and began to extinguish their cigarettes on our faces, hands, stomachs, and ears. After four days, we were transferred to Abakaliki Maximum Prison located between Kpirikpiri and Abakpa areas of the Abakaliki urban city, which by now was like a ghost town. Only the soldiers and their "win-the-war wives" lived in the town. It was like a desert, seeing an Igbo city without Igbos. Muslim infantry soldiers and Hausa-Fulani civilians occupied Igbo homes and drove Igbo cars and controlled Igbo lives and commerce. It was a nightmare and we prayed for the nightmare to end as quickly as it had begun.

23

BOFF

DIPLOMATIC SOLDIERING

IN TODAY'S WORLD, child soldiering has become an urgent humanitarian crisis. The difficult question which people ask is whether or not the child soldier is a hero or a victim of adult abuse. That the child soldier is brutal and wicked is common knowledge. Perhaps what is less known is the fact that a different child soldiering model existed. Many people probably have not heard about the human rights child soldiers known as the Biafran Organization of Freedom Fighters, BOFF. I was a local Unit Commander of BOFF at the Ezza-Abakaliki Sector. As a former commander of BOFF, my friends and students in Kansas still ask me such questions as:

"Did you amputate people's hands and legs in Biafra?"

"Is it true the child soldier is forced to kill civilians?"

"Is it true Biafran children were starved to death by Nigeria?"

My response usually is, "Wait until you read my memoirs, *Never Again.*"

Igbo children are like baby lions. When we, the teenagers, realized that Nigeria had rigged our inalienable right to freedom, we struck.

Before joining the BOFF, I thought about the "Commandos" and the "Rangers." While the two names sound more warrior-like, I had no idea how to communicate with the recruiting officers. I volunteered to join BOFF. In the middle of the Okpoto forest, we had our secret training camp. The villagers knew and saw us but did not come close to the camp. They were aware of what we were doing, but because of their support for Biafra, they dared not report us to the federal troops who, by now, had captured the entire Abakaliki province.

I cannot discuss much concerning the nature of our training and warfare because it brings back horrifying memories of the past. However, our regimental drills as BOFF recruits started at about 4:00 a.m. every morning. Before the cock crowed to announce a new day, we were already warming up. While jogging, we became addicted to the war songs of freedom in Igbo, Ibibio, Efik, English, and various Christian songs such as:

- Enyi Biafra Alaala (Biafra the elephant nation has seceded).

- Gowon ayo Ojukwu, Ojukwu biko egbuzina anyi (Gowon pleads with Ojukwu to stop killing Nigerians).

- Okwute mgbe ebighie ebi kwe kam zoro na ime gi (Rock of ages allow me to hide in thee).

- We are Biafrans, fighting for our freedom, in the name of Jesus we shall conquer.

- Take my bullets when I die, oh Biafrans. If I happen to die or surrender, Biafrans take my bullets when I die.

- Asi mu jebe army mu jebe commando. Asi mu jebe army mu jebe commando, Awusa gba kpaka mu asua wujarara! Eh le-le-uwaoo! Sawam!! (If I am recruited to join the army, I would prefer to join the commando "BOFF" such that when the Hausa Muslims shoot at me, I would dodge their bullets like shadow in guerrilla style)

These songs were empowering and intoxicating enough, such that we did not have to do drugs. BOFF was disciplined. We were constantly reminded that ours was a war of survival or death. We saw the victims of Muslim terrorism, so we believed in a just cause. We believed we were fighting a *just war*. Senior BOFF instructors from Ezza zone went to the Okpoto forest with us. Julius and Gabriel and Daniel and Jude were in command. They were Ezza BOFF warriors.

After training for some weeks, we graduated. We could handle light weapons, Mark 4, grenades, M-16, "Biafran salt," "risky" missions, intelligence gathering, and acts of sabotage against the enemy. In Guerilla Warfare 101, most training of recruits took place in the bushes or in the forests. Such places were usually inaccessible by vehicles. Therefore, while our enemies controlled the captured motor highways of Abakaliki, Izzi, Ezza and Afikpo, the BOFF were the kings of the forest.

The second element was that the guerilla leadership and recruits lived among civilians, dressed in civilian clothes, but carried concealed weapons. Third, as child soldiers, we couldn't terrorize the society because we were deployed to our own villages and communities. Fourth, BOFF believed in *ogu ejiofor* (just war), in which case, our ancestors' spirits and Chineke would protect and guarantee our victory in our struggle.

BOFF came to existence when Biafra had lost its major cities—Abakaliki, Aba, Ahoada, Bonny, Calabar, Enugu, Eket, Ikot Ekpene, Nnewi, Nsukka, Okrika, Onitsha, Owerri, and Umuahia. The war needed a new strategic alternative way of fighting. Between Colonel E. O. Aghanya and the Biafran head of state, Emeka Ojukwu, the idea of mobilizing the civilians was conceived.

The regular Biafran air force, artillery regiments, and navy had become very weak and lacked the logistics to sustain the war. Nigeria, supported militarily by Russia and Britain, had a better fighting force. The BOFF, therefore, was conceptually designed to help lift the low morale of the Biafran fighting forces. Because Biafra had lost the major food-producing provinces to the Nigerian military, it became imperative to introduce a new youth army behind the enemy frontlines of defense. The capture of Abakaliki (my hometown) by the federal troops had the worst impact on Biafra. The whole of Nigeria and Biafra depended on Abakaliki for their food supply, especially as the largest producer of rice, oil, and yam. Due to the loss of this important town regarded as the "food basket" of Biafra, Colonel Aghanya had to introduce "special warfare tactics" to complement the conventional forces.

DIPLOMATIC SOLDIERING

BOFF was involved in diplomatic soldiering in Biafra. Behind enemy lines, when Nigerian troops captured Abakaliki, Izzi, Ezza, and Ikwo clans, the food basket of Biafra collapsed. However, the civilians in the captured area still owed their loyalty to the Republic of Biafra and not Nigeria, which they considered an invading force. Therefore, the BOFF fighters behind enemy lines embarked on a new food aid campaign.

Under my command, the villagers contributed yams, salt, rice, and "win-the-war" donations which we secretly smuggled into Biafra to feed our soldiers and civilians suffering severe hunger and malnutrition. While many Biafran children died of hunger and starvation, the village children in Abakaliki, Izzi, Ezza, and Ikwo did not suffer such plight because our zone was the center of farming and food supply for Biafra, Nigeria, and West Africa. Although our society had been captured by Nigeria, we considered ourselves as diplomats serving the government and people of Biafra behind enemy lines or inside the Nigerian territory. As civilian diplomats and soldiers, we could not indulge in crime, violence, or atrocities that could endanger our families and society. With daring spirit, we smuggled food and money into Biafra, risking our lives because a few unfortunate BOFF members were killed by the federal troops for "violating" the federal sanctions placed on Biafra in order to starve the new nation into submission.

Four decades after the war, I was so lucky to meet and to interview the legendary *Ochi-Agha Biafra,* Colonel Aghanya at Howard University Law School in Washington, DC, in 2011. According to the conceptual and strategic framework, a force to be known as Biafran Organization of Freedom Fighters (BOFF) was to be formed. Second, its area of operation had to be behind the enemy line of defense.

Third, under the laws establishing BOFF, on no account should we fight in any area of the war held by Biafran conventional forces. Fourth, the officers and men of the new force must not assume any known military name or rank. Fifth, all captured conventional weapons by the new force must be made available or surrendered to the conventional Biafran forces. Sixth, all the "operators" in the new BOFF force were not allowed to put on any kind of military uniform. Colonel Aghanya and Major General Alex Madiebo worked together to design the structure of the new BOFF force.

In BOFF's strategic plan, Biafra was divided into *sectors.* Each sector was the highest formation of the BOFF. Next to sector were district, group, cell, and unit formations. The commander of each of the formations was designated as leader. The recruits of the new force received training like the conventional soldiers. Each member, however, was simply called an "operator" to conceal the member's true strategic role.

As a unit commander, I was called "Leader" by my boys. We had become freedom fighters. The Biafran Freedom Fighter was involved in planning and executing operations behind "enemy lines." According to its founding principles, the Biafra Freedom Fighters' primary goal was to "provide information and logistic support to the Biafran conventional forces." Our second duty was to mount ambush attacks and to create obstacles against enemy advancement and mobility.

With the endorsement of BOFF's new strategic agenda by General Emeka Ojukwu, Colonel Aghanya began his audacious strategy of recruiting and training blacksmiths, carpenters, tailors, welders, mechanics, and so many other artisans and professional units of BOFF. With the aggregation of such powerful manpower, uniquely specialized freedom fighters began to fabricate war tools en masse. Young chemistry undergraduates were mobilized to perform research on chemical materials in the forests and in the locality for harnessing and production of war weapons.

Another unique element of BOFF was what Ochi-Agha (Colonel Aghanya) called the "BOFF form B Operation." According to the Colonel, "this involved the mobilization of almost the entire civilian population to carry out Agitation and Propaganda (AGIPROP), with Professor Okonjo, a world-renowned economist and psychologist in charge."

As a unit leader of BOFF at Izzikworo East, I was in charge of the following villages: Amudo, Ntsokara (my village), Amagu, Amaezekwe, Amana, and Ameka. At night, we mounted "sentry" or vigilante checkpoints. We sealed off our communities by monitoring strange activities, strangers, and their movements.

From the intelligence information gathered, we knew the military culture of the federal forces. If one dared attack them from any village or hamlet, the standing order was to wipe out, I mean totally wipe out and destroy the entire village where the attack emanated. To secure the six villages under my command, we slowed down on major offensives that could backfire and bring destruction to the long-suffering rural people. However, if any person or community was perceived to have assisted the federal troops to invade or advance at the warfront, then such person became our target. BOFF had no tolerance for *sabo* (saboteurs).

My unit command headquarters, now located at Ntsokara, my village, forged a military alliance with the village leaders. On our side, BOFF defended the village while the village fed, housed, and supported the cause of Biafra. As a BOFF leader, I could not live in my father's home. The village asked me to choose a secret location as my operational headquarters. I chose Okoro Ngele's compound at Echaraukwu, Ntsokara. I had two bodyguards who lived with me. Ignatius, commonly called IG, was very protective of me. Nwonu Nwomege, Ignatius's father and a respected Echaraukwu elder, had a long friendship with my father. When a freedom fighter or child soldier was posted to his own community, it was less likely that he would rape, kill, or maim his own people. This is because in such a village scenario, everybody knows everybody. And so one could not commit a crime easily and get away with it. Therefore, at the back of my mind was the central issue of the war, the security and survival of the Biafran people. Toward this objective, therefore, the freedom that we sought was indeed different from the dominant or western views of freedom. The Biafran Organization of Freedom Fighters, BOFF, therefore, was a revolutionary arm of Biafra's quest for self-determination, democratic governance, and freedom. The freedom which BOFF sought was essentially different. We sought the following:

- Freedom from genocide and human rights violations
- Freedom from death, torture, and disappearances
- Freedom and right to political and economic justice
- Freedom and right to dignity as human beings
- Freedom and right to self-determination

It was for these natural rights that we dared to fight and die for Biafra. The audacity of freedom and the power to set people free are unstoppable when their time have come. When the time came, nobody could stop the course of the river. The collective power of freedom fighters is like a cleansing flood or deluge. Military force might slow it down, but its unstoppable waves will eventually prevail if the cause is just. The spirit of freedom is an unstoppable, generational force for change.

Characteristic of the BOFF training, today I am still a freedom fighter behind enemy lines involved in transitional justice and subaltern education worldwide. What distinguishes BOFF from the more recent guerrilla movements is the nonbrutal use of force against civilians, children, and women. BOFF had well-educated and intelligent leadership.

When the federal troops changed tactics and began to use food to buy the hearts and minds of the Biafran civilians, Colonel Aghanya said to himself, "Is it not time to stop this war since the civilians for whom I have been fighting to protect...and who have been dying of hunger... are now getting food from the enemy to survive?" Only visionary leadership could ruminate on such a moral idea.

In other sectors, I heard rumors that BOFF girls were extraordinarily trained to handle the federal troops who usually kidnapped Igbo girls. For one strange reason, the federal troops could never keep their eyes off Igbo girls. True or false, Igbo girls were considered very pretty, intelligent, and of a higher breed. Ordinarily, the average Igbo girl would not associate with soldiers who generally were considered as low class, poor, and illiterate, but the war had become a leveler. Many Igbo girls lived with federal troops in order to survive the harsh realities of the war. Others, like the BOFF girls, were on a military mission, while serving the domestic and social needs of the federal troops.

BOFF was a different revolutionary model. We were nationalists. Our revolution was an outcome of insecurity in Nigeria. Most of the fighting forces and BOFF were volunteer citizens. With our minds, bodies, and souls, we fought the enemy, believing in Celestine Ukwu and his philosophers' metaphor that *ilo abu chi* (one's enemy is not one's God).

- *Akalaka anyi nedu anyi* (Our destiny leads us on).

- *Akalaka onye nedu onye* (One's own destiny leads him).

- *Ife ncha sina onyinye Chukwu* (All things happen as gifts from God).

- *Ife ncha sina akalaka* (Everything happens according to our destiny).

The political philosophy of our cause was best articulated in our warrior songs, for example *osondu* (in the race for life). In osondu, we were asked to reflect on this mundane world of vanity which is not our real home. "Let us remember that we are created in this world by Chukwu (God)."

In the musical track *Usondu*, Celestine Ukwu warns the moral society to beware of "living a life of vanity," or a corrupt and immoral life. In peacetime and in wartime, Ndigbo (Igbo people) both dead and living, are in a sacred alliance, which is difficult to understand unless one is Igbo. This covenant is so deeply etched on our minds that when the struggles of life become too unbearable, we can send a petition to God.

I have attempted to state the role of BOFF and my unit leadership in the Biafran revolution for self-determination. Second, I have discussed the nonviolent operations of BOFF under my command. I have also briefly stated what we did, why we did it, and our weaknesses too as freedom fighters, but we never kidnapped school girls or children during our struggle. The idea of kidnapping innocent children might have come from hell.

The secret of our revolution's survival for almost three years was first because of Biafra's audacity, visionary leadership, and the *general will* of the people to survive. The desire to survive helped to mobilize the much traumatized society. As Fredrick Forsyth recalls, "The people contributed everything they had got; poor villages took collections; rich men emptied their foreign accounts and donated dollars and pounds. Tailors made uniforms out of curtain materials, and cobblers turned out army boots from canvas strips. [Abakaliki] farmers donated yams, cassava, rice, goats, chickens and eggs. Taxi drivers and mammy-wagon owners drove troop convoys and priests and school teachers handed over their bicycles." Umuazu, my civilian traders "exported" food, salt, and money donations to our people in Biafra as we stated earlier. Yes, there were also some traitors and cheaters, defectors, profiteers and racketeers, according to Fredrick Forsyth. But our cause was just.

KANSURU

Certain villagers conspired to kill the *kansuru* (councilor), the village leader. When the conspirators asked me and my boys to kill him, I wanted to know what he did. Instead, as I could understand it, the chief conspirator said that the kansuru owed his father some amount of money, which he had refused to pay. There was also a land dispute in question. The irony is that two out of the three major conspirators were the kansuru's own relatives. With the consent of the "chairman," the trio wanted me and my boys to assassinate the kansuru.

"You will never be somebody," Papa explains. "You too will be killed just as you killed him. The worst abomination is to have blood in your head and hands in this world. Blood guilt wrecks one's life permanently. The law of Kamenu must prevail. You reap what you sow in life. It is also known as the law of cause and effect. If one kills, one will also be killed by another person. It is only a matter of time."

On that fateful night, the three men made the unforgettable trip to the Okofia forest. Early in the morning, the trio returned without their victim. My heart sank. One by one, they visited me and repeated how "cowardly" their victim handled his tragic fate.

"He begged and begged and begged for mercy. He resigned his chieftaincy and wanted us to have it just to spare his life," confessed one perpetrator.

"He cried like a baby and reminded us that we were his relatives. That night, we trekked over ten miles and as the victim promised to give us money to spare his life, we dealt the fateful blows that silenced him forever," narrated another conspirator.

As the war came to an end, I remembered our kansuru. I remembered how ordinary people could become such evil men and perpetrators overnight. Someone you think could not harm an ant could indeed become a green snake in a green grass. I can never trust anymore. After the war, one of the perpetrators said to me, "Ewa, your life was saved only because you were the commander of BOFF in our society and we know you'll keep your mouth shut. We were aware that you know, we will come after you if you opened your mouth and exposed us." One after the other, the three perpetrators have all died, tragically too. Life has taught me that we reap what we sow in this world.

For over forty years after our revolution, I sleep deeply, knowing that when I had the power to kill people and get away scot-free, I did not soil my hands with bloodstains. The most painful aspect of this man's death is that he was not murdered by the Muslims, like the many Igbos who lost their lives. Our kansuru might not have been a good leader to his enemies, but he was a great village leader who mobilized Amaokpo women to cut bundles of grass with which the village school roofs were thatched and repaired. The headmasters consulted with him on many issues concerning the villagers and St. Ben's Catholic Primary School. In particular, it was under his village government that we witnessed the building of the first zinc house in the school. He mobilized the villagers to contribute money and gather stones for the construction of the school building. He also organized farm-free workdays for community projects. Such days were set aside for the construction of the school.

As a child, our village kansuru was there when we took our first photographs, when the urban tailor from Abakaliki came to our rural school to take our measurements. He was there when we marched from St. Benedict's to Sacred Heart, Onueke Ezza, to celebrate Nigeria's independence from the British Crown. Our kansuru's legacy is there for all to see. Many times, when Amagu people clashed with our own village on boundary disputes, he courageously mobilized the youth and the elders to fight back. Like Nwiboko Obodo, our kansuru was as brave as a lion.

Once in a while, rumor would have it that the kansuru was a corrupt leader. However, there was not much for any Ntsokara leader to corrupt him with. The villagers had not much money, except animals and land resources. But such was the time.

24

A FORGOTTEN NATION

As THE WAR hastened toward its end, it became important to restate the cardinal principles of our revolution. The Biafran revolution did not mean kidnapping of innocent citizens or destruction of people's lives and property. Rather, the revolution meant *change*—change for a better, greater, and stronger society. In reclaiming the dreams and principles of the Biafran revolution, we need to revisit the Ahiara Declaration.

EXCERPTS FROM AHIARA DECLARATION

I stand before you tonight not to launch the Biafran Revolution, because it is already in existence. It came into being two years ago when we proclaimed to all the world that we had finally extricated ourselves from the sea of mud that was, and is, Nigeria. I stand before you to proclaim formally the commitment of the Biafran State to the Principles of the Revolution and to enunciate those Principles.

Some people are frightened when they hear the word Revolution. They say: Revolution? Heaven help us! It is too dangerous. It means mobs rushing around destroying property, killing people and upsetting everything. But these people do not understand the real meaning of revolution. For us, a revolution is a change–a quick change, a change for the better. Every society is changing all the time. It is changing for the better or for the worse; it is either moving forward or moving backwards; it cannot stand absolutely still. A revolution is a forward movement. It is a rapid, forward movement which improves a people's standard of living and their material circumstance and purifies and raises their moral tone. It transforms for the better those institutions which are still relevant, and discards those which stand in the way of progress.

- The Biafran Revolution believes in the sanctity of human life and the dignity of the human person. The Biafran sees the willful and wanton destruction of human life not only as a grave crime but as an abominable sin. In our society every human life is holy, every individual person counts. No Biafran wants to be taken for granted or ignored, neither does he ignore or take others for granted. This explains why such degrading practices as begging for alms were unknown in Biafran society. Therefore, all forms of disabilities and inequalities which reduce the dignity of the individual or destroy his sense of person have no place in the New Biafran Social Order. The Biafran Revolution upholds the dignity of man.

- The Biafran Revolution stands firmly against Genocide–against any attempt to destroy a people, its security, its right to life, property and progress. Any attempt to deprive a community of its identity is abhorrent to the Biafran people. Having ourselves suffered genocide, we are all the more determined to take a clear stand now and at all times against this crime.

- The new Biafran Social Order places a high premium on Patriotism–Love and Devotion to the Fatherland. Every true Biafran must love Biafra; must have faith in Biafra and its people, and must strive for its greater unity. He must find his salvation here in Biafra. He must be prepared to work for Biafra, to stand up for Biafra and, if necessary, to die for Biafra. He must be prepared to defend the sovereignty of Biafra wherever and by whomsoever it is challenged. Biafran patriots do all this already, and Biafra expects all her sons and daughters of today and tomorrow, to emulate their noble example. Diplomats who treat insults to the Fatherland and the Leadership of our struggle with levity are not patriotic. That young man who sneaks about the village, avoiding service in his country's Armed Forces is unpatriotic; that young, able-bodied school teacher who prefers to distribute relief when he should be fighting his country's war, is not only unpatriotic but is doing a woman's work. Those who help these loafers to dodge their civic duties should henceforth re-examine themselves.

- All Biafrans are brothers and sisters bound together by ties of geography, trade, inter-marriage and culture and their common misfortune in Nigeria and their present experience of the armed struggle. Biafrans are even more united by the desire to create a new and better order of society which will satisfy their needs and aspirations. Therefore, there is no justification for anyone to introduce into the Biafran Fatherland divisions based on ethnic origin, sex or religion. To do so would be unpatriotic.

- Every true Biafran must know and demand his civic rights. Furthermore, he must recognize the rights of other Biafrans and be prepared to defend them when necessary. So often people complain that they have been ill-treated by the Police or some other public servant. But the truth very often is that we allow ourselves to be bullied because we are not man enough to demand and stand up for our rights, and that fellow citizens around do not assist us when we demand our rights.

- In the New Biafran Social Order sovereignty and power belong to the People. Those who exercise power do so on behalf of the people. Those who govern must not tyrannize over the people. They carry a sacred trust of the people and must use their authority strictly in accordance with the will of the people. The true test of success in public life is that the People—who are the real masters—are contented and happy. The rulers must satisfy the People at all times.

- But it is no use saying that power belongs to the People unless we are prepared to make it work in practice. Even in the old political days, the oppressors of the People were among those who shouted loudest that power belonged to the People. The Biafran Revolution will constantly and honestly seek methods of making this concept a fact rather than a pious fiction.

- Arising out of the Biafrans' belief that power belongs to the People is the principle of public accountability. Those who exercise power are accountable to the people for the way they use that power. The People retain the right to renew or terminate their mandate. Every individual servant of the People, whether in the Legislature, the Civil Service, the Judiciary, the Police, the Armed Forces, in business or in any other walks of life, is accountable at all times for his work or the work of those under his charge. Where, therefore, a ministry of department runs inefficiently or improperly, its head must accept personal responsibility for such a situation and, depending on the gravity of the failure, must resign or be removed. And where he is proved to have misused his position or trust to enrich himself, the principle of public accountability requires that he be punished severely and his ill-gotten gains taken from him.

—Emeka Ojukwu

(See Appendix B to read the full text of Ahiara Declaration)

25

IGBO EXCEPTIONALISM

IGBO DI ICHE.

No DOUBT, EVERY society is *unique*. However, the idea that *Igbo di iche* (Igbo is different and unique) has its roots in our strong spiritual and moral laws and in our belief in Chineke (Creation God), and warrior cultures. However, in Ahiara Declaration, the qualities of the Igbo (Biafran citizen) are succinctly stated. The excerpt of the declaration below speaks on the qualities of the Biafran citizen:

> But in talking about the People we must never lose sight of the individuals who make up the People. The single individual is the final, irreducible unit of the People. In Biafra that single individual counts. The Biafran Revolution cannot lose sight of this fact.
>
> The desirable changes which the Revolution aims to bring to the lives of the People will first manifest them-

selves in the lives of individual Biafrans. The success of the Biafran Revolution will depend on the quality of individuals within the State. Therefore, the caliber of the individual is of the utmost importance to the Revolution. To build the New Society we will require new men who are in tune with the spirit of the New Order. What then should be the qualities of this Biafran of the New Order?

1. He is patriotic, loyal to his State, his Government and its leadership; he must not do anything which undermines the security of his State or gives advantage to the enemies of his country. He must not indulge in such evil practices as tribalism and nepotism which weaken the loyalty of their victims to the state. He should be prepared, if need be, to give up his life in defense of the Nation.

2. He must be his brother's keeper; he must help all Biafrans in difficulty, whether or not they are related to him by blood; he must avoid, at all costs, doing anything which is capable of bringing distress and hardship to other Biafrans. A man who hoards money or goods is not his brother's keeper because he brings distress and hardship to his fellow citizens.

3. He must be honorable; he must be a person who keeps his promise and the promise of his office, a person who can always be trusted.

4. He must be truthful: he must not cheat his neighbor, his fellow citizens and his country. He must not give or receive bribes or corruptly advance himself or his interests.

5. He must be responsible: he must not push across to others the task which properly belongs to him, or let others receive the blame or punishment for his own failings. A responsible man keeps secrets. A Biafran who is in a position to know what our troops are planning and talks about it is irresponsible. The information he gives out will spread

and reach the ear of the enemy. A responsible man minds his own business; he does not show off.

6. He must be brave and courageous: he must never allow himself to be attacked by others without fighting back to defend himself and his rights. He must be ready to tackle tasks which other people might regard as impossible.

7. He must be law-abiding: he obeys the laws of the land and does nothing to undermine the due processes of law.

8. He must be freedom-loving: he must stand up resolutely against all forms of injustice, oppression and suppression. He must never be afraid to demand his rights. For example, a true Biafran at a post office or bank counter will insist on being served in his turn.

9. He must be progressive: he should not slavishly and blindly adhere to old ways of doing things; he must be prepared to make changes in his way of life in the light of our new revolutionary experience.

10. He is industrious, resourceful and inventive; he must not fold his arms and wait for the Government to do everything for him; he must also help himself.

IGBO DI ICHE

The uniqueness of the Igbo society is based on the people's achievement motif, arrogance, bravery, courage, competitive spirit, intellectual power, hard work, government without kings, stubbornness, ultrademocratic government, conservative, libertarian and liberal ideologies combined. These contending value systems together with the ten individual qualities of the Biafran citizen constitute what we refer to as *Igbo di iche* or Igbo exceptionalism.

By early January 1970, our artillery soldiers were weak and tired. Biafra's arms and weapons of war had been exhausted. By air, land, and sea, the British-Russian-Egyptian-Nigerian forces had totally circled around what was left of our new country, Biafra. On January 15, 1970, in the presence of the Nigerian military leader, General Yakubu Gowon, the vice head of state of Biafra, Philip Effiong, was forced to make this declaration:

> I, Major General Philip Effiong, Officer Administering the Government of the Republic of Biafra, now wish to make the following declaration:

1. That we affirm we are loyal Nigerian citizens and accept the authority of the Federal Government of Nigeria.

2. That we accept the existing administrative and political structure of the Federation of Nigeria.

3. That any future constitutional arrangement will be worked out by representatives of the people of Nigeria.

4. That the Republic of Biafra hereby ceases to exist.

With these declarations, we lost our freedom and our dignity through the use of force or coercion. Biafran nationalists still ask when *might* has become *right*. When has the global community accepted replacing international *rule of law* with the *use of force* as a democratic and legitimate way to dissolve another nation-state? Or was the Nigerian military junta justified to use force in implementing the slogan, "To keep Nigeria one is a task that must be done?" This is a dangerous precedent in global criminal justice.

For over four decades, the Biafran freedom dream has turned into a nightmare. To us, it is sunset in Biafra. What shall we say to the dead and maimed Biafrans? When the Acting Head of the Biafran State, General Philip Effiong, surrendered power to Nigeria, we said our last prayers. The Muslim mob and soldiers would undoubtedly complete their unfinished jihadist pogrom against Igbo Christians and other fellow Biafrans.

With the brutality of the federal troops and the Biafran propaganda machine, we were almost sure that the Nigerian soldiers would "complete" the genocide which had started on January 15,

May 29, and September 29, 1966. The evidence of their brutality could be seen all around us. One day passed and another day silently followed. We feared that our leaders who were taken to Lagos, the Nigerian capital city, would be lined up and executed by firing squad. It had happened in the past.

At Ntsokara, my operational headquarters, my bodyguard, IG, was playing the Ashigo game when the announcement came over the radio. He paused, stood up, and rushed into the grass hut to give me the unthinkable news. "Leader, Biafra has surrendered. General Effiong is addressing the nation now."

"IG, summon all BOFF boys under my command," I ordered.

"We must wait to hear from Gabriel Nworie," the Idembia-born BOFF leader in charge of the Izzikworo sector. But after a few hours, I made up my mind to address my boys.

I began with our usual BOFF war songs and chants.

"Ole ebe k'unu si (What citizens are you)?"

"Biafrans," my boys echoed.

"Ebe ka unu no (Where are you now)?"

"Biafra."

"Ebe ka unu bi (Where do you live)?"

"Biafra...agaghim arapu Biafra gawa Nigeria ga biri (I would never leave Biafra to become a Nigerian citizen)."

"Biafra gadi ndu (Biafra Will Survive)."

"Fellow BOFF warriors, our leaders have surrendered and the war is now over. From the bottom of my heart, I thank you all for defending our fatherland with your own lives. We will continue to remember and respect our brothers, sisters, and fellow Biafrans who were killed at the war front and in the hands of the northern Muslim civilians and the military.

"With your gallant effort, we were able to protect Ntsokara, Amagu, Amaezekwe, Amana, Ameka villages, and the Ezza people. We are all aware of what happened to the citizens of Okofia village when the federal troops entered and burnt down huts and killed so many helpless civilians.

"Our tactics not to attack federal troops within the Izzikworo East zone have paid off. There was no retaliatory offensive directed at our five villages by the federal troops which is why most of our people survived the war."

At first, Ntsokara people detested "food aid" and argued that the concept of receiving "free" food was like "begging." And in Ezza culture, begging is seen as a curse from God. No normal person should beg or ask for alms. No villager wishes to be associated with "free food," as society would laugh at such recipients. "With your help," I continued, "we were able to meet up the rigid rules which the international food agencies established as pre-conditions to approving and opening a food distribution center at Ntsokara. We mobilized the hungry and starving villagers to construct sheds at St. Benedict's Catholic School, Amaokpo Ntsokara where food distribution took place. Women and children and old people began to receive food aid like others at Amagu and Amaezekwe where people got their own *ration* at St. Patrick's School, Okometa, Amagu.

"When I got food allocation for Ntsokara women and kids from Red Cross Food Aid at St. Patrick's, the crowd was so much that it took a whole day to process and distribute the stockfish, cornmill, milk, and salt allocated to us. While many of the Biafran children died of starvation and kwashiorkor, Abakaliki, Ezza, Izzi and Ikwo people were spared, thanks to the International Food Agencies, thanks to Ezza farmers and you the BOFF who protected both the civilians and the I.G.Os. in the cause of our people.

"Finally, please stay together and report to me at least once a week until further instructions from the BOFF Headquarters.

"If our leaders who have been *invited* to the Supreme Headquarters in Lagos, Nigeria, are executed, we will have no other alternative than to embark on massive and prolonged guerilla warfare until we reclaim our freedom and sovereignty.

"As rumored also, if the winning Nigerian military commanders decide to wipe out our children, women, and people, BOFF will find such a situation UNACCEPTABLE. Whatever is the case, BOFF men and women, remember that we have a blood covenant with our dead citizens, heroes and relatives who were killed either by the federal troops or by the Nigerian Muslim civilians. We vouched to fight till the last Biafran soldier. The Biafra–Nigeria war may be over and we are happy as it prevents the further loss of more lives, but our fight for freedom cannot stop until we are indeed free."

As I saw it then, there would be many phases and many generational wars until freedom comes. Too much blood has been wasted. Too much damage has been done. Too much injustice has occurred which cannot be easily expiated. We can forgive and forget and reconcile the individual atrocities and criminal acts against us, but we do not have the right to forget the perpetrators who planned, mobilized and murdered children and women on January 15, July 29, September 29, 1966, and during the three-year war.

According to Chimamanda Adichie, this is *the thing around our neck*, a blood covenant with the dead Biafran freedom fighters and victims of religious hatred. Ndigbo believe in the Law of *Kamenu*, natural truth telling and justice (you reap what you sow). The continuous bloody campaigns by Islamic jihadists in Northern Nigeria and the kidnappings in eastern states today can be partly attributed to the unresolved consequences of past injustices and karma. Some people do believe and others do not believe in the law of karma, but karma is real. Believe it or not, there is Chineke's invisible hand in every society's struggle for justice and freedom.

Four decades after the war, Ndigbo have not regained their economic and political rights as Nigerian citizens. Four decades after the war, nothing has happened to the war criminals. What have government and society done to hunt down the human rights violators from both Biafra and Nigeria? Since the war ended, all perpetrators have been enjoying the trappings of a solid

Nigerian life—an expensive lifestyle, good paying jobs, and top political positions. Nothing suggests that they have any regrets as agents of a tragic past. Nobody has had the courage to indict the war criminals on the genocide, torture, false imprisonment, and the deaths of over thirty thousand children and women in 1966. Since then, the killing of Christians, Igbos, and Easterners have continued every year for almost five decades in northern Nigeria.

I was kidnapped, tortured, and imprisoned on the false assumption that I was a Biafran soldier. My three brothers were killed in the war. Now that the group has resumed cutting off citizens' heads again, who would ask questions? Who does the *Inweronye* (subaltern) class have to fight for their rights and dignity?

As survivors of the Nigerian genocide in 1966 and subsequently the war, we owe it to the dead victims to hold the perpetrators accountable. No doubt, to research, investigate, and prosecute these long-forgotten criminals will be difficult because of the duration of the crime. Eyewitnesses might not be easy to locate. However, we the survivors ought to spend weeks, months, and even years collecting enough data to prosecute the perpetrators. Because those of us who played active roles in the conflict are aging and dying off, there is not much time to waste in bringing human rights abusers to justice. As *Ochi-Agha*, Aghanya, the BOFF commander advised, "We are no more interested in fighting with guns to actualize Biafra. The phase of the struggle now is that of *agha-uche*. In the twenty-first century, the pen is mightier than the gun."

There is a prediction that the twenty-first century belongs to the subaltern (long-forgotten and voiceless) peoples of the world, such as the young Tunisian, Egyptian, Syrian, and Libyan street protesters who are seeking their political freedom and economic justice. As a freedom fighter, I know there will be more growing demands for youth rights in this century. I know also that Biafra's freedom matters in the reshaping of a new, just, and peaceful global community.

It seems like a travesty of justice to wage an aggressive war against a people who have chosen the path of self-determination. It seems like a violation of international law to use bullets instead of ballots to force one society into another. Biafran nationalists argue that the defeat of Biafra and consequent reunion with the British-engineered political creature called Nigeria has not served the cause of justice for the following reasons:

1. The Nigerian example lays a dangerous precedent in international law.

2. The Nigerian military justice model regrettably promotes *victor's justice.*

3. With Biafra's defeat, Nigeria assumed the role of the judge and jury.

4. The invasion and illegal war deprived Biafrans of their natural right to self-determination.

5. Perpetrators of war crimes have not been tried, pardoned, or punished.

6. The unpunished genocide and crimes against humanity are dangerous precedents that gave rise to the incessant terrorist atrocities taking place in northern Nigeria.

The execution of virtually all Igbo military men and women and the subsequent genocide carried out by the northern mob were a result of a deliberate state policy, which is why the federal military government did not make any efforts to stop the massacre. As of today, no soldier has been court-martialed for the almost total elimination of Igbo officers and civilians in the federal military. As of today, no Nigerian or Biafran soldier has been punished for the atrocities committed against the civilians. The Igbo soldiers who killed our Muslim prime minister, Muslim premier of the north, and finance minister have not been prosecuted either. They too should be prosecuted.

In 1966, every Igbo person was an enemy, whether he or she was a child, woman, old, young, soldier, or civilian. Nigeria singled out the Christian Igbo and killed them all over the country. Their deaths have put blood guilt on Britain, Nigeria, and Russia. However, the "generals" who should have stood in the dock, charged for war crimes, have gone scot-free even after detailing their atrocities in their memoirs. For over forty-five years, after the war, no state or federal legislator or government official has sponsored a National Reconciliation Act or Truth Commission to review the moral implications of the war.

When we continued to witness the murdering of our mothers and sisters and brothers by the federal troops, the children of Biafra were forced to wage a secret shadow war against the enemy. As children fighting within the Biafran Organization of Freedom Fighters, BOFF, we had no stable war front. We had no uniforms and no recognizable military insignia. With the visible evidence of the atrocities against our people, we saw the postcolonial state as a monstrous beast that had gone mad, waging an unwarranted war against the peace-loving and business-minded Igbo people. In our childlike eyes, Nigeria was guilty of killing our fellow children, our mothers, and our fathers.

Later, as an adult, I would learn that Nigeria also violated the Geneva Convention when I was arrested, tortured, and imprisoned as a civilian, thereby violating my right to the "Protection of Civilian Persons in Time of War" clause. Nigeria, I presume, is a signatory to the Geneva Convention. The Nigerian, British, and Russian governments which did the killings of innocent Biafran civilians were expected to comply with the international law as stipulated in the Geneva Convention.

Nigerian-USSR collaborative model is partly responsible for most of the African conflicts in the past four decades. Basically, all African conflicts have been, in reality, proxy wars between European and North American countries. The summary of this conspiracy and collective injustice against Biafra explains why May 30, 1967, is so important to us.

Tuesday, May 30, 1967 is significant in many ways:

1. For the first time, the people of Eastern Nigeria became *aware* that neither their property nor their lives could be protected by any government based outside Eastern Nigeria.

2. The people of Eastern Nigeria, *believing* that they were born free with certain inalienable rights which could best be preserved by themselves, had to take action for self-preservation.

3. Therefore, the Biafran Freedom Declaration was drafted to liberate them from the injustices perpetrated by the Nigerian military and Muslim jihadists.

4. The Biafran Freedom Declaration is a formal document that says, we are no longer safe in Nigeria.

5. The Declaration was a formal statement saying: "We are no more Nigerian citizens. Since peace talks and reconciliation could no longer work, we're now Biafran citizens."

26

NWIGWE

Life is incomplete without Nwigwe Uturu, nwa nshi nnam.

After the war ended, I told my father that I had to try an urban life again. There was nothing at Ntsokara for a primary school graduate to do. I could not and have never been trained in the skills of farming and blacksmithing which comprise my father's professions.

Abakaliki urban was a ghost town immediately after the war. Basically, the town was occupied by only Nigerian soldiers and the few Hausa-Muslim traders who sold provisions, onions, goats, cows, cattle, rice, and other long-deprived items during the war. The conquered Biafrans needed these items badly but had no money to buy them. My kid brother, the last of my mother's three boys, Nwigwe Daniel Unoke (aka "Ocean Diver," "Last Kobo"), had quickly learned how to speak Hausa and became a sales boy for the opportunist traders who occupied each town as soon as the federal troops captured it.

Then there were no jobs, no government, no schools, no police, no rules, and no order. I witnessed a society without a leader, without taxation, without transportation, water, electricity, roads, and food. However, "man must survive" was our motto. I began to make tea every morning in order to give breakfast to the few returning Biafran workers and ex-soldiers who formed the skeletal network of the state civil service. I bought water from *meruwa* (the Hausa water hawker) who hung two tins of water on a long stick across his shoulders and trekked for several miles from the Abakaliki Water Works road back to town.

Through tea making and selling of bread, I made a little money with which to begin a new business. My first trip to Effium garri market was remarkable. I bought about two bags of garri and transported them in a *gwongworo* (lorry) to Ogbete market where I sold them with minimal profit. I had to sell the bags so cheaply because I could neither take them back to Abakaliki nor store them anywhere at Enugu if unsold. I was a novice in the business.

My second trip was different. All my bags of garri were soaked by water in the open lorry and I suffered a total loss. My meager capital melted away with the tropical rain. Just then, something strange happened.

"Okoye Lands" was my greatest tea customer and mentor. Tall and friendly, he never failed to have his cup of tea every morning before trekking to the Ministry of Lands, which only had a skeletal staff immediately after the war ended.

One day, Okoye Lands asked me, "What are your future plans after your BOFF experience?"

"My interest is going back to school."

"Were you in college before the war?"

I told him lies. I narrated how I was a student of Yaba Trade Center in Lagos before the war. The transitional, postconflict government in former Biafra (now East Central State) had a new education policy to absorb and enroll all eastern students who were in colleges in any part of Nigeria before the war. Mr. "Okoye Lands" revealed that he had discussed my case with the principal of Government Trade Center, Abakaliki.

Before the war, Mr. J. C. Ofili was the principal of Government Trade Center, Ahoada, Port Harcourt. He had been forced to return to Awka, his hometown, because of the war. He would be redeployed to head GTC, Abakaliki. As I said earlier, I got admission and began to train in electrical installation, carpentry, metallurgy, and other technical subjects. I was only able to pay for my first semester. There was no money for food and boarding.

Nwigwe Unoke, aka Daniel, my kid brother, rode his bicycle several times from Ntsokara to Abakaliki to bring me firewood, yam, oil, and fruits from my mother and father. During the war years, life was brutal and uncertain. My family lived in constant fear of air riads, Muslim soldiers, and poverty. We had no hospitals, no clean water, no good roads, and no schools in our villages. At the end of the war, therefore, most surviving Biafrans began life afresh. The name of the game was survival. Nwigwe rode about thirty miles to and fro and did it happily throughout the two years I spent going to school at GTC. Nobody in my life has been able to match my brother's love. I can never forget the connection that I had with my mother's last son, Nwigwe, the brother I fondly call *mkparawa*. He cared and he respected "senior," as he called me in acknowledgement of my status as the Okpara, first son of the Unoke family—the prince.

In 2006, when I traveled from the US to bury him, I had received his dying wish, "Nobody should bury me except my senior brother." Mgbom people and I honored his wish. As I asked my nephew Unoke Friday Unoke to "point" at the spot where his father would be buried according to our tradition, I drifted into a deep recollection of the *turning moments* I had shared with my powerful junior brother.

One day, as we sat down to make plans about our future after the war, I had wanted both of us to go back to school. Nwigwe sharply interjected, "Nwunnem, anyi te refuta kwa iya!" meaning it is an unprofitable plan! As my brother's lifeless body lay in that open casket, I thanked Chineke that nobody killed him like Nwiboko Obodo, like kansuru, or like the current terrorist victims. No Muslim civilian or soldier murdered my mother's last son. No Muslim mob murdered "Nwanshi" Unoke Ekirika (Nwigwe Uturu), the oracle that "protected" my father's earthly journey.

When I dropped a handful of sand on the casket bearing my brother's mortal remains, when Mgbom people lowered "mkparawa nnam" into the hallowed ground near my childhood hut, I closed my eyes and told my kid brother, "Mu te refuta diya (I will not come out of this destiny which life has dealt me with any victory without you, my brother)." Nobody can fill the void which his large image has created in my heart. The pain may hide itself as other life issues push in front, but the death of mkparawa (a legendary brother) is something I can never heal from.

On a happier note, his five children call me *father*, and this is a great honor. Life is what Ndigbo call *osondi owendi* (sweet and bitter).

Before our own time comes, how can we as a people, as former child soldiers, as a society and government, free ourselves from what we have done? As individuals, how can we free ourselves from what has been done to us? As victors and victims, how can we set ourselves free from what we have failed to do? From my war experience, a government's ability to build a more just and humane society today primarily depends on its responses to the unfinished injustices of the past. This is true because the basic desire of the postconflict society is durable peace and not war.

When the war ended, we were forced back into "One Nigeria," plagued by corruption, crime, military dictatorship, and blood guilt. In the new federation, there was so much talk about national unity. However, national unity and disarmament of combatants did not cover the BOFF child soldiers. Then, child soldiers were regarded as nonpersons. There was no specific program designed to reintegrate us into the Nigerian society. Furthermore, not all of us could be identified. Therefore, we fizzled out of the country's mind such that today, when one talks of Nigerian national security, people do not remember Biafra. Yet the question of Biafra's right to self-determination remains a major problem to Nigeria and the global community.

In the current dangerous times created by jihadists, Biafran nationalists believe that justice denied is justice delayed.

27

JUSTICE

A NATION WITHOUT justice is a lawless socciety.

In the twenty-first century, atrocities and injustices against children have not received enough national and local attention despite the current global campaign of the United Nations. National governments and communities do not know how to address past human rights abuses that will lead toward a more peaceful and more democratic future. If national governments and international organizations can spend billions of dollars in conducting destructive warfare annually, then prudence demands that world governments should invest more in conflict prevention through citizen diplomacy, peace campaigns, and by establishing transitional justice commissions in postconflict societies worldwide.

Four decades after, we still bear the emotional and physical scars of our unhealed past. After almost three years of war, the end came unexpectedly. General Philip Effiong had surrendered to the Nigerian military government in Lagos. When the fighting ended, it was left with the victorious military government to decide how to deal with the injustices of the past.

Regrettably, today, jihadism is thriving in human rights violations because Nigeria has neither the political culture of punishing perpetrators in order to deter future human rights abuses nor the culture of truth telling in order to reconcile a divided society. The failure of the many transitional governments to deal with historical injustices or to reckon with the socioeconomic and political wrongdoings of the past are the root causes of the current jihad war against the federal government of Nigeria. Without the resolution of the Biafran self-government issue, there will be no peace and security in Africa's most powerful and most populous nation-state. The longer the delay in *recognizing* Biafra as an independent sovereign state, the more costly it would be in human and material resources to Nigeria and the global community.

The good news is that Biafran military leaders led by General Effiong were not executed by General Gowon after their surrender. Otherwise, the Biafran Organization of Freedom Fighters under my command were prepared to wage underground guerrilla warfare against the illegitimate military government. If General Ojukwu or General Effiong of Biafra had been executed for secession by the Nigerian military regime, BOFF would have launched a subterranean guerrilla war throughout Nigeria.

I believe that the Nigerian military leader, General Yakubu Gowon, was a good man. But Gowon's "no victor, no vanquished" amnesty rigged us, the victims of our rights to justice, for the human rights abuses we suffered in the hands of the Muslim soldiers. "Gowon's amnesty" was a fraudulent transitional justice gesture which completely erased the future of Biafra as a sovereign nation-state, recognized under international law despite its defeat in battle. The truth is that Nigeria conquered Biafra and forced the new nation to rejoin the federation. Another truth is that Biafra, having been recognized formerly and informally by certain countries, had automatically become, under international law, a recognized country with a *recognized* government, population, geographical area, and power to enter into treaty relations with other nations. And since recognition is a political act which does not expire, therefore, Biafra remains a sovereign nation despite its captivity status in Nigeria. Political *recognition* does not expire, fade, or vanish with the force of the victor's gun.

What Ndigbo seek in their political life are freedom, justice, peace, happiness, and a just society. Because of the above moral values, Igbo people constantly evaluate how power is used or abused in their society. The result of such examination leads us to know how healthy our political system is at any given period. For example, we collect data to help us understand how our society can be classified on the important issues of poverty, crime, peace, security, maintenance of the rule of law and order, inequality and freedom, hence the need for prudent judgment and political wisdom, which only the wise leader can give.

In a multicultural society like Nigeria, how can society and state reconcile the clash between freedom and power? The Biafra–Nigeria war was a failure of political leadership to reconcile the dispute between power and freedom. The war represented the climax of the failure of leadership and wrong political choices. An unskilled and unwise leadership cannot make wise political choices. Mediocre leadership lacks the capacity to strive for political breakthroughs in political, economic, or moral issues. Biafra bears the burden of freedom today due to colonial economic interests in Nigeria. But in the twenty-first century, the idea that might is right is globally unacceptable.

After the war, my master, Chief Joseph Irukwu, employed me as an insurance claims clerk with the Unity Life and Fire Insurance Company located at Nnamdi Azikiwe Street, Tinubu Square, Lagos. After three years since the end of war, I could not get admission into any Nigerian university. I was not good enough to seek admission because, under the post-British educational system which Nigeria operated, my London City and Guilds Diploma in oxy-acetylene and electric-arc welding is nothing but an artisan certificate which is unacceptable to any local or national university for admission purposes. I ignorantly continued to pay and take numerous national examinations without success. However, I remained hopeful that one day I would get admission.

After seven years, I decided to do self-study since I did not attend any secondary school. I enrolled in the Rapid Results correspondence college and eventually passed four subjects (GED) with honors. This was good news indeed. However, I failed in mathematics, without which I could not be admitted to any Nigerian university.

Vincent Magbo was my greatest mentor at the Unity Life and Fire Insurance Company Limited. He was Chief Irukwu's secretary. One day, Magbo asked me, "What are your plans for the future? Whatever are your plans, I want you to consider this: Insurance is an international business and you are an insurance man married to an international wife. Therefore, I see your destiny as an international person. A new insurance college jointly established by the United Nations and the Anglophone countries of West Africa is opening soon in Monrovia, Liberia. Why don't you apply? Your master, Chief Irukwu, is in charge of establishing and recruiting pioneer students for the college. Discuss it with him." Vincent Magbo had no idea how scared I was of my master.

It took courage for a former houseboy, who still lived with his master to open up discussion concerning his future insurance education. As time drew nearer, I did the unthinkable and braced up for a negative outcome. However, I was shocked when my master asked, "Really? You're interested in enrolling at the new insurance college in Liberia? Very good, then give your name to my secretary at the NigeriaRe office to add to the list of prospective students."

After nine months, I graduated from the West African Insurance Institute, College of Insurance and Risk Management. Subsequently, the University of Nebraska offered me admission to study Business Administration. I was emotionally charged as I celebrated my long anticipated dream of traveling to the United States for a university education, but the dream faded away just as it came—no funds. One day, as I accompanied Melody, my fiancé, to the University of Liberia's main campus to check her results, I perused virtually every news item on the bulletin boards, curious to see if there were any new opportunities for me. I intentionally married Melody in order to set a target for myself. Since she was already a freshman at the University of Liberia, I was motivated and challenged to obtain a university education too so that I did not become inferior in the eyes of our future children.

In 1987, I graduated with a bachelor's degree (Cum Laude) in political science. The University of Liberia's Continued Education Department gave me a provisional admission to do remedial mathematics before carrying a full academic load. This is an opportunity Nigeria did not give me. Liberia, therefore, held the key to my future, without which I would probably never have fulfilled my childhood dream of obtaining a university education.

While continuing my adult education studies, I worked at Intrusco, an American property and casualty insurance company, for two years, before I established the Liberty Insurance Brokers. Later, I upgraded the insurance brokerage agency to a full-fledged insurance company, known as Liberty Life and General Insurance Company.

In 1990, the *Daily Observer* newspaper published a list of prominent citizens and residents marked to be killed by the Charles Taylor-led rebels in Liberia. My name was on the list. I fled to Freetown in Sierra Leone, leaving my six-year-old daughter and wife behind. Leaving my family behind was learning how to live like a bachelor again. Life without my wife and my little daughter was empty and lonesome. It was almost imposible to think of a future without them. Any wonder, I gradually drifted away and became tuffiarable (worthless), drunkard. Liqour almost ruined my life since it became impossible to quit drinking and smoking. Later in life, I would regrettably hear from my personal physicians that my past life of drinking and smoking are partly responsible for most of my health problems currently. The conflict in Liberia continued to get worse. After a few months with my friend, Solomon Samba, in Freetown, I left for Nigeria. For the second time, I had survived war and death.

Back at home, I contested an election for the position of Mayor of Ezza Local Government but I was rigged out. A few years after, I ran for the Ebonyi Central Senate seat and won the primary election under the United Nigeria Congress Party, UNCP. My friend, Pius Anyim, who also contested the senate seat for the Ebonyi South constituency, gave me 20,000 Naira when my campaign ran out of funds. Anyim has since become president of the senate and secretary to the federal government of Nigeria. However, the military leader of Nigeria, Gen. Sanni Abacha, suddenly dropped and died in office. All elections were cancelled and I became jobless, but the Secretary to the Government of Enugu State, Dr. Icha Ituma and Dr. Ozo Nweke Ozo, offered me the position of political editor of *Daily Star Newspaper* at Enugu.

The turning moment for me as political editor was the article I wrote on the "Abakaliki-Enugu Road Closure." The military administrators in charge of the barracks along the road suddenly erected tall walls across the federal road, thereby permanently disrupting all traffic flowing to the Enugu airport and Abakaliki, Ogoja, and Cross River States. The public, economy, school children and business people suffered. I simply wrote asking the military leaders, "Which existed first, the Abakpa military barracks or the Abakaliki-Enugu road?" Since the road had been in existence since the colonial period, the barracks must fold up and move to the top of the Milkin Hill where no civilian dared to trespass.

When I wrote and published the critical article condemning the forced closure of the road, the military sent a team of soldiers to arrest me. I was driving out when the angry soldiers stormed the *Daily Star Newspaper* offices looking for me. After a few days, I was ambushed by the soldiers who ran over me with their military jeep. I was soaked in blood as the skin near my right eye was peeled off my face. I received many stitches in the emergency clinic where a good Igbo man took me along with the second victim, my friend and fellow radical journalist, Thomas Achi Nwakoko, who totally supported my position on the "Abakpagate" issue.

Not long, Rev. Father Evans Nwamadi of the Catholic Dioceses of Enugu offered me a job to "come and serve God." Under Bishop Eneje, I became the Founding Editor of the *Flame Newspaper*. Although I was paid less than my salary at *Daily Star* by the director, Fr. Evans, I stayed on the job in order to serve Chineke, the merciful God who had saved me in all the wars that life had placed on my earthly journey.

As Father Evans got ready to pursue his doctoral studies in the US, I left to take up an appointment with the Institute of Management and Technology, IMT, as an insurance lecturer. A few months later, Mr. Enweruzor went on leave. As the Acting Head of Department, I wrote the first African textbook on insurance in the college, *Foundation Study in Insurance*. The book was remarkably promoted by the IMT rector, Prof. Njeze.

The separation between my six-year-old daughter, my wife, and I began to take a toll. They had gotten asylum in the US while the embassy denied me a visiting visa to reunite with them until after eight years. I became a drunkard and smoked cigarettes helplessly. After my botched UNCP senate attempt, I started the healing process by enrolling in the first-class institution, University of Nigeria, Nsukka, UNN, which had denied me admission during my youthful years. After two years, I graduated and became a Lion, with a master's degree in International Relations. Dreams do fulfill.

After eight years, my wife Melody applied for an asylum for me and on March 13, 1999, I recorded the greatest family moment of my life when the former six-year-old, my only child, Aliuwa, Melody, and I melted into each other at the JFK airport, New York, in tight hugs, fearing to let go. This reunion was a *turning moment* in our lives.

28

EBONYI

A CONTINUUM OF THE BIAFRAN DREAM

IN THE POSTCONFLICT period, we made the transition from being known as Biafrans to Nigerians. Although the war was over, another freedom war resurfaced. The long-marginalized Abakaliki people decided to fight for the creation of a new Ebonyi State in Nigeria. As wawa Igbo, we had been politically dispossessed and excluded for too long. Dr. Offia Nwali, the Harvard-educated senator representing Abakaliki, Congressmen Alo Nwokocha, Andrew Nwankwo, and Hon. Innocent Ugota were the champions and original founding fathers of the Ebonyi State Movement. They introduced the "Ebonyi State" Bill in the Senate and the House of Representatives when they resided at the famous 1004, Victoria Island, Lagos.

First, I was briefed by Hon. Andrew Nwankwo about the campaign to create Ebonyi state. He explained that Abakaliki was the only old colonial province in Nigeria which had not been recognized as a state. In Lagos, Andrew took me to see Senator Offia Nwali, the charismatic, American-educated doctor and politician who urged me to take up the youth leadership of the Ebonyi freedom campaign. I subsequently held several meetings with Offia, Andrew, Alo, and Ugota on the strategic framework of action in our new fight for state freedom. However, there was a problem.

While the initial "Ebonyi State" campaign car stickers were so many, most Abakaliki indigenes did not own cars except the congressmen named above. I discussed the new Ebonyi agenda with my two closest friends, Sylvester Iboko (aka Sly) and Kingsley Edogu (aka Best Endas). The three of us became the founding youth leaders of the national movement on Ebonyi state creation in the federal capital city, Lagos. Since the long dispossessed Abakaliki people did not own cars, we decided to instruct our men to peel and paste the stickers on their room doors and briefcases in creating awareness for the new political campaign.

The creation of Ebonyi state would allow us as defeated Biafran people to govern ourselves on state and local government levels. We would then qualify to get monthly federal funds for wages, salaries, and development like other states. Throughout Lagos, and in our villages, we campaigned for our second freedom after Biafra's defeat. My childhood friends were all involved in the freedom movement we brought home from Lagos.

MY FRIENDS

Francis Nworie Nwoke, aka Darby, was the only friend who knew I was *intelligent*. One day he said to me, "Do you know many Ezza people think you're just an arrogant youth who grows Jackson 5's hairdo? They have no idea you're an honor student. People always judge you by your appearance most times." I wanted to be as smart as Darby in mathematics, science, and social studies, but could not. He graduated from St. Enda's Secondary school with distinction in all his "school cert" subjects. As a statistician and educator, his death has left a vacuum in Ezza and Ebonyi state. His death remains unsolved till today. Darby was a warrior in the campaign for Ebonyi freedom.

Rexy taught me compassion and how to be happy in the face of adversity. When his senior brother, Ezeugwu, mistakenly dismantled a foreign metal ball, it erupted like a volcano and shattered his eyes, rendering him totally blind. Rexy lamented but remained strong and caring after the grenade incident. When I filed my papers to run for the mayor (chairmanship) of Ezza South Local government, Rexy withdrew his application and gave me his support. The first gun I used as a BOFF commander was given to me by Rexy. Part of me died with "Boy Rex," my most humble and deeply caring friend. Each time I see Morgan, Sooky, Kathy, and his other children, I recollect the fond memory of the moments I shared with *Rexy nwokorom*. Rexy died fighting for Ebonyi freedom.

Paulinus Oru (*Nwokorom*) was a big brother and friend. Whatever I lacked as a village lad, like bicycle, money, companion, and social life, were given to me by him. He gave me his junior sister, Nwuguru, to marry, but I was not ready, so my uncle John aka Abamenda married her. Yet my friendship with Nwokorom endured until he died at a very early age. Last year, Camillus, his junior brother, died. Recently, Samuel, the last child of Paully's mother, died. I have pledged to care for Nwokorom's mother as long as life endures. Life is a series of turning moments.

Marcel Nwichita Nwokporo taught me many lessons as a surrogate senior brother and best friend. After the war, Marcel took me to live with him at Nkalagu Cement Factory. He taught me discipline and freedom to do what I liked that was not unlawful. None of us, his boys, could smoke in his car without him kicking out the offender. Later, he provided me shelter with my family as a returnee and survivor of the Liberian Civil War. A few years ago, he became the Mayor of Ezza South local government. Later, Hon. Nwokporo was elected as a member of the State House of Assembly. This radical warrior remains my best surviving Ezza brother and friend.

A memorable moment occurred during Nwichita's marriage to Rose Nwankwo. While Hon. Andrew Nwankwo endorsed the union, Chris Nwankwo, the senior brother, was "silently" opposed to the idea and refused to even grant us audience. Since Chris did not wish to set his eyes on either Marcel or Rose, I became the Nwokporo family's peace ambassador. At the eve of the wedding, my two long trips to the Nwankwo's village home at Izzi yielded no success. However, with our characteristic Ezza stubbornness, we dared and married Rose, not minding the consequences. Love conquers prejudice. The marriage has been a blessing despite its manifest challenges. Marcel, the politician, loves reading, politics, and friends. He is a radical advocate for freedom, justice, and community peace building.

My friend, Alphonsus Ibeogu (aka Pontius), was a radical lawyer. He named his law firm Inweronye Law Chambers. As a fellow Ebonyi inweronye advocate, I have attempted to develop further the political theory of the subaltern society to honor Pontius. I campaigned for him and we discussed among others the conceptual agenda for the new Ebonyi state: small government, great society with first class political institutions, roads, services, and social welfare for the long-neglected Abakaliki and Ebonyi people. Any future leadership of our people which does not remember the history of our long-suffering people must not lead. Kidnapping, corruption, and violence were not part of our strategic agenda for the new Ebonyi State which we fought so hard to establish.

My outspoken friend and critic of military despotism was silenced a few years ago in a fatal plot, leaving his wife and children without husband and fatherless. Pontius's death reminded me of how the military attempted to assassinate me at *Daily Star* for challenging the closure of the Abakaliki-Enugu Road. One way or the other, the victor nation had become too dangerous for inweronye or human rights advocates like us.

Akam Alo, like the rest of my friends, was also known as an Abakaliki radical. In reality, we were not troublemakers. Rather, we were Inweronye advocates fighting for the long-silenced, long-forgotten citizens of Ebonyi State. During our informal discussions after the creation of Ebonyi State, Alo, Ibeogu, Iboko, Edogu, Nwokporo, Unigwe, Rexy, John Williams, Darby, and I developed a forward-looking strategic agenda for the newly created Ebonyi State. Our objective was to apply the principles of the Biafran Revolution (Ahiara Declaration) to the new state:

1. A small government in Ebonyi State in order to save funds for development.

2. High quality ring roads connecting all the local governments in Ebonyi State.

3. Investing in Inweronye welfare and education.

4. Severe punishment for corruption and fraud in Civil Service.

5. Ending crime and violence in Ebonyi State.

6. Transformational leadership with vision, justice, and an action agenda.

7. Our collective resolve was that "our populist agenda affirms that any democratically elected politician can govern in Ebonyi State provided that such leader adheres to the above principles of our freedom agenda. Like in northern Nigeria, our road contracts must be awarded to experts who would be supervised by Ebonyi civil engineers to ensure that *Ebonyi standard* is maintained and assured." I am not sure that Ebonyi State's past governments and politicians are aware of our youth freedom manifesto.

Paul Unigwe, tall and handsome, was another friend and fellow radical warrior. An aspiring politician, he was murdered in a remote hotel near Abakaliki urban city. Paul was less than thirty years when he was assassinated. During his funeral, Ezza youth surged forward in warrior mood chanting and mourning in readiness to avenge his death. Like the rest of the Abakaliki

Troublemakers, as we were sometimes tagged, Paul was audacious and fearless.

Ike Anaga, with a PhD in music, was invited by the state government to return from Norway to assume the CEO position of the Enugu State TV station. However, sectional politics derailed his chances and he sat in socioeconomic limbo for a long time. In adversity, I empathized and developed a strong bond with Shagasha. Dr. Anaga depended on me to develop his management strategy when he was finally appointed the CEO of the *Daily Star*. But Shagasha, as we fondly called him, had internal opposition from the past leadership and was found one day dead in his hotel room. His brother was with him that fateful night. Rumor has it Shagasha was poisoned. "There goes another fellow warrior, another Abakaliki radical, another freedom fighter," I cried.

Nnachi Enwo Igariwey and I are still best friends. He was my best teenage friend. When he got admission into the University of Nigeria, he advised me to ensure I obtained a university education. Otherwise there could be a crack in our friendship. After about twenty years he was surprised to see me at Abakaliki when I returned from the USA. Garry said, "Ewa, so I can call you a doctor?" I said, "Sure you can." Then he asked again, "So I can also call you a professor, and I said, "Sure Nwokorom, why are you so surprised? Recall you advised me to go to school?" Garry said, "Yes, indeed, to obtain a degree like myself. I never asked you to go for a PhD then."

Nnachi Enwo Igariwey

Kingsley Ike Edeogu, aka Best Endas, was appointed Director of Ebonyi State Sanitation Agency but after a brief illness, he died. We were best friends. He was a member of BOFF whose records of war were quite different from mine. We were very close and did many social activities together at Lagos with Sly. Every Friday was our birthday since we did not know our exact birth dates. Our parents did not know how to read and write, therefore, they did not keep our birth dates. Best Endas and I played hard and enjoyed our freedom. My friend had a tough attitude about life. When he was dying, he had told a close friend that only me has an idea of what killed him. And I surely do but will not disclose it.

Sylvester Iboko remains my closest surviving childhood friend who campaigned for the creation of Ebonyi state. He lives at Abakaliki with his caring wife and children. Life and war have taught Sly to turn to Jesus for redemption. Ebonyi political leaders have not recognized the pioneering campaigns which I ignited with Best and Sly for the emancipation of our long-silenced Ebonyi people. On October 1, 1986, when General Sanni Abacha created Ebonyi state, Sly reminded me of the five cartons of Gulder beer I bought for the Abakaliki members of the House of Representatives at their Mile Two, Lagos, residence then. Sly, Best, and I got drunk while celebrating the creation of Ebonyi State of which the three of us were the youth civil rights pioneers in Lagos and at home in Abakaliki. But, as the saying goes, "the gun that liberates shall not rule."

After the war, Bassey Ekpenyong taught me lessons in public relations and to see that kindness to others has rich rewards. He taught me the art of friendship, excellence in service, and good work ethics. "Oye, my man" is unforgettable. I am convinced he was born to be great in life.

Chiemela Ndubisi and I took a Liberian girl to the Reflections and Hibiscus night clubs in Monrovia for the very first time. Six months later, Bassey and Chiemela and John Osaje bore witness as I slid my engagement ring on "Slim's" finger. Melody, aka Slim, aka Lady, and I have remained married for over thirty-three years now.

In reflecting on the agony of defeat in war, we see in the Biafran example, both triumphant freedom and the failure of freedom. In our captive Nigerian federation, our friends and family members have continued to die in the hands of the Muslim jihadists. As compared to other major ethnic nations, our federal employment statistics pale in comparison to others. Because of this insecurity which has lasted for nearly five decades, most Biafran nationalists have naturalized in the United States and Europe, preferring alien citizenship to that of a country where the Christian is not allowed to marry a Muslim, where the Christian is automatically tagged an infidel, where Islamic fundamentalism has established a permanent state of terror and bloodbath against innocent civilians.

On the contrary, Biafra's fight for freedom has led the federal government of Nigeria to create more states in order to weaken the Igbo and Biafran political base and power to secede or to seek any further right to self-determination. When I looked into the closed eyes of my dead friends and radical Biafran freedom fighters, I saw what the Nigerian authoritarian regime did not want the world to see or to hear—*the truth*. The truth is that Biafra does not wish to conquer or to rule Nigeria. The truth is that Biafrans were forced out of Nigeria. The truth is that the crimes against humanity committed by Nigerian soldiers have not been punished. The truth is that Biafra is still a legally recognized nation-state conquered and forced to "reunite" with the over three hundred other ethnic nations that make up the colonial political creature called Nigeria.

29

AMERICA

WHAT LIFE HAS taught me.

America, the great land of freedom, magic, and wonderland of my childhood dreams, has been good to me. First, the Bill Clinton government granted me asylum when my name showed up among the list of people to be killed in Liberia by Charles Taylor's National Patriotic Front.

Second, at JFK airport, I received my permanent resident permit, social security number, and the legal status to work in America and enjoy most privileges reserved for the citizens of the United States. But getting a job in Philadelphia was as difficult as climbing Mount Kilimanjaro. In January 2000, I decided to plunge into the uncharted waters of the doctoral studies at Howard University, Washington, DC.

Coming from a postcolonial nation of Nigeria with a British educational background, I felt like a fish out of water in the American academic system. I recall my first writing assignment and the failing grade I made under Professor Maye King, an

African American political scientist and Africanist. She simply remarked on my paper, "I do not think you are prepared for graduate studies at Howard. You wrote without any theoretical or ideological framework." I got it. If I am good in theories, doctrines, and ideologies today, it is partly because I received the baptism of fire from this radical female scholar, Dr. King.

After five hectic but rewarding years of reading, writing, testing, and research work, the prestigious Howard University that produced Nigeria's first president, Nnamdi Azikiwe, Thurgood Marshall, Ralph Bunche, and Montana L. Morton awarded me its highest degree, a PhD in political science with majors in international relations and comparative politics and Africa as my regional study concentration. To be known as a "Bison" is one of the greatest honors an *inweronye* (subaltern) scholar can receive.

In 2005, Prof. Levi Nwachuku created another *turning moment* in my American journey when he offered me an adjunct faculty position in Lincoln University at Oxford, Pennsylvania. Teaching at Lincoln is unique because Dr. Nnamdi Azikiwe, a fellow Igbo and great nationalist, who pioneered the fight for independent Nigeria, attended both Howard and Lincoln and lectured in the latter. However, my Lincoln journey was very brief. After two semesters, Cheney University, Ohio State University, and Kansas City Kansas Community College made job offers to me. However, I chose KCKCC, a junior college, where my life's story could inspire and motivate my students to dare to dream.

At Kansas City, I have learned many lessons from many people: Prof. Chieke Ihejirika, Prof. Henry Louis, Karen (my sis), Gene Hernandez, Dr. Ugo Mgbike, Mike Ofokansi, Prof. Melanie Jackson-Scott, Professors John Ryan, Charles Reitz, Chuck Wilson, Mehdi Shariati, Brian Bode, Barbara Clark-Evans, Karalin Alsdurf, AHSS colleagues, KCKCC friends, and the Igbo community in Kansas.

30

AFRICA

TELLING AN AUTHENTIC African story matters to Igbo people. The primary causes of the anger, hate, terror, and violence we face today are rooted in the difficulty of imagining other people who are different from our religion, race, ethnicity, tribe, gender, ideology, culture, country, and continent. For example, listen to Evelyne Gacii, my former political science student in Kansas, USA, bare her mind on our ignorance about Africa:

> Why are we so ignorant about Africa?
> Do you wear clothes back home?
> Do you have lions and tigers in your backyard?
> Did you just learn how to speak in English?
> These are some of the questions posed to people from the great continent of Africa, the origin of mankind, by Americans or other people from the so called *First World*. To me, this is the greatest level of ignorance. Who in the twenty-first century asks these things? I think it is not only disrespectful to ask someone such questions, but also insulting.

"I was born and raised in Kenya," says Evelyne. "I tell that to some Americans and they get puzzled or wait for me to elaborate because they have never heard of such a place. What a pity! Their next reaction is [that of] great sympathy for me written all over their faces. I can almost read what is going through their minds; maybe trying to picture me in one of the poor slums as seen on the television, hoping I can even understand what they are saying to me, since they think I probably do not know how to speak English. [Next on their minds] is trying to help me and my poor family in Africa. The list is endless, as if it is the worst place on Earth to be born in, as if it is a place which is unfit for human existence.

Who is to blame for all these false beliefs about Africa? I would say the media, missionary misrepresentations, and mis-educated European theorists.

Every country has both good culture and bad culture. There are very nice places to live in the United States, and there are some places one would not give a second look. There are hungry children in America just as there are hungry children in Africa. I am not saying that what is on TV is a lie, I am just saying as much as our continent is less developed, as much as there is escalating poverty in Africa, not everything is bad about Africa. We have way too many good things to offer.

Africa is as good as any other place in the world if not better. I really thank God that I wasn't born anywhere else. I am so proud of my country and my continent because I know we have so much potential and a lot of good things to offer such as great people, great culture, and breathtaking tourist attraction sites just to mention a few.

I challenge people to open up their minds and learn more about Africa as a whole because it matters. Americans should tour some parts of Africa and when they come back, they will have a totally different view of the continent of Africa, the original home of humanity. It will really be worth their time and money!

Ewa's Note: Evelyne Gacii was a political science student and my mentee at KCKCC. Ignorance misleads, robs us of our dignity and makes us look like fools. Beware of the danger of imagining Africa and "others' who are different from us.

31

RECLAIMING THE BIAFRAN DREAM

BIAFRA IS A symbol of our long-lost and original freedom which colonialism took away. The spirit of our people's ancient freedom was betrayed again when Nigeria, Britain, Egypt, and Russia recolonized our original nation. The new victor government after the war has also betrayed the promise of our revolution. As child warriors of the Biafran Organization of Freedom Fighters, we dreamed and believed in recreating a great and just society founded in the history of the past. Igbo people believe that the past is the foundation for *nkiruka* (a greater future).

As a child soldier, prince, hawker, houseboy, and political scientist, I believe that the future will be better than the past. However, for this to happen, we must recognize that visionary leadership, wisdom, virtuous lifestyle, and big ideas matter. Ideas are more important than material possession. While bad political ideas have done much evil in the past, for example, colonial dispossession, slavery, and Adolf Hitler's genocide against the Jews, the United States of America was established through a revolution, a good idea (good politics). Can any nation-state declare the US an illegal government today? Why, then, is Biafra not *recognized* by the international community as an independent nation-state?

Historically, a lot of subaltern scholars do go into exile like most Igbo intellectuals today (including me) because of the frustrations of authoritarian politics at home and the danger it poses to any opposition, for example, the many friends I have lost to political killings. It is, at once, amazing and exasperating to note that one of Africa's greatest nations with most intellectual giants "selects" the worst political miscreants for the executive, legislative, and judicial leadership of the country.

A transformational leadership ought to know that when extreme poverty of the many clashes with the extreme wealth of the few, the result becomes an invitation to revolution. Why does the government legitimize stealing the taxpayers' money by "elected" officials and public servants? Most of these politicians and officials have through their actions stolen the citizen's freedom, future, and dignity.

Today, Nigerians have lost their citizen power to terrorism. Fear, politics, and terror have combined to polarize the people. If fundamentalist Muslims continue to kill other citizens who are different, how can peace return to that country? In the conflict between peace and terror, poor and rich, Christianity and Islam, bad leadership is on top controlling and misleading. The ruling class has recolonized the three branches of government; therefore, the reputation of today's politician is down to zero.

The noble virtues, principles, and values of the Biafran dream in the Ahiara Declaration are centered on building the first "great society" in Africa that guarantees durable peace, security, abundance, technology, equality, justice, freedom, and happiness.

In this transitional era of the human spirit, we are experiencing an improved freedom and liberty worldwide, despite few challenges here and there. Political principles are getting better as compared to when English people lived in caves and fought end-less wars. Yet, progress is said to be a gift of the African people to the rest of the world. The advances made by the US, Europe, and Africa demonstrate that man can progress morally.

Progress is linked to freedom and self-determination. Biafran people fight for the common good of all people living in a just and happy society like their ancestors did in Africa before the colonial dispossession which "interrupted" that original freedom.

As an Inweronye freedom advocate, I fight against political exclusion, economic injustice, and human rights abuses on behalf of the subaltern society worldwide. Inweronye, as an Igbo politi-cal ideology, is concerned with the socioeconomic and political conditions of the long-silenced, long-forgotten, and long-dispos-sessed society in which Biafra belongs.

32

HEALTH

My body still bears the scars of my past.

LATE IN 2011, Dr. Sabato Sisillo looked me in the eyes and asked, "Has any other doctor told you you have COPD?"

"What is that?" I inquired.

Chronic obstructive pulmonary disease (COPD) is a lung disease "characterized by chronic obstruction of lung airflow that interferes with normal breathing and is not fully reversible." As one of the last surviving child soldiers of the BOFF, I had earlier been diagnosed with asthma and high cholesterol, among others.

With this new addition, I think, indeed, that my own life is short, hence, the need to record and pass on the story of BOFF and our fight for freedom to a new generation.

In the speech which I gave at the Intercultural Center in 2005, I did not talk about my poor health or about dying. Rather, I spoke about my childhood dreams and *Never Again* in the face of colonial and postcolonial injustices. I argued that, together, we have the power to set the subaltern society free from injustice and prebendal politics.

Abakaliki people, Biafrans, and Igbo people have suffered long dispossession and human rights abuses. Justice to them is an unfinished business. People who dream and hope to build a great future cannot forget their past.

When I am gone, I wish to remind my children and their generation that people who fight for freedom cannot rest until it comes. If the people of the United States, India, Nigeria, and all African nation-states have the right to self-determination, why is Biafra not a functional sovereign nation today even after diplomatic recognition by five countries?

The tale of the child soldier is a sad theme in human morality. However, what distinguishes the Biafran child soldier from the rest is his moral sagacity in protecting and not abducting or killing innocent civilians.

Life is a series of turning moments. In trying to unlock the puzzles on my journey in this lifetime, I want my children to know that I have exceeded my childhood dreams, despite the challenges life has placed on my path.

Radhika Coomaraswanmy, the United Nations undersecretary general and special representative for children and armed conflict asked me to write my memoirs as a child soldier. Radika believed that "the world needs to hear [my] story, especially, now when children are so much abused in many global conflicts."

The continuous abduction and killing of Nigerian children is unacceptable to the moral world. For example, on the night of April 14, 2014, about 230 innocent girls were abducted from their boarding school in Chibok, Borno State, Nigeria, by a group of Islamist militants.

Radhika is right. The world needs to hear the story of a different group of Biafran teenage freedom fighters who were involved in human rights and diplomatic soldiering and not terror, kidnapping, or amputation of limbs. The Biafran Organization of Freedom Fighters is different. Consequently, the post-9/11 world has much to learn from the BOFF humanitarian model. Transitional justice has been recognized as an important moral tool in helping postconflict societies deal with the issues of reconciliation, rehabilitation, reconstruction, and national recovery globally.

33

GLOBAL SECURITY

FROM A CHILD soldier's experience, I feel there are five major new global security challenges facing humanity in the twenty-first century:

1. Political exclusion
2. Lawlessness
3. Terror
4. Violence
5. Danger of imagining "others"

Both Rama Mani, an expert in global security and post-conflict societies, and I share almost similar views about the new global threats to humanity.

POLITICAL EXCLUSION

When a society suffers from political exclusion, the result, most times, is *inequality* and *poverty*. In an excluded society, there is usually a collective feeling of political, economic, religious, and judicial injustice against the excluded citizens. Such a society gradually becomes a breeding ground for recruiting poor children as jihadists.

LAWLESSNESS

When people have been long exploited and their civil rights abused without respect for international law, when sanctions are broken and governments use illegal means to bypass the law, when the three branches of government are corrupt, stealing public funds and resources with impunity, then, such an exploited society becomes a breeding ground for recruiting poor children for suicidal attacks. Their limbs and lives are the limbs and lives of nobody.

In most societies, the worst cases of lawlessness, for example, corruption, come from politicians, corporate executives, and civil servants who loot the taxpayers' money for personal use. These people are "pen robbers." Political corruption and corporate fraud are more deadly than the militants or street criminals that the mass media show us on national television.

The United Nations and human rights advocates ought to make new laws to ensure that politicians and jihadists are not committing human rights abuses against citizens and especially children.

When the military governor of Enugu State was looking for five honest citizens to constitute a committee to probe financial fraud in the State's Department of Finance, the Secretary to Government Dr. Itcha Ituma and Dr. Ozo Nweke Ozo nominated me as the most honest person to represent the Abakaliki people in the fraud committee. I subsequently served as the secretary to the panel and custodian of the committee's records and under the protection of one policeman until the panel completed its work.

Therefore, if I die today, my greatest regret is that I did not have the chance to show transformational leadership to my long-muted, long-dispossessed, and long-forgotten Abakaliki, Ebonyi, and my original ethnic nation of Biafra.

When I die, let the society know that I was not a perfect person. I made mistakes in life. But let society also know that I abhorred any form of injustice, corruption, and human rights abuses.

When I die, let my children and family inscribe this on my head epitaph: "Mkparawa." Let *Eluwa* (the world) remember me as the freedom fighter who was committed to freedom, kamenu, and peace in the cause of the Inweronye's right to dignity and happiness.

This postconflict world urgently needs to establish an Ethnic United Nations as a global parliament to resolve past and present injustices that threaten global security, especially the question of self-determination for the Palestinian people, northern Nigerian Muslims, and Biafra. The global minority has a natural right to freedom.

Therefore, let the UN establish a department to advocate for the Rights of the First and Original Peoples of the global ethnic nations.

TERROR

This sense of exclusion and lawlessness provoke the excluded peoples of the world to lose hope in life and to feel that the only option left for them is to break society's laws in order to survive. Inweronye or the subaltern or the excluded person will therefore begin to use violence to gain power since society and corrupt government have blocked all avenues to seek legal or judicial remedy for past injustices.

VIOLENCE

As a former child soldier, I ask the moral world, especially the ethnic nations, to reclaim the dreams of their great past. I warn governments and societies that terror is becoming more widespread now more than ever, due to better access to advanced weaponry in a post-9/11 world that is at once globalizing and polarizing. Since the jihadist militants and nationalist movements have access to better weapons of war and the ability to wage and spread terror, there is a cloudy climate of fear worldwide.

DANGER OF IMAGINING "OTHERS"

The poor children of the world who are most vulnerable are regarded by government and the adult fundamentalists as non-persons. When I was abducted by the Muslim soldiers in Biafra, I was treated as an object, a nonperson. The over-three hundred Nigerian school girls who were kidnapped by Muslim militants since April 2014 are regarded by their captors as the children of nobody. To the perpetrators, the innocent Nigerian school girls are imagined objects. The moral world needs to wake up and reimagine our daughters and sons who bear the burden of adult abuse and exploitation. Together, we can set our children free.

WORKING TOGETHER

Exclusion: Every country, every society, and every visionary leader should ensure that you do not exclude the minority people in your society. If any particular group is politically, economically, or judicially excluded, they would lose power. Next, such minority or majority would attempt to reclaim its lost dignity and freedom. "The thing around our neck" in the twenty-first century, *according to the great storyteller on Biafra, Chimamanda Ngozi Adichie,* is self-government for the ethnic minority. The basic issue is survival. How can the long-marginalized minority survive? There is need to establish an Ethnic United Nation in order to protect the original nations and their peoples.

34

DEPENDABLE MYSTERY

THE SPIRITUAL PERSPECTIVE

On Sunday, April 24, 2011, I watched my friend Rev. Kevin Olsen, deliver his last sermon at the Zion United Church of Christ under the theme "Dependable Mystery." During the sermon, Kevin assured his congregation that "God is still speaking to us." Then I remembered Biafra, the unfinished nation and the invisible hand of God in our struggle for freedom.

THE LAST SERMON

"Where were you the day John F. Kennedy was shot? Where were you when the World Trade Center buildings were attacked? The next question that comes to mind is where was God? Where is God? These are no easy questions, there is *mystery* involved. When healthy young adults die in wars, God is present." Kevin explains.

According to my friend, Kevin, even in the face of doom and death and pain, God is still present in this *dependable mystery*. "We encounter this mystery every day; Zion welcomes 104 people; Haitians continue to pray in spite of the recent earthquake which nearly destroyed their society."

There are no God-forsaken people.

There is no God-forsaken place.

We gathered during JFK's death.

We gathered during the World Trade Center attack.

We gathered during the Biafra-Nigeria War, I thought.

"It is during these dark *moments* that we see God's love. In the face of our personal struggles and tragedies, we remember the mystery–the dependable mystery," says Kevin.

As Kevin spoke, my inner-self silently chanted:

> There are no God-forsaken people.
> The Muslims are not God-forsaken people.
> The Jihadists are not God-forsaken people
> The Christians are not God-forsaken people.
> There is no God-forsaken society on Earth.
> Nigeria is not a God-forsaken place.
> Biafra is not a God-forsaken place.

In my final e-mail to Kevin, I wrote:

"I need your explanation on why Biafra lost a *just war*? "Why are Muslims incessantly committing genocide against Igbo Christians in Nigeria? Why did God allow this to happen?"

Kevin: "Your [questions are] not so easy...my first thought is that often our image of God is based on our human understanding of justice (judicial system...who is right, who is wrong, evil vs. good, etc.) So I'm not sure that's a good starting place. Also I'm not sure God uses force to intervene...and put things right. I think that's what we want God to do...but as I reflect I'm not certain God does this...Jesus didn't?

"I agree that too many oppressed people die at the hands of their unjust oppressors. But I think my sermon reflects where

God is when we suffer and die unjustly and that's all we get. I think God invites us to work for peace and reconciliation (restorative justice as my friend Ewa would say) that's how we and God right our wrongs...in non-violent ways. But, unfortunately it doesn't always happen as we wish. The *dependable mystery* is that no matter what happens...God is with us and for us as we all struggle to become fully human."

Like Southern Sudan and Scotland, Biafra's fierce campaign to leave Nigeria is real and supported by Biafran nationalists at home and abroad. Like Azania and the African National Congress, ANC, only Biafrans will decide on their independence. The long unstoppable beheading of "infidels" and kidnnaping of school girls help the nationalist cause to mobilize citizens for an awakening—a true freedom awakening. It's all about our future and our children. Aghauche, such is the time. Biko Chineke (Dear God), give me another dream.

This one is over!

APPENDIX A

DEPENDABLE MYSTERY

By Rev. Kevin Olsen
April 24, 2011
Matthew 28:1–10

Let us pray…

Has your worldview ever been changed by new discoveries or new insights because of the way you experienced life? In 1493 Christopher Columbus returned to Spain to report the discovery of the New World. In 1929 Edwin P. Hubble came down from the observatory on Mt. Wilson with an astounding message: The universe is expanding; space stretches uniformly in all directions, carrying the galaxies with it. These are discoveries that changed our view of the world and the cosmos.

And then there are those earthquake moments when the ground we stand on shakes us to the core. They are images burned into our minds. A pretty, young, dark haired woman in a pill box hat sits beside her sandy haired, attractive young husband in a convertible. They smile and wave to the crowds of people lining the streets.

Then comes the sound of gun shots, there is chaos and frenzy. There is the young woman clutching her husband who is dying from gunshot wounds.

Where were you the day they told us President Kennedy had been shot?

There is a countdown and a blast off and the space shuttle lifts off the pad, soars into brilliant blue sky. The shuttle climbs and climbs and then . . .an explosion leaves gigantic trails of smoke. Confusion and uncertainty reign. Where is the shuttle? Where are the astronauts? Are they dead or alive? Where were you that day?

It was early in the morning on the west coast; I was in seminary and had just finished breakfast when I turned on my computer to begin another day of research and writing. I couldn't believe my eyes.

"Jan, turn on the television! An airplane has just flown into the World Trade Center tower in New York." We watched in horror as we saw the towers collapse in real time. Where were you that day?

Each time we experience these kinds of tragedies in our nation, or witnessed disasters: earthquakes, tsunamis, floods, volcanic explosions, fires, here and around the world, in the days and weeks that follow, we ask one another, "Where were you when you heard the news?" And so often in the days and weeks that follow, we hear another question asked," Where was God?"

In the face of pain and loss and tragedy, we may well know where we were but we wonder, "Where was God?"

Our question is not unlike Mary Magdalene's who goes to the tomb looking for Jesus. The experiences of the last several days were difficult for Mary. She watched as her teacher, friend, and Lord was arrested, crucified, and buried.

She watched as all his disciples deserted him, as he suffered and bled and died. Although she can recall the details, the last several days seem like a bad dream, a nightmare. Now she comes to the tomb, sad and grieving.

She asks our question, "Where is God?"

In the midst of tragedy, we ask with Mary, "Where is God?"

The answer to that question is not an easy one.

There is mystery involved and yet it seems we need the mystery to believe that even in the face of terrible loss, God is present. We need the mystery to know for certain that there are no God forsaken places...or God forsaken people.

When a country mourns the death of a leader, when healthy young adults are lost in a tragic accident, when our children die through senseless violence, when unimaginable death and destruction prevail, we need to know God is present.

It is not something we can easily explain. There is no spreadsheet or blueprint or computer program to explain the mystery. But we know by following Jesus there are no God forsaken places...there are no God forsaken people. This is dependable mystery.

The two Marys find the answer to their question. In an earthquake moment the Marys get a glimpse into the end of the age, God's eternal future, is revealed and the risen Christ meets them and says Greetings!"

Yes, Mary discovers the answer to her question.

She finds that even the tomb is not a God forsaken place. She touches and sees and hears that God is present, even here, in the face of pain and death, God is present. This is dependable mystery.

God's presence in the face of death is mystery, but a mystery that we can trust. Jesus reveals the presence of God at work in the world, healing, loving, forgiving, feeding, reconciling drawing us into God's holy love. In Christ there are no God forsaken places...no God forsaken people.

I encounter this mystery every day in my work as parish pastor. It is a mystery to me why a small German congregation in Kansas City, Kansas has welcomed 140 Micronesian people into their space and hearts, sharing God's love by providing them a place to worship. Where God is…there is hospitality and love.

It is a mystery to me why, the people of Haiti in spite of all the odds being against them continue to worship, pray, study, fellowship, and sing their hearts out. And yet it's a dependable mystery. Where God is…there is resurrection hope and love.

God is present in this community of faith. This is no God forsaken place. There is no God forsaken people. There is Holy mystery and love here.

Can we get to the bottom of this mystery?

Can we understand the mystery in even a small way?

The foundation of the mystery of God's presence among us is love. Where there is God, there is selfless love.

In *moments* of sadness, in the midst of our community, there is love…remember how we all gathered following President Kennedy's death. Or how we all gathered in our sanctuaries during that first week following 9/11.

Perhaps the hardest place for us to believe in God's presence among us is when we stand at the graves of our loved ones.

We join Mary in her weeping.

We wonder with her, "Where is God?"

It is often at these darkest moments when God's love becomes most visible to us as Easter resurrection, hope and joy.

Because Mary goes to the tomb, only to discover a risen Christ, we believe that death does not conquer life. As Jesus is raised from the dead, as we are raised from the waters of baptism, so are we raised to new life in Christ Jesus.

Here, the *dependable mystery* and revelation of God's love for us give us hope and Easter joy.

In the face of tragedy, in our community of faith, in our personal struggles in life and in death, there is an answer, a *mysterious* answer to our question, Mary's question, "Where is God?"

In Jesus, in his life, in his death, in his resurrection, God is with us always, present in life, present in death, present in love, present in Easter hope and joy.

There are no God forsaken places. There are no God forsaken people.

APPENDIX B

BIAFRA: THE ORPHAN CHILD OF FREEDOM

(For the Genocide Scholars Annual Conference in Argentina)

Genocide, Justice, Truth, Memory, and Recovery

By Ewa Unoke PhD

Associate Professor of Political Science, Kansas City Kansas Community College, Kansas City, Kansas. Formerly, Biafran Child Soldier and Freedom Fighter, currently, Director, Henry M. Louis Center for Global Transitional Justice and Founder, Students for Global Peace.

INTRODUCTION

The past has refused to lie down quietly and rest in most post-colonial societies. In the current Nigerian federation for example, internal integration has neither fully evolved nor become the dominant characteristic of the post-colonial state. This paper investigates, and analyzes the defunct *Republic of Biafra* as a post-conflict society in political transition from military defeat to forced reintegration with the Nigerian amalgam. The amalgamation of over 250 different ethnic nations into one political union in 1914 by the colonial British Empire has its inherent problems. The forced union sparked off the beginning of an intensive ethnic rivalry and competition for political power and the sharing of national resources. The African post-colonial state has inherited an alien political culture which is not only amoral and oppressive but also violent. Conceptually, the United Nations was established to help in maintaining both internal and international peace and security. However, the UN Security Council's veto power robs the global organization of its liberal attributes and strength. This conceptual dilemma interrupts the genuine collective quest for global peace and security. Due to the demands and challenges of the African and Arab world populist movements, there is need for a new World Order.

The quest for power, justice and happiness is a universal phenomenon. Most societies worldwide desire to live in a just and democratic society. Most people also desire to enjoy peace, prosperity, happiness and not war. However, the waves of African conflicts and the recent Arab world democratic awakening have created new challenges and new threats to world peace, prosperity and security. But, the greatest threat to global peace and security today is neither terror nor tyranny, but *global silence* over unresolved historical and current injustices as the current populist Arab uprisings reveal. For how long, therefore, should freedom and human rights be allowed to perish in the vortex of political realism and its assumptions? As the current uprisings indicate, power politics, in the 21st century can succumb to the moral forces of freedom.

As a former freedom fighter, victim and child soldier in Biafra, I remain optimistic that truth telling, justice, and reconciliation could herald a new beginning in human relations. Biafra fought a three-year-war and surrendered to Nigeria in January, 1970. However, Nigeria is not a foreign occupier like Britain and Belgium. Four decades after the Biafra–Nigeria war, why do peace and justice still elude the multi-national Nigerian state which had enshrined in its national anthem the dictum, "though tongue and tribe may differ, in brotherhood we stand?" Both Western and African Sages have attempted to illuminate what *freedom* and *justice* mean, and through their thoughts, they bequeathed to us a profound heritage to help us reflect on the true meanings and importance of freedom and justice. Akputa Nwunoke an ancient Ezza Sage and Plato, for example, believe that justice is the harmonious ordering of the citizens who live within a particular political community according to their natural endowments and talents. While Akputa argued that justice could be achieved in the political community when wise citizens are allowed to rule, Plato concurred that justice was achievable when city-states were ruled by philosopher-kings who would use their wisdom to do "what is right." Both agreed that intelligence, education and public campaigns could resolve the constant conflict between power and justice.

TRANSITIONAL JUSTICE

We start with a brief definition and the theoretical framework of transitional justice. First, transitional justice refers to how societies, governments and victims deal with the past and present injustices and social wrongdoings. The question of how oppressed people reckon with their unpleasant past is both difficult and perplexing. TJ's central concerns revolve around the themes of healing, catharsis, epuration, human rights, justice, lustration, pardon, punishment, truth telling, reconciliation and national recovery. The theme of transitional justice is relatively a new theoretical framework in both international relations and comparative politics. However, in most indigenous political cultures, the doctrine of transitional justice is usually interwoven with traditional morality.

The primary concerns of the TJ theories rest on post-conflict reconstruction, rehabilitation and reconciliation. Few obvious examples of transitional justice models include; The Nuremberg Trials after Hitler, Nelson Mandela's Truth and Reconciliation Commission of South Africa, TRC, International Criminal Tribunal of Rwanda, ICTR, International Criminal Tribunal of Yugoslavia, ICTY, TRC of Chile, and the CONADEP of Argentina. *disappeared@yendor.com.*

"Formed after democracy was restored in Argentina in 1983, the National Commission on the Disappeared was chartered to investigate the fates of the thousands who disappeared during the junta rule. The commission was to receive depositions and evidence concerning these events, and pass the information to the courts, in those cases where crimes had been committed. The commission's report would not extend, however, to determine responsibility, only to deliver an unbiased chronicle of the events."

The Liberian TRC ran into a serious conflict of interests with the government of Ellen Johnson-Sirleaf because unlike the Argentinian TRC, it went ahead to "determine responsibility," and as such was considered to have delivered a biased "chronicle of events," especially when the TRC recommended that former Liberian politicians including the incumbent president should be banned permanently from active political participation.

But, if transitional justice is a reliable conflict-resolution mechanism for seeking post-conflict justice and forgiveness, what therefore, is the place of transitional justice in the international system? How does TJ focus on the micro level of analysis–within the state. How does TJ focus on the macro level–within the global community? And most importantly, what is the role of TJ in international law?

How do transitional governments deal with the victims of post-conflict societies and oppressive regimes? How do societies and governments deal with past injustices that have refused to lie down quietly and rest? Should criminal perpetrators be pardoned, punished or forgiven and forgotten? If so how? These questions become especially, more important to societies making the transition from dictatorship and monarchy to freedom, for example, Britain and France sometime in history had to execute their absolutist monarchs. What about countries moving from dictatorship to democracy? How did the following societies come to terms with their historical injustices: the Romans against the Jews; Israel vs. Palestinian population; Germany following Nazism; South Africa after Apartheid; Reparations for African Americans; Blood Feud in the Balkans; Democratization in Latin America and East-Central Europe. How do societies, governments and victims deal with blood guilt in political transitions?

Some political scientists and historians argue that society cannot remedy the injustices of history. In indigenous political cultures, religion is rather suggested as an alternative solution, as seen in the doctrine of Kamenu, the natural law of cause and effect or karma. If one sowed the seeds of conflict or injustice, one must be prepared to reap what one has sowed. On the contrary, Western societies believe in both punishment and pardon in dealing with both past and present injustices. However, the ordinary passive citizen can survive authoritarian or military dictatorship through consent or silence. In authoritarian regimes, citizens can get along with despotic regimes by whispering, intrigues, back-stabbing and through corrupt alliances. On the TJ example, one can come to terms with the unhealed past by speaking out against injustice.

This essay investigates and analyzes the effects of an imposed "peace" without justice. Biafra is an example of what happens when a stronger state conquers and re-absorbs a weaker state through the use-of-force. How durable is this type of transitional power politics?

Equally important, is the issue of reverse injustice. As the victims of political, social and economic wrongdoings demand justice, how far can they pursue reparative or restorative justice without creating new zones of injustice against innocent citizens who were not directly involved in such past injustices? Take the case of the African-Americans and the descendants of the Anglo-Americans, or the Israeli-Palestinian conflict, for example. Has the occupation of the West Bank created a historic wrong or true justice? Since every human society has the warrior political culture, transitional justice in the 21st century has become one of the most important tools in post-conflict resolution theory and practice.

A FUNDAMENTAL DUALITY

There are a number of substantive distinctions and dualities that do exist between the western and ethno-African theories and practices of transitional justice.

1. Whereas, the dominant *western* transitional justice model is primarily concerned with, or takes up an orientation towards survival and moral probity;

2. The mkparawa or *ethno-African* transitional justice model does not only encompass survival and moral uprightness, but also includes several community-building features such as the ethos of freedom, purification, an ethic of care, a communal worldview and restorative justice features.

The primary concerns of the post-conflict society include; peace, survival, justice, healing, reconciliation and national recovery. The above indigenous values constitute the building blocks that render the mkparawa, *ethno-African* transitional justice brand more effective and more cathartic in healing the wounds of the past. The cultural differences above also help to explain why the African or traditional model seems more successful than the western model in promoting post-conflict reconciliation. Let us examine three brands of the *ethno-African* or indigenous models of transitional justice; kamenu, *(Nigeria)* ubuntu *(South Africa)* and gacaca *(Rwanda)*. The following narrative on the Rwandan gacaca further explains this phenomenon.

"Kagame didn't rely on outsiders to build his crucial success, which was political reconciliation. He started out by following the standard model in which perpetrators of violence were prosecuted and then jailed," [western model]. "But soon we had 130,000 in jail—and many more [suspects] outside," Kagame said. "The genocide in our country involved a huge percentage of our population, both in terms of those who were killed and those who killed." So Kagame arrived at the idea of using an indigenous system—*gacaca* courts, essentially local village councils where people confessed and were punished but, mostly forgiven and "reintegrated into the communities from which they came…this has led to a unique situation among post-genocide countries…in Rwanda, killers and the relatives of their victims live side by side, in every village in the country and together are rebuilding their future." Fareed Zakaria, "Africa's New Path: Paul Kagame Charts a Way Forward," *Newsweek*, July 27, 2008. Kamenu is another traditional or ethno-African TJ example.

People seek success and happiness through many avenues such as jobs, wealth, fame, hobbies, and religion. Kamenu is both a political theology and an ideology of liberation; a set of ideas and a way of life for the Ezza nation and its puritan-like worldview of society. Kamenu is an ancient doctrine which has been passed on from generation to generation only by word of mouth. It speaks to the cardinal issues of human rights, justice, peace, conflict resolution, and democratic political culture. Kamenu has no founder and no desire to convert people. The kamenuist, rather seeks the ultimate truth of natural justice and happiness through reason. Kamenu is also called *karma.*

Ubuntu simply means interdependence. It is a Zulu people's worldview. It means "I am, because you are, I am nothing without you, and you are nothing without me." Archbishop Desmond Tutu offered this definition: 1999.

A person with Ubuntu is open and available to others, affirming of others, does not feel threatened that others are good, for he or she has a proper self-assurance that comes from knowing that he or she belongs in a greater whole and is diminished when others are humiliated or diminished, when others are tortured or oppressed.

Tutu further explained Ubuntu in 2008: "One of the sayings in our country is Ubuntu–the essence of being human. Ubuntu speaks particularly about the fact that you can't exist as a human being in isolation. It speaks about our interconnectedness. You can't be human all by yourself, and when you have this quality–Ubuntu–you are known for your generosity. We think of ourselves far too frequently as just individuals, separated from one another, whereas you are connected and what you do affects the whole World. When you do well, it spreads out; it is for the whole of humanity."

Given the rich cultural and political values in gacaca, Ubuntu and Kamenu, therefore, I contend that the above sensibilities which are essentially African are superior to their western elements of pardon or punishment. I would also argue that these traditional sensibilities evidence a paradigmatic shift. The traditional model shifts emphasis from survival, morality and other more prosaic concerns to the more substantive issues of liberation, restoration and community vitality. Such a paradigmatic shift requires the utilization of resources not typically available through western academic scholarship. The brief comparative focus on Rwanda, South Africa and Ezza societies allow us to benefit from such TJ comparativist cultures of the ubuntu, gacaca and kamenu doctrinal perspectives. The trio highlight the benefits of the African transitional justice models as compared to the Western perspective which has failed to promote post-conflict healing and reconciliation in Africa or worldwide.

TRUTH TELLING AND A FORGOTTEN GENOCIDE

Truth cannot be suppressed forever. Confessions and Truth telling constitute some of the major characteristics of the African ancestral traditions. Forty-four years ago, Biafra fought a *civil war* with Nigeria and lost. Biafra is sometimes regarded as the world's most forgotten genocide. Today, the name Biafra symbolizes a collective guilt, and shame on the conscience of the world. Fear is real. And peoples' response to such fear is human. The remote and proximate causes of the conflict would soon culminate into the first ethno-religious genocide in West Africa. The conditions and threats which precipitated the war in 1967 still exist today. As Biafra exemplifies, post-conflict societies and governments that ignore the issue of transitional justice have only postponed the conflict until another day. The Biafran story is an epic narrative of a society under recovery in the aftermath of genocide without true justice. Yet, the plight of the Biafran people is not getting much attention in the world media today. As people long-enmeshed in the ashes of a brutal war, their experience shows that *victor's justice* cannot be imposed on the vanquished society for too long. Rather, true justice and true freedom must either be negotiated or adjudicated under the rule of law. But, this was not the case with Biafra.

LESSONS LEARNED

Can the human society learn any lessons from Biafra, (Africa's first and most brutal genocide) in dealing with the new global security challenges of terrorism, populist revolution and post-conflict recovery in the 21st century?

The renewed struggle for the *actualization* of the Biafran nation-state, the oil-rich Niger Delta violence, and rampant kidnappings within the Eastern States (former Biafra) are true indicators to prove that the three pillars of truth, memory, and justice constitute the foundation on which durable peace, reconciliation and national recovery can be anchored. The Biafran story is an unforgettable crime against peace and humanity. And as such, the perpetrators, and the silent moral majority should ask the dead for forgiveness.

PAST INJUSTICES AND TRUTH

"How could they kill children and pregnant women?" Truth telling is an essential TJ mechanism from the African post-conflict worldview. When citizens speak the *truth*, and governments do *justice*, societies will *reconcile*. Western human rights theories and practice, though, well-meaning in purpose, lack the efficacy in helping transitional societies such as Biafra or Nigeria in their fight for freedom and against terrorist attacks respectively. Many examples abound, such as the Arab world and North African Uprisings, the Rwandan, Congolese, Angolan, Liberian, Sierra Leonean, Sudanese and Nigerian conflicts. Between September 18, and 24, 1966, over 30,000 Igbo people were murdered by Muslims in Northern Nigeria. More than 600,000 fled back to their ethnic homelands in Eastern Nigeria; maimed, raped, and defiled. Igbo children, youth, women and men stood up to bear witness, but, the world turned its back and looked away while *Ndigbo* (Igbo people) and other Easterners were murdered by their Muslim neighbors. The victims lamented, "ihe emebiwo," (things have gone wrong). The genocide wiped out millions of innocent Biafran infants, children, women, and men. In the genocidal campaign against Ndigbo, the aggressor believed that starvation was a legitimate instrument of warfare. Therefore, the Federal military government's economic blockade starved the Biafran children to death in their hundreds and thousands. How could a military government institute a deliberate strategic policy to kill innocent children, pregnant women and senior citizens whom it was supposed to protect?

Such was the time. It was a time when being identified as an Igbo person became a death sentence. Up till today, the complete truth about the Biafran genocide has not been told. As former child soldiers, and victims, how can we eat, drink, and sleep well, knowing that Biafran victims and wounded veterans are starving and forgotten without healthcare or shelter? Time after time, those who have the power to stop genocide do not. As former prisoners of war, life has taught us that there are times when society has to use force in order to stop people from committing evil.

Sometimes, we do not choose the battles we fight in life. Sometimes, the battle just comes to us, whether we like it or not. What boggles the mind is the difficulty in understanding why the aggressor nation should be allowed to conquer and rule an innocent, but weaker and vanquished society? Might is not right in international law.

January 15, 2011 marked the 41st anniversary of the end of the Biafra–Nigeria conflict. In 1967, the Nigerian federal military government launched a brutal war against the Eastern region which had seceded on May 30, 1967, and declared its independence as the **Republic of Biafra**. After the 1966 genocide against them, Igbo people no longer felt secured in any other part of Nigeria. For nearly three years of war, Biafra surrendered in January 1970, and got re-assimilated into the Nigerian federation. The focus of this essay, therefore, is on the Biafran perspective of the war which Biafrans call the "Biafra–Nigeria war between two sovereign states," while Nigerians call it the, "Nigerian civil war."

The declaration that the war ended with "No Victor" and "No Vanquished" was a "melodrama" according to Phillip Effiong Jr., for indeed there was a victor and a vanquished people. For example, state creation during the conflict was a masterful act from the military government to divide and rule the Biafran territory. This strategy is triumphant. To further punish the vanquished Biafran society, the Nigerian military leadership refused to promote any Igbo or Eastern Nigerian officers. Rather, Brigadier Njoku was dismissed, while Major Ekanem was killed among others.

Paul Bartrop, Australian-born professor points out that while the Biafran genocide was going on, the United Nations did not heed the humanitarian appeal to save or to recognize Biafra. According to the United Nations, it was an internal matter and the UN does not have the power to intervene in the domestic affairs of member states. "Nobody said genocide was happening in Biafra." The military government's intention was to destroy Igbo people. Forty one years after the massacre, nobody has been punished for war crime violations. Furthermore, no transitional justice mechanism has been put in place for the prevention of future crimes of similar magnitude. The result is the escalation of legitimate and illegitimate freedom and terrorist movements now terrorizing the Nigerian nation and its people. But, Professor Bartrop is not alone in his observations.

Prof. G. N. Uzoigwe also advises Igbo intellectuals to keep the Biafra story alive. "If it is wrong for Ndigbo, (Igbo people) to dominate and rule Nigeria in the past, why is it right for Ndiawusa, (Hausa-Muslims) to dominate and rule Nigeria for four decades?" Furthermore, "if the July 1966 counter coup was a revenge coup against Ndigbo for their January 1966 coup, why did the Muslim soldiers stage another massive massacre and genocide in September 1966 against the same Igbo civilians?" The moral world remembers and condemns the death of 6 million Jews; the disappearances in Argentina; 46 years of Apartheid rule in South Africa; the Rwanda genocide; Yugoslavia, Chile, Sierra-Leone and Liberia; but no international organization, no humanitarian organization, no global media remembers the Biafra–Nigeria genocide which claimed over 3 million lives. Four decades after, the world has continued to turn its back on the Igbo people and their cause in seeking truth and justice and freedom.

Today, the Southeastern states (former Biafra) is under siege. There is fear and uncertainty as waves of kidnapping hold the society by the jugular. It is unthinkable to imagine that in the Southeast, especially, within the Igbo society, people are continuously being abducted and thousands of dollars demanded for their release. In the Niger Delta where the nation's oil wells are located, the militants have continued to take people hostage, and to demand ransom. This criminal act of kidnapping has suddenly become a very lucrative business for the jobless youth. According to the *Daily Sun*, "Today, there is hardly any day that passes without any case of kidnapping in any of the five states of the Southeast, (former Biafra). At the last count, no fewer than 250 people have been kidnapped in Anambra, Imo, Abia, Ebonyi and Enugu states (former Biafra). Also millions of Naira have been paid as ransom to kidnappers..." (Daily Sun: Voice of the Nation, June 12, 2009) www.sunnewsonline.com/webpages/news/nation al/2009/13national-13-06-200... 6/12/2009).

KIDNAPPED VICTIMS

Michael Aguowo and his Liberian wife were abducted by a gang of twenty gunmen the night after their wedding at Nibo in Awka South Local Government Area. The kidnappers demanded $100 million ransom. On November 16, 2008, Dr. Joseph Dimobi was abducted and later released after the payment of $5 million. November 3, 2008, Dr. Tochukwu Mbachu, Chair, Nigerian Medical Association (NMA) was abducted from his hospital. Two Chinese expatriates employed by Innoson Industries Nigeria limited were also abducted.

The latest incident is the kidnapping of the Coordinator of the United Nations Development Programme (UNDP), Uchenna Ani. Why are Igbo people kidnapping fellow Igbo people?

Many oil workers from the United States and Europe are kidnapped almost every month in the Niger Delta Area. It has become quite difficult to separate the criminals from the militants who are fighting for the actualization of the Biafran state. The Biafra–Nigeria conflict therefore, remains a very toxic and an unfinished war of justice, human rights and self-determination. Biafra's independence and recognition by other nations cannot be wished away.

JUSTICE: NO NUREMBURG TRIALS, NO MEDALS

According to Max Soillun, when the war ended, Igbo people expected that their defeat would be followed by "their wholesale massacre." However, the Nigerian military leader, General Yakubu Gowon, "the leader of the victorious Nigerian military refused to proclaim victory;" rather, he "declared a general amnesty for all those who fought against him, and invited members of the defeated side to join his administration. He refused to conduct trials, or execute the defeated..." The Igbos quietly accepted their fate in a "united" Nigeria without any thoughts of sabotage or guerilla warfare.

GENOCIDE, WAR, AND STARVATION

According to Max, all this happened without a United Nations resolution or peacekeeping force, international peace plan and conferences, or the protected negotiations that it usually takes to resolve modern conflicts." What Marx's shallow analysis failed to capture is that, in the aftermath of genocide, Gowon's "no victor, no vanquished" amnesty was a strategic blunder. His blanket pardon means that perpetrators of war crimes and crimes against humanity would never be punished in order to deter future violations. In the aftermath of genocide, peace without justice guarantees neither durable peace nor sustainable security.

In "The Dawn of National Reconciliation," Gomu pays homage to the fallen, and to the heroes who have made the supreme sacrifice that we may be able to build a nation great in justice, fair play and industry. "They will be mourned forever by a grateful nation. There are also the innocent men, women, and children who perished not in battlefield but as a result of the conflict. We also honor their memory. We honor the fallen of both sides of this tragic fratricidal conflict. Let it be our resolution that all those dead should not have died in vain." *Gowon's "The Dawn of National Reconciliation"–a speech to the nation on January 15, 1970. p.3.* "Let the greater nation we shall build be their proud monument forever..."

Forty-one years after the dawn of national reconciliation speech, what progress has Nigeria made towards human rights justice, healing and reconciliation?

First, the so called "guarantee[d]" right of every Nigerian to reside and work wherever he chooses in the Federation," has failed. Since 1970, the killing of Biafrans in the Northern states has never stopped.

Gowon's so called amnesty or national "reconciliation" was a mere interregnum that slowed down the hands of justice. So many military commanders and ordinary ranks who committed atrocious crimes of kidnapping, killing, maiming, raping and defiling innocent children, women and men have not been brought to justice. Forty one years after, no soldier, or civilian has been prosecuted for war crimes. There has also been no form of transitional justice; to speak truth, to do justice or to reconcile or integrate the Biafran society within the Nigerian Federation. For forty one years, past injustices have been swept under the carpet and forgotten. However, the past has refused to lie down quietly and rest.

Today, alarmed at the frequent outbreaks of violence in Northern Nigeria, the United Nations mandated it's Special Advisor on the prevention of genocide, Francis Deng to visit Nigeria in order to ensure the prevention of future occurrences of genocide, especially in the Plateau state.

Indeed, the incessant and callous killings in Plateau State could be said to qualify as genocide, since, in the main, people have been targeted for elimination based on their tribal and religious backgrounds or based on indigence-settler divide. The attacks are carefully planned, and often, professional and murderous militias are retained by one group or the other to ambush and attack their enemies with vulnerable women, children, the old and infirm becoming the primary victims.

The mass-killing in the North, especially, Plateau State is not quite different from the Rwanda, Sierra Leonean and Darfur tragedies. Nigeria does not seem to have learned any lessons from the Biafran conflict. The same Plateau State had become the zone of the worst horror and savagery against Igbo people and Eastern minority groups during the 1966 genocide. In Jos area of Plateau State an Igbo man's head was chopped off with an axe. His stomach was ripped open and his intestines flowing out. Six-foot Onwuamaibe Anyaegbu was travelling by train from Pankshin near Jos (in Plateau state) and met his tragic end at the Oturkpo Railway station in Northern Nigeria where he was beheaded by the Plateau Muslim mob. This scenario summarizes the grief of Eastern Nigeria in 1966. Onwuamaibe was beheaded along with over 30,000 fellow Eastern Nigerian children, women, old people and others. Igbo people in Nigeria cried and cried for freedom, justice, and appealed to the United Nations for intervention and for recognition. But, the UN looked away. The current killings and kidnappings in the Plateau, Northern States and former Biafran territories prove that a deferred injustice is a justice postponed.

Genocide killings against the Igbo people first occurred during the 1952 Kano riots. It re-occurred in July 1966 after the first military coup (January) presumed to have been organized by Igbo officers against Northern and Western leaders. The genocide and near total elimination of all Igbo military officers in July and subsequent massacre of thousands of Igbo civilians in the Northern Region were all regarded as revenge attacks. "It is a pity that the international community kept a blind eye to these genocides in which no one ever got punished for the dastardly wastage of human lives. The Nigerian authorities and the world looked the other way while religious fanatics and ethnic bigots freely attacked people and burnt down places of worship and private and property... [until] it speedily snowballed into the civil war."

The war ended four decades ago, but the religions and ethnic killings have flared up from time to time. Forty four years later, the UN and the global community are still not ready to hear the truth, in order to do justice to the Biafran cause. The UN must be prepared for another Rwanda, another holocaust, another bloodbath if the voices of freedom are forcefully silenced again.

The central theme in the Biafran case study is the necessity for societies emerging from conflict not to ignore the human rights violations on the both sides of conflict. Sometimes, perpetrators are granted blanket amnesty, but, "reconciliation" without justice is an attempt to transform themselves into survivors. For many years after the Biafra–Nigeria war, Igbo survivors who stumbled into long lost friends and relatives greeted each other,"happy survival." While the survivors' human rights had been violated, it becomes an irony for the perpetrators to transform themselves also into "survivors." Their nearly acquired survivors' status, therefore transforms the criminals into becoming victims too. In this scenario, ALL are victims, and as such, nobody will be prosecuted for war crime violations on both the Nigerian and Biafran sides. Yet, certain Biafran officers were executed after the war by the victors.

General Gowon, under military law may not have the right to forgive crimes against the state. But, Gowon has no right to forgive human rights crimes against individual Igbo persons and families. According to Aryeh Neier, criminal prosecutions not only give a voice to the victims, providing an opportunity for public acknowledgement of their suffering, they provide an opportunity to obtain justice, justice not just for the victims themselves but on behalf of the whole humankind.

The lesson which Biafra teaches the world is this: when victims of injustice have suffered long unaddressed repression and political exclusion, then, revenge and the unleashing of the spirit of freedom become unavoidably unstoppable. Sometimes, it is important to heed the warning of Jose Zalaquett that "by merely sounding more righteous, you may end up delivering worse than you started to your people and their nation." Forty one years after the war, Gowon's "no victor, no vanquished" conflict resolution model has violated the Zalaquett principle, as the current kidnappings and killings in Nigeria portray. Perpetrators should be punished for their human rights violations against innocent children during the war. Surviving infants and children witnessed the gross violations, such as the killings of their parents, siblings among other victims. The current Jihadism is reproducing the same crime of genocide that led to Biafra's secession.

Because of their vulnerability, Biafran children were the very first victims of the federal military government's blockade and strategic tactics that, "starvation is a legitimate instrument of warfare." Biafran children were also recruited as child soldiers, while many Igbo women were raped and abducted as sex objects.

Biafra is an unfinished nation. There is need to setup truth commissions in order to tell the truth, to do justice and to reconcile the Biafra–Nigeria society. International criminal courts have documented several war crimes, crimes against humanity and genocide in Liberia, South Africa, Chile, Argentina, Yugoslavia and Rwanda except Biafra. It seems there is no need for accountability for the over 30,000 civilians murdered in a planned mob action in Northern Nigeria in 1966. The question of Biafran self-determination and justice will not go away because there is a covenant between the living and the dead, the past and the future. There is a duty to remember and to continue the struggle in the cause of the heroes who died to give the living their freedom and justice.

Igbo secession was a statement sent loud and clear to the international community that oppression, brutal killings, and unjust wars could no longer be tolerated. The message was heard and understood, but international apathy contributed in the death of over 3 million Biafran children, women and people. When the federalists argue that Biafra would not be able to sustain itself as an independent nation, they miss the point. The central issue which caused the war was the federal military government's sponsored genocide against Igbo people and Eastern minorities. Nigeria's oil wells are located in Biafran territory. Like in Chiapas and Chechnya, the oil which was considered a natural endowment had become a curse to the oil-producing native peoples.

Biafra's self- determination struggle has its roots in Nigeria's inability to understand the fears and hopes of the Easterners. Easterners or Biafrans were fighting a nationalist war of survival. It was the killing of virtually all Igbo military officers in the Nigerian military, (July 1966) and the subsequent mob massacre of over 30,000 Igbo civilians by the Hausa-Fulani Muslims that facilitated the urgent quest for Igbo self-determination. Nigeria was no longer safe for any Igbo person. It was a period when being Igbo was a death sentence in Nigeria. Britain and the USSR provided the arms and weapons with which Nigeria used to nearly exterminate the Igbo people, while the world kept silent without condemning such acts. The national interest of these two countries rested on Nigeria's oil wealth and how they benefited from it. One of the major causes of the war was the British colonial empire's amalgamation of disparate ethnic-nations to create a multinational Nigerian federation. But, Nigeria's over 250 ethnic-nations existed as separate, autonomous political entities with individual self-governments before the British came and for obvious political convenience decided to coercively forge a common federation for all the ethnic nations. One wonders when the illegality of colonial border creation has become a legitimate principle of law. Which one existed first, an ancient autonomous

Igbo nation with its self-governing democratic institutions or the 1914 political creature known as Nigeria? As affirmed by a scholar, "When basic freedoms are infringed upon and millions of lives are infringed upon and millions of lives are at stake, arbitrarily imposed colonial boarders must not be allowed to prevail."

Justice was done, however, when the new Republic of Biafra was recognized by Tanzania, Gabon, Ivory Coast, Haiti and Zambia. Other countries which gave informal recognition through various forms of support to Biafra include, The Vatican City, France, Ireland, Israel, Benin, Portugal, and Red China. While Britain supported Nigeria, the United States remained disturbingly neutral. However, the majority of American public donated and supported the cause of Biafra.

Political pundits believed that Biafra and the Igbo people were hated by the West because of racism. According to them, black people are viewed as subhuman; therefore, they do not have the constitutional rights and privileges of normal human-beings.

Human Rights movement was the response to inequality, oppression, lynching and other injustices that plagued the African Americans since slavery. After nearly a decade of non-violent protests and marches, ranging from the Montgomery boycott to the student-led sit-ins of the 1960's, to the march on Washington D.C. in 1963, basic civil rights were finally guaranteed to blacks. This scenario is an eerie resemblance to the Biafran war experience – long dispossessed and voiceless people who were fighting for justice, civil rights and freedom.

THE US FACTOR

In seeking justification for its actions against Biafra, the Commander-in-Chief of the Armed Forces of Nigeria, Major General Yakubu Gowon drew an analogy between the Nigeria-Biafra war and the U.S. Civil War. Like the American war, Nigeria had to prove that its military was trying to maintain unity like the American Federalists. According to the West Africa magazine, these were many similarities between the two historical wars. First, both sides in the conflict believed they would be able to defeat their opponent in weeks. Second, Southern secessionists and Biafran secessionists were labeled "rebels."

Aliuwaoma Unoke, Biafra's struggle for Independence, (Oxford, PA: Lincoln University, PoL410- Senior Seminar, February 18, 2005, 5)

Third, the Confederates believed that the Unionists were fighting them for their cotton, while the Biafrans believed Nigeria was after their oil. Fourth, there was an obsession with taking the secessionist capital of Richmond as with taking the capital of Enugu in Eastern Nigeria. Fifth, Southern secessionists would have labeled the Union war atrocities as genocide, same as the Biafran Government.

After the U.S. civil war, the confederate money became useless, same predicament as Biafra. But, Levi Nwachuku contends that history never exactly repeats itself. It would, therefore, be inappropriate to draw such a comparison in order to satisfy political aims. "The Nigerian-Biafran war, primarily because it had an element of "secession" should not be regarded as the 19th century American Civil war repeating itself in a 20th century Black African Nation." According to Levi, the comparison of the U.S. Civil war and the Biafran-Nigerian war is faulty in many respects. First, a military coup d'état did not facilitate the outbreak of the U.S. civil war. Second, the Southerners Levi A. Nwachuku, "U.S./ Nigeria: An analysis of U.S. Involvement in the Biafran war 1967- 1970. UMI Dissertation Services. 1973,188 were not massacred by the North in the civil war: neither did the U.S. federal government blockade Southern boundaries before the war. Third, the secessionist south initiated the war and the U.S. government was drawn in to defend its integrity. In contrast, it was the Nigerian government that waged war on Biafra. Fourth, Biafrans felt that Nigeria forced them out, not that they wanted to leave. Fifth, in the American Civil War the South seceded because its citizens wanted to continue with slavery, whereas Igbo people seceded because they wanted to free themselves from ethnic hatred and slavery. These differences show how invalid Nigeria's arguments had become. Furthermore, Southern secession was about the preservation of the institution of slavery, while the Igbo case was about freedom and survival.

Four decades after the war, justice has not been done to the Igbo society. Forty one years after, national reconciliation and recovery have not occurred.

NATIONAL RECOVERY

Nigeria is a nation in recovery. Forty years after its debilitating civil war the multinational nation-state is still in transition from its history of ethnic and religious divide towards political cohesion and national integration. As part of its national identity, the country's human rights abuses against fellow Igbo citizens cannot help in advancing the cause of national recovery. Four decades of victor's justice have fueled ethnic revenge and mass movements for change. Like the U.S. civil war example, post-war reconstruction was a form of victor's justice that impeded reconciliation between the two antagonistic regions. When Gowon's so-called "reconciliation" occurred, it came at the cost of abandoning any serious efforts to achieve any semblance of justice for the victims of the war and their descendants.

For nearly one-half of a century, justice for the war victims on both sides remains an unfinished business today.

Rather than using the rule-of-law to punish perpetrators of war crimes against defenseless civilians, Gowon's "amnesty" denied the victims of their constitutional rights to justice and freedom. Like Lincoln, Gowon's *no victor, no vanquished* "amnesty" identified the perpetrators also as "victims" of war. Gowon's reinterpretation of international law was an attempt to facilitate national healing and recovery. Four decades after, Nigeria remains a victor nation without any form of national reconciliation, justice or cohesion. No lessons have been learned, forty years later. The idea of collective guilt is absurd if the burden of guilt is shared equitably by both the perpetrators and their victims.

Forty-years later, neither Nigerians nor the vanquished people of Biafra have been able to heal from the wounds of the past. Gowon's emphasis on national unity degrades and finally denies the victims their human rights. If Gowon's "no victor" strategy is a peace plan, then Igbo people have waited, far too long, at the periphery of national power, since the war ended forty years ago. According to Robert Meister, "In the aftermath of civil war or revolution amnesty is always an appealing alternative to purges, political prosecutions, and lustration laws. But amnesties are generally based on both a desire to forgive and a need to remember."

In this case, Nigeria forbade anybody to remember or to preserve any memories of the Biafran past. In reconstructing the moral foundation of Gowon's "no victor" theory, the General created a "victor's truth" as an authentic truth to replace human rights trials. In his theory of national recovery, the authoritarian leaders' priority was "national unity" but, the important issues of truth telling, justice and the future freedom of Biafra were ignored. Yet, four decades after the war, the movements for the recognition of Biafra continue to wax stronger worldwide. The Biafran question is not yet behind us because truth, justice and freedom cannot be suppressed forever.

Nigeria matters in global politics and security, but its future is precariously uncertain. Why? In the environmentally damaged Niger Delta, which is part of the defunct Republic of Biafra, well-armed freedom fighters demand a greater share of the oil revenue and political independence. The Nigerian federation faced with various movements fighting for self-determination could fall apart in future because Nigeria does not know how to deal with its past.

Nigeria is an important nation-state with the largest population in Africa. However, the country is split between two alien religions. Islam came by land from Asia, while Christianity came by ship from Europe. The country produces about ten percent of the world's oil needs as one of the major oil exporting countries of the world. Oil production is frequently disrupted by frequent violence from the well-armed "rebels." Nigeria has experienced three waves of political transition towards democratic consolidation and national recovery. But, military coups, corruption and violence have become the definitive political culture of the state.

Nigeria is an unfinished nation-state. Forty-one years after the repressions and serious human rights abuses during the Biafra–Nigeria war, the central issues of justice and freedom have been deliberately ignored. A muted United Nations considered the Biafran genocide an internal affair of the Nigerian state. Western transitional justice as an international human rights tool, therefore, has failed in helping victims deal with their healing process and recovery.

THE IGBO PAST

The British colonial creature known as Nigeria was home to quintessential civilizations many centuries before the coming of Europeans. The famous Nok culture is legendary for farming and iron smelting skills of which Ndigbo (Igbo people) were adepts. While most African societies built and lived in city-states, Ndigbo lived in egalitarian, self-controlled villages. There was never a single kingdom called Nigeria or a Nigerian nation-state. Nigeria, therefore, is a product of European voyages of "discovery." Due to Portuguese, Spanish, French and English Atlantic slave trade, many Americans, Brazilians, Cubans and Caribbeans are of the Igbo ancestry.

NIGERIA: A COLONIAL CREATURE

As we have seen, the Igbo nation had been in existence from ancient times before Frederick Lugard, the English colonial ruler merged the Yoruba and Igbo ethnic nations into a "British Southern Protectorates" and later forced the Muslim North into the so called "British Northern Protectorate." The final merger of the north and south protectorates gave birth to the country called "Nigeria." Pan-Africanists label the postcolonial state as an illegitimate political child of its colonial creator.

With the waves of political self-determination in the 1960s, the new African leaders were afraid to alter the artificial colonial boundaries. The question now is, since when in international law did an illegitimate, colonial state become a legal persona? If colonization was a crime against humanity, why should the moral world recognize the colonially engineered state but refuse to recognize the viable, original, ethnic nations of the world, especially, Biafra?

From a legal perspective, the colonial state seems to lack authority, legitimacy and sovereignty. Nigeria, as a post-colonial state is a political aberration. While London controlled the "laws" of the Anglophone societies, Paris controlled the "laws" of the Francophone nations in Africa. Exploitation and dispossession became the center of imperial national interests. Where, in international law did the imperial powers obtain the legal right to conquer and rule and dispossess the ethnic nations? Nigeria, like its British creator conquered and rules Biafra now for almost five decades and the world remains silent? The UN and the West do not know how to deal with the injustices of the past. Does the West listen only when the liberation guns begin to bark and bite?

The roots of the current cultures of corruption, religious conflicts arise from the British divide-and-rule colonial strategy. This is why the country is so badly fragmented and continues to lack cohesion. Recall the important pledge, "Though tribe and tongue may differ, in brotherhood we stand." The hope in the words of Nigeria's first national anthem has been dashed.

Fifty years after self-determination, national integration has not occurred. "The north is especially different: poor, isolated, underdeveloped and Muslim. Muslim North has never liked being ruled by Christians, either British or Southern Nigerians. If they had to be in a single country, the northerners always sought to be its own rulers. The fundamentalist Islamic movement of Nigeria, dubbed the "Black Taliban" is alleged to have ties with al Qaeda and Iran. The U.S. counterterrorist officials now closely scrutinize Northern Nigeria as a major center of terrorist recruitment and fund-raising. However, African Muslims argue that Islam is the continental religion for Africa because it pays no attention to skin color and has deep roots in Africa, whereas Christianity is a recent arrival brought by Europeans with an implicit racism.

But, Indigenous faith adherents dismiss both Islam and Christianity as alien, Arab and European spiritual paths which conflict with the indigenous and ethnic doctrines of the Native African. Nigeria's major political problems such as corruption, ethnic politics, and election rigging are perpetuated, not by the indigenous citizens but by the Christian and Muslim politicians in both Africa and Nigeria. The trouble with Nigeria has a cleft political culture, which means that the country is split between two cultures, Islam and Christianity, displaying what Samuel Huntington calls "intercivilizational disunity." From historical examples, Christian and Islamic cultures rarely co-exist peacefully within the same sovereign state. Muslims have been known to secede from such sovereign states for examples:

Upon independence in 1947, Muslim Pakistan split from Indian which is a majority Hindu. In Yugoslavia, Muslims in Bosnia and Kosovo refused to be ruled by Serbs. The Muslim Central Asian republics of the Soviet Union separated in the late 1991. Muslim Turks broke away [from] the north of Cyprus in 1974... In parallel with Nigeria, Christians of south Sudan where oil had been discovered, tried and succeeded to break away from the Muslims north.

Nigeria is a weak nation-state, but not yet a failed state likes Afghanistan and Somalia where national governments no longer exist. "If Nigerian state authority declines further, however, it could turn into a failed state. The Nigerian elitist group has strong incentive *to keep Nigeria one*–graft from oil revenues. "If Nigeria falls apart, only the Niger Delta would have the oil. This was one of the roots of the Biafran war." According to Roskin, crime is astronomical in Nigeria. Even university students go into crime. Secret student fraternities, to make sure they pass their courses, intimidate professors by burning their cars and even kidnapping their children. Some students then become members of gangster cults, murdering members of rival cults and selling their services to politicians, thugs, and militants trying to seize the Niger Delta. Nigeria has become infamous for internet scams that get you to reveal your bank account numbers. For many, crime is a good job, the only one they can get." (Michael G. Roskin. *Countries and Concepts: Politics, Geography, Culture* (Boston: Pearson/Longman, 2011, 517 Ibid, 520 (22-23) IBID 522)

The lesson which humanity learns from the Biafran experience is this: Transitional governments should not ignore human rights violations in dealing with a traumatic past. Without justice and truth telling, national recovery and reconciliation cannot take place. As Biafra proves, a long forgotten, politically excluded society degenerates into poverty. And, joblessness and poverty create a fertile climate for the recruitment of jobless youth into gangster cults which unleash terror, and fear within the post-conflict society. As we have seen, continued political exclusion of the former Biafran territory is a grave danger to Nigeria, West Africa and the world.

MEMORY

Forty years is long enough time to remember Biafra. It is time to remember the heroes, and to advocate for the victims' rights, especially for the long-abandoned and disabled veterans of the Biafran revolution who are fast dying off at their Oji River solitary shelter. According to Frederick Forsyth, "Nothing can or ever will minimize the injustice and brutalities perpetuated on the Biafran people, nor diminish the shamefulness of a British government's frantic, albeit indirect, participation...It seems quite logical and imperative to keep alive, the mood of the Biafran people who watched their entire society shattered and destroyed, "their children waste away and die, their young men cut down in thousands."

It is equally important to remember the more complex position of the Nigerian people during the war. While the Muslim Nigerians committed the genocide against Easterners, a few dissenting intellectuals like Peter Enahoro, Tai Solarin and Wole Soyinka were either exiled or jailed for speaking truth to power. During the war, the Nigerian people were muted, and their real views on the war might never be known. In a military dictatorship, survival and the law of self-preservation sometimes take precedent over truth telling and justice. For several years, the military government banned the use and public display of any Biafran memorabilia such as; money, flag, motto, anthem, car stickers or T-shirts.

In recent times, however, things have changed. On August 26, 2004, the movement for the actualization of the sovereign state of Biafra (MASSOB) called for a one-day boycott of all economic and social activities in remembrance of the Biafran revolution. Three decades prior to this event, Igbo people had remained politically apathetic because they had been marginalized and forgotten for a very long period. They had lost their identity within the post-conflict Nigerian society. Despite the Nigerian governments' attempts or suppressing activities, MASSOB's nationalist mobilization shows that the Igbo audacity and spirit of freedom are still alive. Another pro-Biafran group known as the "Rising Sun" in Sierra Leone has emerged and empathizes with Biafrans. While the "old Biafra" used force in self-defense, the new nationalist groups basically operate on non-violence principles in their campaign to seek international recognition for the Republic of Biafra.

Most nation-states are multi-ethnic societies. Like Nigeria, most of them have gone through certain transitional stages. Sometimes, in the course of these evolutionary stages, some states have had high levels of violence. After 300 years of existence, the United States is still striving to remedy those basic injustices and needs of its core-periphery clashes.

Political scientists argue that nationalism and self-determination have not matured in Africa, hence, ethnicity still holds strong. Igbo people and other minority Biafrans are convinced that their welfare will be better served in their own ethno-national setting than in the politically murky and uncharted waters of multinational identity. Many new states emerge because of similar fear and uncertainty. But experiences cannot be the same. While the Jews and Israelis share a common identity, African-Americans do not totally share a common identity with the rest of the 54 countries of Africa. If the Nigerian citizen cannot live and get elected from any place in Nigeria outside his or her ethnic homeland, then, there is little or no bases for a common national identity. In this dysfunctional relationship, the political engineering of basic institutions; religious, economic, social and political spheres which can satisfy the needs of all citizens have become impossible.

Nationalism and self-determination, therefore, are associated with freedom. However, nationalism is also a disintegrating force. The question of who rules who, who is inside and who is outside the political system begin to set in? Then, those who do not share the identity of the ruling ethnic identity begin to react.

The war ended in January 1970. In order to weaken Biafran collective identity and unity, the military regime split Nigeria into thirty six states. The Biafran nation-state is now further split into eight states, thereby confining the Igbo speaking states to five land-locked states. "Surrounded on all sides by Nigeria," there is little hope that the five Igbo-speaking states without the rest of the Eastern states could constitute a viable Biafran nation-state, some Igbo people argue. But this argument is hollow. To become eligible for recognition as a state in international law, the entity claiming statehood must satisfy certain legal standards:

1. Effective and independent government.

2. Possession of defined territory.

3. Capacity to freely engage in foreign relations.

4. Effective control over a permanent population.

After satisfying the above criteria, Biafra was recognized by several nation-states including Gabon, Haiti, Ivory Coast, Tanzania and Zambia, while France, Belgium, Netherlands and the Vatican gave various support to the Biafran government and people. I, therefore insist that Biafra was a legitimate, sovereign state and remains a recognized, *de jure* nation-state, under international law, despite its *de facto* status as a defeated and reabsorbed region of the Nigerian state. When would Biafra obtain justice in order to voluntarily reunite with Nigeria or to reclaim its long-lost freedom and self-determination? Only time will tell.

THE QUESTION OF GENOCIDE

Genocide is an ugly word. It is the name given to the biggest crime man is capable of committing. What constitutes genocide in the modern world? What degree of violence towards a people justifies the use of the word? What degree of intent is necessary to justify the description? After years of study, some of the world's best legal brains have assisted in drawing up the definition written into the United Nations Convention on Genocide and adopted on 9 December 1948. Article Two specifies that: In the present Convention genocide means any of the following acts committed with intent to destroy, in whole or in part, a national, ethnical, racial or religious group, as such:

1. Killing of members of the group;

2. Causing serious bodily or mental harm to members of the group;

3. Deliberately inflicting on the group conditions of life calculated to bring about its physical destruction in whole or in part;

4. Imposing measures intended to prevent births within the group;

5. Forcibly transferring children of the group to another group.

Article 1 states that genocide, whether committed in time of peace or war, is a crime under international law, and Article 4 makes plain that constitutional rulers, public officials or private individuals may be held responsible.

Obviously, in time of war men get killed, and as they belong to a national, ethnical, racial or religious group this paragraph is perhaps too wide to be practicable. It is the use of the phrase 'with intent' that separates the usual casualties inflicted during war from the crime of genocide. The killing party must be shown to have had, or to have developed, intent to destroy, and the victims must be a national, ethnic, racial or religious group.

There are two other points about genocide that have become habitually accepted in law; one is that intent on behalf of the Head of State of the inflicting party needs not be proved. An Army General can direct his troops to commit genocide, and the Supreme Commander is held responsible if he cannot control his armed forces. Secondly, the deliberate decimation of the leadership cadres of a racial group, calculated to leave that group without the cream of its educated manpower, can constitute genocide even if the majority of the population is left alive as a helpless mass of semi-literate peasantry. The society may then be presumed to have been emasculated as a group.

The Biafran charges against the past federal military government rest on their behavior in five fields: the pogroms of the North, the West and Lagos in 1966; the behavior of the Nigerian Army towards the civilian population they encountered during the course of the war; the behavior of the Nigerian Air Force in selection of its targets; the selective killings in various captured areas of chiefs, leaders, administrators, teachers, technicians and the deliberate imposition of hunger, which starved to death an estimated 500,000 children between the ages of one month to ten years.

About the massacres of 1966, enough have been said. It is generally admitted that the size and scope of the killings gave them "genocidal proportions" and there exists ample evidence to show that mob action against the Easterners were planned, directed and organized by both Muslim military personnel and Muslim civilians. Furthermore, that no inquiry was ever instituted by the central government, nor any punishment, compensation or restitution paid.

The widespread killing of Biafran civilians and of Igbo inhabitants of the Midwest State is equally incontrovertible. After the withdrawal of the Biafran forces from the Midwest in late September 1967 during a six- week occupation, a series of massacres started against Igbo residents. The explanation that it was difficult to differentiate between soldiers and civilians cannot hold water, for as had been explained, the armed forces were withdrawn in almost every case before the Second Division of the Federal Army came within firing range. These massacres were witnessed by numerous foreign residents of the various Midwestern towns concerned, and widely reported in the international press. Some examples will suffice:

> *New York Review*, 21 December 1967, "In some areas outside the East which were temporarily held by Biafran forces, as at Benin in the Midwestern region, Ibos were killed by local people with at least the acquiescence of the Federal forces. About 1000 Ibo civilians perished at Benin in this way."
>
> *Washington Morning Post*, 27 September, 1967, "but after the Federal takeover of Benin Northern troops killed

about 500 Ibo civilians in Benin after a house to house search."

London Observer, 21 January 1968, "the code [Gowon's code of conduct] has all but vanished except for Federal propaganda. In clearing the Midwest state of Biafra forces Federal troops were reported to have killed, or stood by while Muslims killed more than 5,000 Ibos in Benin, Warri, Sapele, Agbor, Asaba."

Asaba, which lies on the Western bank of the River Niger, was a small riverside township. Here the massacre occurred after the Biafran troops had crossed the bridge back into Biafra. Later, Monsignor Georges Rochiau, who traveled on a fact finding mission, as directed by his Holiness the Pope, visited both Biafra and Nigeria. At Asaba, by then in Nigerian hands, he talked with priests who had been there at the time. On 5 April, 1968, he was interviewed by the French evening newspaper *Le Monde*, to whom he said: "There has been genocide, for example on the occasion of the 1966 massacres... Two areas had suffered badly [from the fighting]. Firstly the region between the towns of Benin and Asaba where only widows and orphans remained, Federal troops having for unknown reasons massacred all the men."

According to eye witnesses of the massacre, the Nigerian commander ordered the execution of every Ibo male over the age of ten years old.

The Midwest killings had nothing to do with the prosecution of the Nigerian war efforts. The pogrom against Biafran citizens was widely interpreted as a taste of things to come. Despite the gravity of the Biafran conflict, the world continued to turn its back to Biafra, forty four years after the war.

CONCLUSION

A winnable war against the forces of power politics, terrorism and authoritarian rule is possible. The spirit of freedom seems to be calling upon us to become anti-terror warriors, nuclear war abolitionists, human interest advocates, freedom awakening activists and to campaign for the restructuring of the United Nations. The African *transitional justice* model like Kamenu, the belief in the natural law of cause and effects, ubuntu doctrine of interdependence and the gacaca community spirit of reconciliation, have more healing and cathartic effects on the victims of past traumatic injustices than their western counterparts. We can remedy the injustices of history through the mkparawa model which recognizes, economic justice and moral justice. There are deep ethical and political values in seeking reconciliation and in coming to terms with the past. *Restorative justice* is the motive of the *ethno-traditional* model while the *Western model* emphasis is to deter future wrongdoing. Political transition to a more durable peace and security must be founded on *truth* and *justice*. When truth telling establishes the facts, and restorative justice provides remedy, then, reconciliation and national recovery can be possible.

WORKS CITED

- The National Commission on the Disappeared (CONADEP) *disappeared@yendor.com*, 5/29/2011

- (*Daily Sun: Voice of the Nation*, June12,2009) www.sun-news online.com/webpages/news/national/2009/13natio nal-13-06-200...6/12/2009.) STOPPED

- Max Soillun, Forty Years After Biafra—Forgiveness and Beyond, March 2010 pl www.thepogrom-war-starvation. Blogspot.com/2010_03_01_archive.html12/28/2010 warface.

- (New Jersey: Goldline and Jacobs Publishers, 2010, 115)

- Carla Hesse and Robert Post, (Ed) Human Rights in Political Transitions: Gettysburg to Bosnia, (New York: Zone Brooks, 1999, 11)

- The U.S. Civil (10. Geoffery Birch, *Biafra: The case for Independence*, (London: The British- Biafra Association, 1968.)

- Aliuwaoma Unoke, *Biafra's struggle for Independence*, (Oxford, PA: Lincoln University, PoL410- Senior Seminar, February 18, 2005, 5).

- Aliuwa Unoke Ibid, 10-14 Then, those who do not share the identity of the ruling ethnic identity begin to react.

- Levi A. Nwachuku, "U.S./Nigeria: An analysis of U.S. Involvement in the Biafran war 1967-1970. UMI Dissertation Services. 1973,188

- Michael G. Roskin. *Countries and Concepts: Politics, Geography, Culture* (Boston: Pearson/Longman, 2011, 517 Ibid, 520(22-23) IBID.

- *New York Review*, 21 December 1967:

- *Washington Morning Post*, 27 September, 1967:

- *London Observer*, 21 January 1968:

- Fareed Zakaria, "Africa's New Path: Paul Kagame Charts a Way Forward," *Newsweek*, July 27, 2008

APPENDIX C

THE AHIARA DECLARATION

THE PRINCIPLES OF THE BIAFRAN REVOLUTION

By CHUKWUEMEKA ODUMEGWU OJUKWU

General of the People's Army

PROUD AND COURAGEOUS BIAFRANS,

FELLOW COUNTRY MEN AND WOMEN,

I salute you. Today, as I look back over our two years as a sovereign and independent nation, I am overwhelmed with the feeling of pride and satisfaction in our performance and achievement as a people. Our indomitable will, our courage, our endurance of the severest privations, our resourcefulness and inventiveness in the face of tremendous odds and dangers, have become proverbial in a world so bereft of heroism, and have become a source of frustration to Nigeria and her foreign masters. For this and for the many miracles of our time, let us give thanks to Almighty God. I congratulate all Biafrans at home and abroad. I thank you all the part you have played and have continued to play in this struggle, for your devotion to the high ideals and principles on which this Republic was founded.

I thank you for your absolute commitment to the cause for which our youth are making daily, the supreme sacrifice, and a cause for which we all have been dispossessed, blockaded, bombarded, starved and massacred. I salute you for your tenacity of purpose and amazing steadfastness under siege.

I salute the memory of the many patriots who have laid down their lives in defense of our Fatherland. I salute the memory of all Biafrans—men, women and children—who died victims of the Nigerian crime of genocide. We shall never forget them. Please God, their sacrifice shall not be in vain. For the dead on the other side of this conflict, may their souls rest in peace. To our friends and well-wishers, to the growing band of men and women around the world who have, in spite of the vile propaganda mounted against us, identified themselves with the justice of our cause, in particular to our courageous friends, officers and staff of the Relief Agencies and humanitarian organizations, pilots who daily offer themselves in sacrifice that our people might be saved; to Governments, in particular Tanzania, Gabon, Ivory Coast, Zambia and Haiti. I give my warmest thanks and those of our entire people.

THE STRUGGLE

Fellow country men and women, for nearly two years we have been engaged in a war which threatens our people with total destruction. Our enemy has been unrelenting in his fury and has fought our defenseless people with a vast array of military hardware of a sophistication unknown to Africa. For two years we have withstood his assaults with nothing other than our stout hearts and bare hands. We have frustrated his diabolical intentions and have beaten his wicked mentors in their calculations and innovations. Shamelessly, our enemy has moved from deadline to deadline, seeking excuses justifying his failures to an ever credulous world. Today, I am happy and proud to report that, all the odds notwithstanding, the enemy, at great cost in lives and equipment, is nowhere near to his avowed objective.

In the Onitsha sector of the war, our gallant forces have kept the enemy confined in the town which they entered 15 months ago. Despite the fact that this sector has great strategic attraction for the vandal hordes, being a gate-way, as it is, to the now famous jungle strip of Biafra, and the scene of the bloodiest encounters of this war, it is significant that the enemy has made no gains throughout this long period.

In the Awka sector of the war, the story remains the same. The enemy is confined only to the highway between Enugu and Onitsha, not venturing north or south of that road.

In the Okigwe sector, from where the enemy made the thrust that brought him into Umuahia, the situation remains unchanged, with our troops making the entire enemy route from Okigwe to Umuahia no joy ride. In Umuahia town itself, fighting has continued in the township.

In the Ikot Ekpene, Azumini and Aba sectors of the war, the vandals, whilst maintaining their positions in Ikot Ekpene and Aba with our troops surrounding them, have continued to suffer heavy casualties in their attempt to hold firmly on to Azumini.

We now come to the Owerri/Port Harcourt sector. After the clearing of Owerri township and our rapid move towards Port Harcourt, our gallant forces are holding positions in Eleele town, in the outskirts of Igirita and forward of Omoku.

Across the Niger, the successes of our troops have been maintained despite numerous enemy counter-attacks. Our Navy has continued to support all operations along the Niger with good results. Our guerrillas have continued their magnificent work of harassing the enemy and giving him no respite on our soil. I salute them all.

In the air, the Biafran Air Force has made a most dramatic re-entry into the war, and in a brilliant series of raids has all but paralyzed the Nigerian Air Force. In four days' operations, eleven operational planes of the enemy were put of action, three control towers in Port Harcourt, Enugu and Benin were set ablaze, the Airport building in Enugu, and the numerous gun positions were knocked out. The refinery in Port Harcourt was set on fire. And, more recently, three days ago, the Ughelli Power Station was put out of action. The brilliance of this performance, the precision of the strike, the genius of target selection, have left Nigeria in a daze and her friends bewildered. Another way of looking at this is that in four days of operation, the Biafran Air Force has destroyed more military targets than what the Nigerian Air Force has been able to do for two years.

In cost, probably twice what the Nigerian air raids have cost us in military equipment and installations. The only superiority left in the record of achievement of the Nigerian Air Force is the number of civilians and civilian targets their cowardly raids have destroyed. Proud Biafrans, I have kept my promise.

Diplomatically, our friends have increased and have remained steadfast to our cause; and despite the rantings of our detractors, indications are that their support will continue.

At home, our sufferings have continued. Scarcity and want have remained our companions. Yet, with fortitude, we seem to have overcome the once imminent danger of mass starvation and can now look forward to a period after the rains of comparative plenty. Our efforts in the Land Army program give visible signs all over our land of imminent victory in the war against want.

Fellow countrymen and women, the signs are auspicious, the future fills us with less foreboding. I am confident. With the initiative in war now in our own hands, we have turned the last bend in our race to self-realization and are now set on the home straight in this our struggle. We must not flag. The tape is in sight. What we need now is a final burst of speed to breast the tape and secure the victory which will ensure for us, for all time, glory and honor, peace and progress.

Fellow compatriots, today, being our Thanksgiving Day, it is most appropriate that we pause awhile to take stock, to consider our past, our successes notwithstanding; to consider our future, our aspirations and our fears. For two long years we have been locked in mortal combat with an enemy unequalled in viciousness; for two long years, defenseless and weak, we have withstood without respite the concerted assault of a determined foe. We have fought alone, we have fought with honor, we have fought in the highest traditions of Christian civilization. Yet, the very custodians of this civilization and our one-time mentors, are the very self-same monsters who have vowed to devour us.

Fellow Biafrans, I have for a long time thought about this our predicament—the attitude of the civilized world to this our conflict. The more I think about it the more I am convinced that our disability is racial. The root cause of our problem lies in the fact that we are black. If all the things that have happened to us had happened to another people who are not black, if other people who are not black had reacted in the way our people have reacted these two long years, the world's response would surely have been different.

In 1966, some 50,000 of us were slaughtered like cattle in Nigeria. In the course of this war, well over one million of us have been killed; yet the world is unimpressed and looks on in indifference. Last year, some blood-thirsty Nigerian troops for sport murdered the entire male population of a village. All the world did was to indulge in an academic argument whether the number was in hundreds or in thousands. Today, because a handful of white men collaborating with the enemy, fighting side by side with the enemy, were caught by our gallant troops, the entire world threatens to stop. For 18 white men, Europe is aroused. What have they said about our millions? 18 white men assisting the crime of genocide! What does Europe say about our murdered innocents? Have we not died enough? How many black dead make one missing white? Mathematicians, please answer me. Is it infinity?

Take another example. For two years we have been subjected to a total blockade. We all know how bitter, bloody and protracted the First and Second World Wars were. At no stage in those wars did the white belligerents carry out a total blockade of their fellow whites. In each case where a blockade was imposed, allowance was made for certain basic necessities of life in the interest of women, children and other non-combatants. Ours is the only example in recent history where a whole people have been so treated. What is it that makes our case different? Do we not have women, children and other non-combatants? Does the fact that they are black women, black children and black non-combatants make such a world of difference?

Nigeria embarked on a crime of genocide against our people by first mounting a total blockade against Biafra. To cover up their designs and deceive the black world, the white powers supporting Nigeria blame Biafrans for the continuation of the blockade and for the starvation and suffering which that entails. They uphold Nigerian proposals on relief which in any case they helped to formulate, as being "conciliatory" or "satisfactory." Knowing that these proposals would give Nigeria further military advantage, and compromise the basic cause for which we have struggled for two years, they turn round to condemn us for rejecting them. They accepted the total blockade against us as a legitimate weapon of war because it suits them and because we are black. Had we been white the inhuman and cruel blockade would long have been lifted.

The mass deaths of our citizens resulting from starvation and indiscriminate air raids and large despoliation of towns and villages are a mere continuation of this crime. That Nigeria has received complete support from Britain should surprise no one.

For Britain is a country whose history is replete with instances of genocide.

In my address to you on the occasion of the first anniversary of our independence, I touched on a number of issues relevant to our struggle and to our hope for a prosperous, just and happy society. I talked to you of the background to our struggle and on the visions and values which inspired us to found our own State.

THE MYTH ABOUT THE NEGRO

On this occasion of our second anniversary, I shall go further in the examination of the meaning and import of our revolution by discussing the wider issues involved and the character and structure of the new society we are determined and committed to build. Our enemies and their foreign sponsors have deliberately sought by false and ill-motivated propaganda to becloud the real issues which caused and still determine the course and character of our struggle. They have sought in various ways to dismiss our struggle as a tribal conflict. They have attributed it to the mad adventurism of a fictitious power-seeking clique anxious to carve out an empire to rule, dominate and exploit. But they have failed. Our cause is transparently just and no amount of propaganda can detract from it.

Our struggle has far-reaching significance. It is the latest recrudescence in our time of the age-old struggle of the black man for his full stature as man. We are the latest victims of a wicked collusion between the three traditional scourges of the black man–racism, Arab-Muslim expansionism and white economic imperialism. Playing a subsidiary role is Bolshevik Russia seeking for a place in the African sun. Our struggle is a total and vehement rejection of all those evils which blighted Nigeria, evils which were bound to lead to the disintegration of that ill-fated federation. Our struggle is not a mere resistance–that would be purely negative. It is a positive commitment to build a healthy, dynamic and progressive state, such as would be the pride of black men the world over.

For this reason, our struggle is a movement against racial prejudice, in particular against that tendency to regard the black man as culturally, morally, spiritually, intellectually, and physically inferior to the other two major races of the world–the yellow and the white races. This belief in the innate inferiority of the Negro and that his proper place in the world is that of the servant of the other races, has from early days colored the attitude of the outside world to Negro problems. It still does today.

Not so long ago the fashion was to question the humanity of the Negro. Some white theorists attributed the creation to the Devil, others even identified the Devil as the first Negro. Later they derived the Negro from the accursed progeny of Ham. Nearer to us still in time, it became a topic for serious debate in learned circles in Europe whether the Negro was in fact a man; whether he had a soul; and if he had a soul, whether conversion to Christianity could make any difference to his spiritual condition and destination. By the nineteenth century it had been reluctantly conceded that the Negro is in fact human, but a different kind of man, certainly not the same kind of man as the white. Pseudo-intellectuals went to work to prove that the Negro was a different kind of man from the white. They uncovered the abundant so-called anthropological evidence from archaeology which "proved" to them conclusively that the Negro was no more the same kind of man as the European than a rat was a rabbit.

It is this myth about the Negro that still conditions the thinking and attitude of most white governments on all issues concerning black Africa and the black man; it explains the double standards which they apply to present-day world problems; it explains their stand on the whole question of independence and basic human rights for the black peoples of the world. These myths explain the stand of many of the world governments and organizations on our present struggle.

Our disagreement with the Nigerians arose in part from a conflict between two diametrically opposed conceptions of the end and purpose of the modern African state. It was, and still is, our firm conviction that a modern Negro African government worth the trust placed in it by the people, must build a progressive state that ensures the reign of social and economic justice, and of the rule of law. But the Nigerians, under the leadership of the Hausa-Fulani feudal aristocracy preferred anarchy and injustice.

Since in the thinking of many white powers a good, progressive and efficient government is good only for whites, our view was considered dangerous and pernicious: a point of view which explains but does not justify the blind support which these powers have given to uphold the Nigerian ideal of a corrupt, decadent and putrefying society. To them genocide is an appropriate answer to any group of black people who have the temerity to attempt to evolve their own social system.

When the Nigerians violated our basic human rights and liberties, we decided reluctantly but bravely to found our own state, to exercise our inalienable right to self-determination as our only remaining hope for survival as a people. Yet, because we are black, we are denied by the white powers the exercise of this right which they themselves have proclaimed inalienable. In our struggle we have learned that the right of self-determination is inalienable, but only to the white man.

SELF-DETERMINATION

The right to self-determination was good for the Greeks in 1822, for the Belgians in 1830, and for the Central and Eastern Europeans and the Irish at the end of the First World War. Yet it is not good for Biafrans because we are black. When blacks claim that right, they are warned against dangers trumped up by the imperialists—"fragmentation" and "Balkanization," as if the trouble with the Balkans is the result of the application of the principle of self-determination. Were the Balkans a healthier place before they emerged from the ruins of the Ottoman Empire? Those who sustained the Ottoman Empire considered it a European necessity, for its Eastern European provinces stood as a buffer between two ambitious and mutually antagonistic empires—the Russian and the Austrian. For the peace and repose of Europe, it therefore became a major concern of European statesmen to preserve the integrity of that empire. But when it was discovered that Ottoman rule was not only corrupt, oppressive and unprogressive, but also stubbornly irreformable, the happiness and well-being of its white populations came to be considered paramount. So by 1918 the integrity of that ancient and sprawling empire had been sacrificed to the well-being of the Eastern Europeans. Fellow Biafrans, that was in the white world.

But what do we find here in Negro Africa? The Federation of Nigeria is today as corrupt, as unprogressive and as oppressive and irreformable as the Ottoman Empire was in Eastern Europe over a century ago. And in contrast, the Nigerian Federation in the form it was constituted by the British cannot by any stretch of imagination be considered an African necessity. Yet we are being forced to sacrifice our very existence as a people to the integrity of that ramshackle creation that has no justification either in history or in the freely expressed wishes of the people. What other reason for this can there be than the fact that we are black?

In 1966, 50,000 Biafrans—men, women and children—were massacred in cold blood in Nigeria. Since July 6, 1967, hundreds of Biafrans have been killed daily by shelling, bombing, strafing and starvation advised, organized and supervised by Anglo-Saxon Britain. None of these atrocities has raised enough stir in many European capitals. But on the few occasions when a single white man died in Africa, even where he was a convicted bandit like the notorious case in the Congo, all the diplomatic chanceries of the world have been astir.; the whole world has been shaken to its very foundations by the din of protest against the alleged atrocity and by the clamor for vengeance. This was the case when the Nigerian vandals turned their British-supplied rifles on white Red Cross workers in Okigwe. Recently this has been the case with the reported disappearance of some white oil technicians in the Republic of Benin. But when we are massacred in thousands, nobody cares, because we are black.

Fellow countrymen and women, the fact is that in spite of their open protestations to the contrary, the white peoples of the world are still far from accepting that what is good for them can also be good for blacks. The day they make this basic concession that day will the non-Anglo-Saxon nations tell Britain to her face that she is guilty of genocide against us; that day will they call a halt to this monstrous war.

Because the black man is considered inferior and servile to the white, he must accept his political, social and economic system and ideologies ready made from Europe, America or the Soviet Union. Within the confines of his nation he must accept a federation or confederation or unitary government if federation or confederation or unitary government suits the interests of his white masters; he must accept inept and unimaginative leadership because the contrary would hurt the interests of the master race; he must accept economic exploitation by alien commercial firms and companies because the whites benefit from it. Beyond the confines of his state, he must accept regional and continental organizations which provide a front for the manipulation of the imperialist powers; organizations which are therefore unable to respond to African problems in a truly African manner. For Africans to show a true independence is to ask for anathemization and total liquidation.

ARAB-MUSLIM EXPANSIONISM

The Biafran struggle is, on another plane, a resistance to the Arab-Muslim expansionism which has menaced and ravaged the African continent for twelve centuries. As early as the first quarter of the seventh century, the Arabs, a people from the Near-

East, evolved Islam not just as a religion but as a cover for their insatiable territorial ambitions. By the tenth century they had overrun and occupied, among other places, Egypt and North Africa. Had they stopped there, we would not today be faced with the wicked and unholy collusion we are fighting against. On the contrary, they cast their hungry and envious eyes across the Sahara on to the land of the Negroes.

Our Biafran ancestors remained immune from the Islamic contagion. From the middle years of the last century Christianity was established in our land. In this way we came to be a predominantly Christian people. We came to stand out as a non-Muslim island in a raging Islamic sea. Throughout the period of the ill-fated Nigerian experiment, the Muslims hoped to infiltrate Biafra by peaceful means and quiet propaganda, but failed. Then the late Ahmadu Bello, the Sarduana of Sokoto tried, by political and economic blackmail and terrorism, to convert Biafrans settled in Northern Nigeria to Islam. His hope was that these Biafrans on dispersion would then carry Islam to Biafra, and by so doing give the religion political control of the area. The crises which agitated the so-called independent Nigeria from 1962 gave these aggressive proselytizers the chance to try converting us by force.

It is now evident why the fanatic Arab-Muslim states like Algeria, Egypt and the Sudan have come out openly and massively to support and aid Nigeria in her present war of genocide against us. These states see militant Arabism as a powerful instrument for attaining power in the world.

Biafra is one of the few African states untainted by Islam. Therefore, to militant Arabism, Biafra is a stumbling block to their plan for controlling the whole continent. This control is fast becoming manifest in the Organization of African Unity. On the question of the Middle East, the Sudanese crisis, in the war between Nigeria and Biafra, militant Arabism has succeeded in imposing its point of view through blackmail and bluster. It has threatened African leaders and governments with inciting their

Muslim minorities to rebellion if the governments adopted an independent line on these questions. In this way an O.A.U that has not felt itself able to discuss the genocide in the Sudan and Biafra, an O.A.U. that has again and again advertised its ineptitude as a peace-maker, has rushed into open condemnation of Israel over the Middle East dispute. Indeed in recent times, by its performance, the O.A.U. might well be an Organization of Arab Unity.

AFRICA EXPLOITED

Our struggle, in an even more fundamental sense, is the culmination of the confrontation between Negro nationalism and white imperialism. It is a movement designed to ensure the realization of man's full stature in Africa.

Ever since the 15th century, the European world has treated the African continent as a field for exploitation. Their policies in Africa have for so long been determined to a very great extent by their greed for economic gain. For over three and half centuries, it suited them to transport and transplant millions of the flower of our manhood for the purpose of exploiting the Americas and the West Indies. They did so with no uneasiness of conscience. They justified this trade in men by reference to biblical passages violently torn out of context.

When it became no longer profitable to them to continue with the depopulation and uncontrolled spoliation of Negro Africa, their need of the moment became to exploit the natural resources of the continent, using Negro labor. In response to this need they evolved their informal empire in the 19th century under which they controlled and exploited Negro Africa through their missionaries and monopolist mercantile companies. As time went on they discarded the empire of informal sway as unsatisfactory and established the direct empire as the most effective means of exploiting our homeland. It was at this stage that with cynical imperturbability they carved up the African continent, and boxed up the native populations in artificial states designed purely to minister to white economic interests.

This brutal and unprecedented rape of a whole continent was a violent challenge to Negro self-respect. Not surprisingly, within half a century the theory and practice of empire ran into stiff opposition from Negro nationalism. In the face of the movement for Negro freedom the white imperialists changed tactics. They decided to install puppet African administrations to create the illusion of political independence, while retaining the control of the economy. And this they quickly did between 1957 and 1965. The direct empire was transformed into an indirect empire, that regime of fraud and exploitation which African nationalists aptly describe as Neo-Colonialism.

Nigeria was a classic example of a neo-colonialist state, and what is left of it, still is. The militant nationalism of the late forties and early fifties had caught the British imperialists unawares. They hurried to accommodate it by installing the ignorant, decadent and feudalistic Hausa-Fulani oligarchy in power. For the British, the credentials of the Hausa-Fulani were that not having emerged from the Middle Ages they knew nothing about the modern state and the powerful forces that now rule men's minds. Owing their position to the British, they were servile and submissive. The result was that while Nigerians lived in the illusion of independence, they were still in fact being ruled from Number 10 Downing Street. The British still enjoyed a stranglehold on their economy.

The crises which rocked Nigeria from the morrow of "independence" were brought about by the efforts of progressive nationalists to achieve true independence for themselves and for posterity. For their part in this effort, Biafrans were stigmatized and singled out for extermination. In imperialist thinking, only phony independence is good for blacks. The sponsorship of Nigeria by white imperialism has not been disinterested. They are only concerned with the preservation of that corrupt and rickety structure of Nigeria in a perpetual state of powerlessness to check foreign exploitation. I am certain that if tomorrow I should promise that Biafra is going to be a servile and sycophantic state, these self-appointed upholders of the territorial integrity of African states will sing a different tune. No...I shall not oblige them. Biafra will not betray the black man. No matter the odds, we will fight with all our might until black men everywhere can, with pride, point to this Republic, standing dignified and defiant, as an example of African nationalism triumphant over its many and age-old enemies.

Fellow countrymen and women, we have seen in proper perspective the diabolical roles which the British Government and the foreign companies have played and are playing in our war with Nigeria. We now see why in spite of Britain's tottering economy Harold Wilson's Government insists on financing Nigeria's futile war against us. We see why the Shell-BP led the Nigerian hordes into Bonny, pays Biafran oil royalties to Nigeria, and provided the Nigerian Army with all the help it needed for its attack on Port Harcourt. We see why the West African Conference Lines readily and meekly co-operate with Gowon in the imposition of total blockade against us. We see why the oil and trading companies in Nigeria still finance this war and why they risk the life and limb of their staff in the war zones.

RUSSIAN IMPERIALISM

And now, Bolshevik Russia. Russia is a late arrival in the race for world empire. Since the end of the Second World War she has fought hard to gain a foothold in Africa recognizing, like the other imperialist powers before her, the strategic importance of Africa in the quest for world domination. She first tried to enter into alliance with African nationalism. Later finding that African nationalism has been thwarted, at least temporarily, by the collusion between imperialism and the decadent forces in African society, Russia quickly changed her strategy and identified herself with those very conservative forces which she had earlier denounced. Here she met with quick success.

In North Africa and Egypt, Russian influence has taken firm root and is growing. With her success in Egypt and Algeria, Russia developed even keener appetite for more territory in Africa, particularly the areas occupied by the Negroes. Her early efforts in the Congo and Ghana proved still-born. The Nigeria-Biafra conflict offered an opportunity for anther beach-head in Africa.

It is not Russia's intention to make Nigeria a better place for Nigerians or indeed any other part of Africa a better place for Africans. Her interest is strategic. In her challenge to the United States and the Western World, she needs vantage points in Africa. With her entrenched position in Northern Nigeria, the Central Sudan of the historians and geographers, Russia is in a position to co-ordinate her strategy for West and North Africa. We are all familiar with the ancient and historic cultural, linguistic and religious links between North Africa and the Central Sudan. We know that the Hausa language is a lingua franca for over two-thirds of this area. We know how far afield a wandering Imam preaching Islam and Bolshevism can go. When Russia gives the Nigerians Illyushin jets to bomb us, the MiGs to strafe and rocket us and AK-47 rifles to mow us down, we should see all this in proper light that Russia, like other imperialist powers, has no regard for the Negro. To her, what is important is to gain a vantage point in Negro-land from which to challenge American and Western European world power and influence. The Arabs also in this find further attraction in that it gives to them a back-door entry eventually into Israel. In this jungle game for world domination and black man's life, let alone his well-being, counts for nothing.

Fellow Biafrans, these are the evil and titanic forces with which we are engaged in a life and death struggle. These are the obstacles to the Negro's efforts to realize himself. These are the forces which the Biafran Revolution must sweep aside to succeed.

ANGLO-SAXON GENOCIDE

If the white race has sinned against the world, the Anglo-Saxon branch of that race has been, and still is, the worst sinner of all. The Anglo-Saxon British committed genocide against the American Indians. They committed genocide against the Caribbs. They committed genocide against the Australian Blackfellows. They committed genocide against the native Tasmanians and the Maoris of New Zealand. During the era of the slave trade, they topped the list and led the genocidal attempt against the Negro race as a whole. Today, they are engaged in committing genocide against us. The unprejudiced observer is forced in consternation to wonder whether genocide is not a way of life of the Anglo-Saxon British. Luckily, all white people are not like the Anglo-Saxon British.

NEGRO RENAISSANCE

Luckily too, all African states not like Nigeria, Algeria, Egypt and Sudan, sworn enemies of the Negro, willing tools of white racism, white economic imperialism and Arab-Muslim expansionism. We salute the shining and enduring examples of Negro renascence throughout the world. To Tanzania, to Gabon, to the Ivory Coast, to Zambia and Haiti, we wish more success in their soldiering for all that is right, just and honorable.

We do not claim that the Biafran Revolution is the first attempt in history by the Negro to assert his identity, to claim his right and proper place as a human being on a basis of equality with the white and yellow races. We are aware of the Negro's past and present efforts to prove his ability at home and abroad. We are familiar with his achievements in prehistory; we are familiar with his achievements in exploring and taming the African and American continents; we are familiar with his achievements in political organizations; we are familiar with these contributions to the world store of art and culture. The Negro's white oppressors are not unaware of all these.

But in spite of their awareness they are not prepared to admit that the Negro is a man and a brother. This is why we in Biafra are convinced that the Negro can never come to his own until he is able to build modern states (whether national or multi-national) based on a compelling African ideology, enjoying real rather than sham independence, able to give scope to the full development of the human spirit in the arts and sciences, able to engage in dialogue with the white states on a basis of transparent equality and able to introduce a new dimension into international statecraft.

In the world context, this is Biafra–the plight of the black struggling to be man. From this derives our deep conviction that the Biafran Revolution is not just a movement of Igbo, Ibibio, Ijaw and Ogoja. It is a movement of true and patriotic Africans. It is African nationalism conscious of itself and fully aware of the powers with which it is contending. From this derives our belief that history and humanity are on our side, and that the Biafran Revolution is indestructible and eternal. From here derives the support we enjoy from the brave and proud peoples of Tanzania, Gabon, the Ivory Coast, Zambia and Haiti who share these ideals and visions with us and who are already engaged in realizing them.

We have indeed come a long way. We were once Nigerians, today we are Biafrans. We are Biafrans because on 30th May, 1967, we finally said no to the evils and injustices in which Nigeria was steeped. Nigeria was made up of peoples and groups with very little in common. As everyone knows, Biafrans were in the fore-front among those who tried to make Nigeria a nation. It is ironic that some ill-informed and mischievous people today will accuse us of breaking up a united African country. Only those who do not know the facts or deliberately ignore them can hold such an opinion. We know the facts because we were there and the things that happened, happened to us.

NIGERIAN CORRUPTION

Nigeria was indeed a very wicked and corrupt country in spite of the glorious image given her in the European press. We know why Nigeria was given that image. It was her reward for serving the economic and political interests of her European masters. Nigeria is a stooge of Europe. Her independence was and is a lie. Even her Prime Minister was a Knight of the British Empire! But worse than her total subservience to foreign political and economic interests, Nigeria committed many crimes against her nationals which in the end made complete nonsense of her claim to unity. Nigeria persecuted and slaughtered her minorities; Nigerian justice was a farce; her elections, her census, her politics–her everything–was corrupt. Qualification, merit and experience were discounted in public service. In one area of Nigeria, for instance, they preferred to turn a nurse who had worked for five years into a doctor rather then employ a qualified doctor from another part of Nigeria; barely literate clerks were made Permanent Secretaries; a university Vice-Chancellor was sacked because he belonged to the wrong tribe.

Bribery, corruption and nepotism were so widespread that people began to wonder openly whether any country in the world could compare with Nigeria in corruption and abuse of power. All the modern institutions–the Legislature, the Civil Service, the Army, the Police, the Judiciary, the Universities, the Trade Unions and the organs of mass information–were devalued and made the tools of corrupt political power. There was complete neglect and impoverishment of the people. Whatever prosperity there was, was deceptive. Unemployment was growing. Thousands of young school-leavers were drifting away from the villages which had nothing to offer them into towns with no employment openings. There was despair in many hearts and the number of suicides was growing every day. The farmers were very hard-hit, their standard of living had fallen steeply. The soils were perishing from over-farming and lack of scientific husbandry. The towns like the soils were wastelands into which people put in too much exertion for too little reward. There were crime waves and people lived in fear of their lives. Business speculation, rack-renting, worship of money and sharp practices left a few extremely rich at the expense of the many, and these few flaunted their wealth before the many and talked about sharing the national cake. Foreign interests did roaring business spreading consumer goods and wares among a people who had not developed a habit of thrift and who fell prey to lying advertisements. Inequality of the sexes was actively promoted in Nigeria. Rather than aspire to equality with men, women were encouraged to accept the status of inferiority and to become the mistresses of successful politicians and business executives, or they were married off at the age of fourteen as the fifteenth wives of the new rich. That was the glorious Nigeria, the mythical Nigeria, celebrated in the European press.

Then worst of all came the genocide in which over 50,000 of our kith and kin were slaughtered in cold blood all over Nigeria, and nobody asked questions, nobody showed regret, nobody showed remorse. Thus, Nigeria had become a jungle with no safety, no justice and no hope for our people. We decided then to found a new place, a human habitation away from the Nigerian jungle. That was the origin of our Revolution.

REDISCOVERING INDEPENDENCE

From the moment we assumed the illustrious name of the ancient kingdom of Biafra, we were re-discovering the original inde-pendence of a great African people. We accepted by this revolu-tionary act the glory, as well as the sacrifice of true independence and freedom. We knew that we had challenged the many forces and interests which had conspired to keep Africa and the Black Race in subjection forever. We knew they were going to be ruth-less and implacable in defense of their age-old imposition on us and exploitation of our people. But we were prepared and remain prepared to pay any price for our freedom and dignity.

And in this we were not mistaken. Five weeks after we had proclaimed our independence Nigeria, goaded by her foreign masters, declared war on us.

For two years now we have fought a difficult war in defense of our Fatherland. From the beginning we have never been in doubt about our ultimate victory. But, seeing the odds ranged against us, the world did not believe that we had any chance of success whatever the merit of our case. Perhaps our determination and persistence are making the world think again. Biafra today is no longer a lost cause. For us, Biafra's eventual triumph has never been in doubt: Biafra has always been the shining light at the end of our dark tunnel. In the two years of our grim struggle, we have learned important lessons about ourselves, about our society and about the world. In some ways this struggle has been a journey in self-discovery and self-realization.

Our Revolution is a historic opportunity given to us to establish a just society; to revive the dignity of our people at home and the dignity of the Black-man in the world. We realize that in order to achieve those ends we must remove those weaknesses in our institutions and organizations and those disabilities in foreign relations which have tended to degrade this dignity. This means that we must reject Nigerianism in all its guises.

THE PEOPLE

Fellow countrymen, are we going to say no to Nigerianism and then let a few unpatriotic people among us soil our Revolution with the stain of Nigeria? Are we going to watch the very disease which caused the demise of Nigeria take root in our new Biafra? Are we prepared to embark on another revolution perhaps more bloody to put right the inevitable disaster? I ask you, my countrymen, can we afford another spell of strife when this one is over to correct social inequalities in our Fatherland? I say NO. A thousand times no. The ordinary Biafran says no. When I speak of the ordinary Biafran I speak of the People. The Biafran Revolution is the People's Revolution. Who are the People? you ask. The farmer, the trader, the clerk, the business man, the housewife, the student, the civil servant, the soldier, you and I are the people. Is there anyone here who is not of the people? Is there anyone here afraid of the People—anyone suspicious of the People? Is there anyone despising the People? Such a man has no place in our Revolution. If he is a leader, he has no right to leadership because all power, all sovereignty, belongs to the People. In Biafra the People are supreme; the People are master; the leader is servant. You see, you make a mistake when you greet me with shouts of "Power, Power." I am not power—you are. My name is Emeka. I am your servant, which is all.

SHAKING OFF NIGERIANISM

Fellow countrymen, we pride ourselves on our honesty. Let us admit to ourselves that when we left Nigeria, some of us did not shake off every particle of Nigerianism. We say that Nigerians are corrupt and take bribes, but here in our country we have among us some members of the Police and the Judiciary who are corrupt and who "eat" bribe. We accuse Nigerians of inordinate love of money, ostentatious living and irresponsibility, but here, even while we are engaged in a war of national survival, even while the very life of our nation hangs in the balance, we see some public servants who throw huge parties to entertain their friends; who kill cows to christen their babies. We have members of the Armed Forces who carry on "attack" trade instead of fighting the enemy. We have traders who hoard essential goods and inflate prices thereby increasing the people's hardship. We have "money-mongers" who aspire to build hundreds of plots on land as yet unreclaimed from the enemy; who plan to buy scores of lorries and buses and to become agents for those very foreign business-men who have brought their country to grief. We have some civil servants who think of themselves as masters rather than servants of the people. We see doctors who stay idle in their villages while their countrymen and women suffer and die. When we see all these things, they remind us that not every Biafran has yet absorbed the spirit of the Revolution. They tell us that we still have among us a member of people whose attitudes and outlooks are Nigerian. It is clear that if our Revolution is to succeed, we must reclaim these wayward Biafrans. We must Biafranize them. We must prepare all our people for the glorious roles which await them in the Revolution. If after we shall have tried to reclaim them and have failed then they must be swept aside. The people's revolution must stride ahead and like a battering ram, clearing all obstacles in its path. Fortunately, a vast majority of Biafrans are prepared for these roles.

When we think of our Revolution, therefore, we think about these things. We think about our ancient heritage, we think about the challenge of today and the promise of the future. We think about the changes which are taking place at this very moment in our personal lives and in our society. We see Biafrans from different parts of the country living together, working together, suffering together and pursuing together a common cause. We see our doctors, scientists, engineers and technologists responding to the demands of the Revolution with brilliant inventions and innovations. We see our Armed Forces with their severely limited resources holding back an aggressor who is massively equipped by the neo-imperialist enemies of African freedom. We see men of learning and mass information spreading with patriotic zeal the true story and significance of the Biafran struggle. We see our farmers determined to win the war against starvation imposed on us by the enemy. We see our ordinary men and women–the people–pursuing, in their different but essential ways, the great task of our national survival. We see every sign that this struggle is purifying and elevating the masses of our people. Every day of the struggle bears witness to actions by our countrymen and women which reveal high ideals of patriotic courage, service and sacrifice; actions which show the will and determination of our people to remain free and independent but also to create a new and better order of society for the benefit of all.

In the last five or six months, I have devised one additional way of learning at first had how the ordinary men and women of our country see the Revolution. I have established a practice of meeting every Wednesday with a different cross-section of our people to discuss the problems of the Revolution. These meetings have brought home to me the great desire for change among the generality of our people. I have heard a number of criticisms and complaints by people against certain things; I have also noticed groups forming themselves and trying to put right some of the ills of society. All this indicates both that there is a change in progress and need for more change. Thus, the Biafran Revolution is not dreamt up by an elite; it is the will of the People. The People want it. They are fighting and dying to defend it. Their immediate concern is to defeat the Nigerian aggressor and so safeguard the Biafran Revolution.

THE PRINCIPLES OF THE REVOLUTION

I stand before you tonight not to launch the Biafran Revolution, because it is already in existence. It came into being two years ago when we proclaimed to all the world that we had finally extricated ourselves from the sea of mud that was, and is, Nigeria. I stand before you to proclaim formally the commitment of the Biafran State to the Principles of the Revolution and to enunciate those Principles.

Some people are frightened when they hear the word Revolution. They say: Revolution? Heaven help us! It is too dangerous. It means mobs rushing around destroying property, killing people and upsetting everything.

But these people do not understand the real meaning of revolution. For us, a revolution is a change—a quick change, a change for the better. Every society is changing all the time. It is changing for the better or for the worse; it is either moving forward or moving backwards; it cannot stand absolutely still. A revolution is a forward movement. It is a rapid, forward movement which improves a people's standard of living and their material circumstance and purifies and raises their moral tone. It transforms for the better those institutions which are still relevant, and discards those which stand in the way of progress.

- The Biafran Revolution believes in the sanctity of human life and the dignity of the human person. The Biafran sees the willful and wanton destruction of human life not only as a grave crime but as an abominable sin. In our society every human life is holy, every individual person counts. No Biafran wants to be taken for granted or ignored, neither does he ignore or take others for granted. This explains why such degrading practices as begging for alms were unknown in Biafran society. Therefore, all forms of disabilities and inequalities which reduce the dignity of the individual or destroy his sense of person have no place in the New Biafran Social Order. The Biafran Revolution upholds the dignity of man.

- The Biafran Revolution stands firmly against Genocide—against any attempt to destroy a people, its security, its right to life, property and progress. Any attempt to deprive a community of its identity is abhorrent to the Biafran people. Having ourselves suffered genocide, we are all the more determined to take a clear stand now and at all times against this crime.

- The new Biafran Social Order places a high premium on Patriotism—Love and Devotion to the Fatherland. Every true Biafran must love Biafra; must have faith in Biafra and its people, and must strive for its greater unity. He must find his salvation here in Biafra. He must be prepared to work for Biafra, to stand up for Biafra and, if necessary, to die for Biafra. He must be prepared to defend the sovereignty of Biafra wherever and by whomsoever it is challenged. Biafran patriots do all this already, and Biafra expects all her sons and daughters of today and tomorrow, to emulate their noble example. Diplomats who treat insults to the Fatherland and the Leadership of our struggle with levity are not patriotic. That young man who sneaks about the village, avoiding service in his country's Armed Forces is unpatriotic; that young, able-bodied school teacher who prefers to distribute relief when he should be fighting his country's war, is not only unpatriotic but is doing a woman's work. Those who help these loafers to dodge their civic duties should henceforth re-examine themselves.

- All Biafrans are brothers and sisters bound together by ties of geography, trade, inter-marriage and culture and their common misfortune in Nigeria and their present experience of the armed struggle. Biafrans are even more united by the desire to create a new and better order of society which will satisfy their needs and aspirations. Therefore, there is no justification for anyone to introduce into the Biafran Fatherland divisions based on ethnic origin, sex or religion. To do so would be unpatriotic.

- Every true Biafran must know and demand his civic rights. Furthermore, he must recognize the rights of other Biafrans and be prepared to defend them when necessary. So often people complain that they have been ill-treated by the Police or some other public servant. But the truth very often is that we allow ourselves to be bullied because we are not man enough to demand and stand up for our rights, and that fellow citizens around do not assist us when we demand our rights.

- In the New Biafran Social Order sovereignty and power belong to the People. Those who exercise power do so on behalf of the people. Those who govern must not tyrannize over the people. They carry a sacred trust of the people and must use their authority strictly in accordance with the will of the people. The true test of success in public life is that the People—who are the real masters—are contented and happy. The rulers must satisfy the People at all times.

- But it is no use saying that power belongs to the People unless we are prepared to make it work in practice. Even in the old political days, the oppressors of the People were among those who shouted loudest that power belonged to the People. The Biafran Revolution will constantly and honestly seek methods of making this concept a fact rather than a pious fiction.

- Arising out of the Biafrans' belief that power belongs to the People is the principle of public accountability. Those who exercise power are accountable to the people for the way they use that power. The People retain the right to renew or terminate their mandate. Every individual servant of the People, whether in the Legislature, the Civil Service, the Judiciary, the Police, the Armed Forces, in business or in any other walks of life, is accountable at all times for his work or the work of those under his charge. Where, therefore, a ministry of department runs inefficiently or improperly, its head must accept personal responsibility for such a situation and, depending on the gravity of the failure, must resign or be removed. And where he is proved to have misused his position or trust to enrich himself, the principle of public accountability requires that he be punished severely and his ill-gotten gains taken from him.

THE TASK OF A LEADER

Those who aspire to lead must bear in mind the fact that they are servants and as such cannot ever be greater than the People, their masters. Every leader in the Biafran Revolution is the embodiment of the ideals of the Revolution. Part of his role as a leader is to keep the revolutionary spirit alive, to be a friend of the People and protector of their Revolution. He should have right judgment both of people and of situations and the ability to attract to himself the right kind of lieutenants who can best further the interests of the People and of the Revolution. The leader must not only say but always demonstrate that the power he exercises is derived from the People. Therefore, like every other Biafran public servant, he is accountable to the People for the use he makes of their mandate. He must get out when the People tell him to get out. The more power the leader is given by the People, the less is his personal freedom and the greater his responsibility for the good of the People. He should never allow his high office to separate him from the People. He must be fanatical for their welfare.

A leader in the Biafran Revolution must at all times stand for justice in dealing with the People. He should be the symbol of justice which is the supreme guarantee of good government. He should be ready, if need be, to lay down his life in pursuit of this ideal. He must have physical and moral courage and must be able to inspire the people out of despondency.

He should never strive towards the perpetuation of his office or devise means to cling to office beyond the clear mandate of the People. He should resist the temptation to erect memorials to himself in his life-time, to have his head embossed on the coin, name streets and institutions after himself, or convert government into a family business. A leader who serves his people well will be enshrined in their hearts and minds. This is all the reward he can expect in his life-time. He will be to the People the symbol of excellence, the quintessence of the Revolution. He will be BIAFRAN.

SOCIAL JUSTICE

One of the corner-stones of the Biafran Revolution is Social Justice. We believe that there should be equal opportunity for all, that appreciation and just reward should be given for honest work and that society should show concern and special care for the weak and infirm. Our people reject all forms of social inequalities and disabilities and all class and sectional privileges. Biafrans believe that society should treat all its members with impartiality and fairness. Therefore, the Biafran State must not apportion special privileges or favors to some citizens and deny them to others. For example, how can we talk of Social Justice in a situation where a highly-paid public servant gets his salt free and the poor housewife in the village pays five pounds for a cup? The State should not create a situation favorable to the exploitation of some citizens by others. The State is the Father of all, the source of security, the reliable agent which helps all to realize their legitimate hopes and aspirations. Without Social Justice, harmony and stability within society disappear and antagonisms between various sections of the community take their place. Our Revolution will uphold Social Justice at all times. The Biafran State will be the Fountain of Justice.

PROPERTY AND THE COMMUNITY

In the New Biafra, all property belongs to the Community. Every individual must consider all he has, whether in talent or material wealth, as belonging to the community for which he holds it in trust. This principle does not mean the abolition of personal property but it implies that the State, acting on behalf of the community, can intervene in the disposition of property to the greater advantage of all. Over-acquisitiveness or the inordinate desire to amass wealth is a factor liable to threaten social stability, especially in an under-developed society in which there are not enough material goods to go round.

This creates lop-sided development, breeds antagonisms between the haves and the have-nots and undermines the peace and unity of the people.

While the Biafran Revolution will foster private economic enterprise and initiative, it should remain constantly alive to the dangers of some citizens accumulating large private fortunes. Property-grabbing, if unchecked by the State, will set the pattern of behavior for the whole society which begins to attach undue value to money and property. Thus a wealthy man, even if he is known to be a crook, is accorded greater respect than an honest citizen who is not so well off. A society where this happens is doomed to rot and decay. Moreover, the danger is always there of a small group of powerful property-owners using their influence to deflect the State from performing its duties to the citizens as a whole and thereby destroying the democratic basis of society. This happens in many countries and it is one of the duties of our Revolution to prevent its occurrence in Biafra.

Finally, the Biafran Revolution will create possibilities for citizens with talent in business, administration, management and technology to fulfill themselves and receive due appreciation and reward in the service of the State, as has indeed happened in our total mobilization to prosecute the present war.

AN EGALITARIAN SOCIETY

The Biafran Revolution is committed to creating a society not torn by class consciousness and class antagonisms. Biafran society is traditionally egalitarian. The possibility for social mobility is always present in our society. The New Biafran Social Order rejects all rigid classifications of society. Anyone with imagination, anyone with integrity, anyone who works hard, can rise to any height. Thus, the son of a truck-pusher can become the Head of State of Biafra. The Biafran Revolution will provide opportunities for Biafrans to aspire and to achieve their legitimate desires.

Those who find themselves below at any particular moment must have the opportunity to rise to the top.

Our New Society is open and progressive. The people of Biafra have always striven to achieve a workable balance between the claims of tradition and the demand for change and betterment. We are adaptable because as a people we are convinced that in the world "no condition is permanent." And we believe that human effort and will are necessary to bring about changes and improvements in the condition of the individual and of society. The Biafran would thus make the effort to improve his lot and the material well-being of his community. He has the will to transform his society into a modern progressive community. In this process of rapid transformation he will retain and cherish the best elements of his culture, drawing sustenance as well as moral and psychological stability from them. But being a Biafran he will never be afraid to adapt what needs to be adapted or change what has to be changed.

PUTTING THE REVOLUTION INTO PRACTICE

The Biafran Revolution will continue to discover and develop local talent and to use progressive foreign ideas and skills so long as they do not destroy the identity of our culture or detract from the sovereignty of our Fatherland. The Biafrans Revolution will also ensure through education that the positive aspects of Biafran traditional culture, especially those which are likely to be swamped out of existence by introduced foreign influences, are conserved. The undiscriminating absorption of new ideas and attitudes will be discouraged. Biafrans can, in the final analysis, only validly express their nation's personality and enhance their corporate identity Biafran culture, through Biafran art and literature, music, dancing and drama, and through peculiar gestures and social habits which distinguish them from all other people.

Those then are the main principles of our Revolution. They are not abstract formulations but arise out of the traditional background and the present temper of our people. They grow out of our native soil and are the product of our peculiar climate. They belong to us. If anyone here doubts the validity of these principles let him go out into the streets and into the villages, let him ask the ordinary Biafran. Let him go to the Army, ask the rank and file and he will find, as I have found, that they have very clear ideas about the kind of society we should build here. They will not put them in the same words I have used tonight but the meaning will be the same. From today, let no Biafran pretend that he or she does not know the main-spring of our national action, let him or her not plead ignorant when found indulging in un-Biafran activities. The principles of our Revolution are hereby clearly set out for everyone to see. They are now the property of every Biafran and the instrument for interpreting our national life.

But principles are principles. They can only be transformed into reality through the institutions of society, otherwise they remain inert and useless. It is my firm conviction that in the Biafran Revolution principles and practice will go hand in hand. It is my duty and the duty of all of you to bring this about.

Looking at the institutions of our society, the very vehicles for carrying out our Revolutionary principles, what do you find? We find old, jaded and rusty machines creaking along most inefficiently and delaying the People's progress and the progress of the Revolution. The problem of our institutions is partly that they were designed by other people, in other times and for other purposes. Their most fundamental weakness is that they came into being during the colonial period when the relationship between the colonial administrators and the people was that of master and servant. Our public servants, as heirs of the colonial masters, are apt to treat the People today with arrogance and condescension. In the New Biafran Social Order, we say that power belongs to the People, but this central principle tends to elude many of the public servants who continue to behave in a manner which shows that they consider themselves masters—the People their servants.

The message of the Revolution has tended to fly over their heads. Let them beware, the Revolution, gathering momentum like a flood, washes clear all impediments on its way.

Take any of the institutions and the history is the same. First, it was fashioned for the British Colonial Service, then it saw service in that ill-fated country called Nigeria. It would be a miracle, fellow countrymen, if it should be found to be adequate for the need of revolutionary Biafra. What is surprising is not that these institutions fail us today but that there should be Biafrans, and some of them apparently very intelligent people, who sit back and expect good results from them. The fact is that one does not require extraordinary common-sense or insight to see the need for overhauling these machines and discarding those that are obsolescent.

THE LEGISLATURE

For example, the Legislature, which should be the primary instrument for effecting the will of the People, was too often in the past used to frustrate the People. As I have said over and over again, power derives from the People. Ideally, all the People should be involved in the actual process of law-making. As a matter of fact, in our traditional society all adults who had attained the age of reason were directly involved in discussion, debate and decision-making on all things affecting the whole people. That was the original government by consensus. That was possible when the community was small and compact. With the emergence of the nation-state which is larger and heterogeneous, this ideal procedure became impracticable. Therefore, the process of delegation of power was evolved to meet a practical need. But this does not invalidate the original principle that power belongs to the People. A man who is delegated by the People to represent their interests, therefore, is acting on behalf of the People and ceases to act for them the moment they withdraw their mandate. Like the ideal leader, the People's representative should get out when the People tell him to get out. He must constantly reassure the People that he is acting in their best interest.

In the past, the People's representatives, while paying lip-service to the primacy of the People and the supremacy of their interest, made sure that in actual practice their own personal will prevailed over the will of the People and their own personal interest over the interest of the nation. Thus we had politicians who spent their time amassing wealth, who did everything conceivable to remain in office, who would kill, loot, throw acid and do anything to remain in power. The will of the People meant nothing to them.

In the New Biafra, the Legislature must be constituted to reflect the spirit and the Principles of the Revolution.

Legislators must understand that responsibility goes with power. Those who wield power must appreciate the responsibility attached to that power. The legislator is a servant of the People given special powers to enable him discharge special responsibilities. Power is not given to him to turn him into a big man, to enable him sit inside huge American cars and build himself palaces. The conscientious legislator who strives to carry out his responsibility will find no time to pursue his own lucrative interests. He will find no time for membership of boards of corporations and directorships of public and private companies, or for doing deals with foreign business interests.

POLITICS AND THE REVOLUTION

In revolutionary Biafra, certain basic reforms in politics and political institutions are necessary in order to safeguard the liberty of the People and protect their interest. For example, it will be imperative to separate the functions of the Legislature from those of the Executive. A member of the Legislature cannot at the same time be a member of the Executive. In the past, it was possible for a legislator to be a minister of state which is an executive post, in which case he neglected either his duty to his constituency or his duty to the state. Very often he neglected both.

In revolutionary Biafra there will be an executive leader elected by the people with full powers to choose his lieutenants. If he chooses a legislator or a public servant, such a person must resign his original appointment.

Another important principle is that people should be free to vote and be voted for wherever they live in Biafra. An Ikot Ekpene man living at Etiti should be free to vote and be voted for at Etiti. He does not have to go to Ikot Ekpene to vote or be voted for as happened in the past.

The principle of delegation of power from the People is so important that every revolutionary government of Biafra must encourage Democratically organized groups of youths, students, women, workers, farmers, professional bodies, managerial and business organizations, traders and others to participate actively in political debate and discussion. The Revolution belongs to them.

Then, let us look at our Civil Service. It is too rigid and inflexible, too slow and ponderous for the needs of today. Too often when quick action and initiative are called for, what the public gets is cold, formal and aloof treatment. What is required in the future is a modernized and energized Civil Service, a Service which will fit into our Revolution and become the instrument of change. Its members must embody the spirit of the New Order by identifying with the values of change and progress and promoting these values in the conduct of public affairs.

THE JUDICIARY

Since our Revolution has its foundation in the Rule of Law, the Judiciary becomes a most important arm of the State. It is the instrument for the protection and defense of our people's liberties, for interpreting the will of our Revolution and for promoting the values of the New Order. It will be necessary, in the first place, to review our body of laws and bring it into line with the values and concepts of the New Order. It will be essential to stream-line this machinery so as to facilitate its processes and make legal redress available to all citizens. Every Biafran should find it possible and easy to have recourse to law courts when his rights or liberties are interfered with or threatened. In this he should be able to count on the support of his fellow citizens.

In the past, justice and its processes were often very remote from the life of the ordinary citizen. The ways of justice were beyond his understanding. And yet justice was meant to exist for his benefit. In revolutionary Biafra, the citizen should understand what law and justice are about. Our Revolution, therefore, aims at involving the citizen in the process of justice so that he will participate actively in the protection of his life and liberties and in the defense of the integrity, stability, and moral health of the nation.

THE POLICE FORCE

Like the Judiciary, the Police Force is a very important institution, very important because it is given the special responsibility of maintaining law and order and guarding the security of the People and the nation. Like other institutions of our society, the Police Force needs to be reformed so that it can better fulfill its function in the Revolution. Its members must absorb the ideals of the New Biafran Social Order. The Police have often been criticized by the public. They have been accused of corruption, bribery and inefficiency. We say that some of these evils and weaknesses can be traced to the fact that the Police Force, like many other institutions of our society, had a colonial beginning and was vitiated in Nigeria. Today we are involved in a task of building a New Society with new values and new outlooks. Our Police Force must be part of this New Order. It must promote the ideals of the New Order–ideals of change and progress. The conduct of its members must, in the spirit of the Revolution, be scrupulously honest. The Biafran Police must be a People's Police, that is to say, a champion of the People's rights. The Policeman is not there simply to arrest criminals. He is also there to help people avoid going wrong. He must never exploit the People's ignorance of their civic rights. On the contrary, it is his duty, where such ignorance exists, to teach the citizen his rights. Above all, he must be a dedicated patriot fanatically devoted to prosecuting the safety and security of the State. Fortunately, we know there are members of our Police Force who are imbued with these ideals. It is on them that the Force will be rebuilt.

THE ARMED SERVICES

The Biafran Armed Forces hold a key position in the Biafran Revolution. They have been rightly in the front-line defense of the Biafran nation and the People in the past two years. They have performed this task creditably, for which the Nation is indebted to them. But like the others, our military institutions carry the stamp of their Colonial and Nigerian origin. For our Revolution, the Biafran Armed Forces must be transformed into a true People's Army.

The New Biafran Armed Forces should have love, unity and co-operation between the officers and other ranks, between them and the People.

They must rid themselves of the starchiness and rigid class distinctions which are the hall-mark of an establishment army; they should always ensure that their members never maltreat fellow citizens; that they never loot or "liberate" the People's property; that they treat Biafran womanhood with respect and decorum; and that they pay fair price for whatever they buy and return whatever they borrow from the People.

The Biafran Armed Forces must unite with the People to build the New Society and must share with the People the Biafran ideology which sustains the Revolution.

THE PUBLIC SERVICES

What emerges from our examination of the public services is that the public servant is yet to learn that he is a servant of the People, not their master; that he must love the People and seek their welfare. There is no room in the New Biafra for the public servant who is arrogant, insolent and overbearing. The Public Service is created to provide an efficient service for the People. It is the responsibility of the public servant to provide this efficient service. There is no room in evolutionary Biafra for the inefficient or indolent public servant, for that man who sits at his desk filling out football coupons; for that woman who makes endless telephone calls, or for that worker who comes late and watches the clock for an hour before closing time. There is no room for the public servant who is corrupt or who uses public facilities to promote his private ends. I think of that man who uses official transport to evacuate his personal belongings and abandons the property of the State to the enemy. I think of that public servant in the Ministry of Lands who allocates State land to himself, his wife and his friends. I think of that Army officer who drives past in any empty car, leaving a wounded soldier to bleed to death. I see these things and I say to myself: these men have yet to grasp the lesson of our Revolution or else sooner or later the Revolution will grasp them.

I ask myself: what can be done to bring the lesson home to them? Nothing at all, unless they are ready to do something for themselves. The revolution cannot wait for the indolent, inefficient and corrupt public servant. He has to catch up with the Revolution, or the Revolution will catch up with him. The public servant who cannot, or will not, do the work for which he is hired, will be fired. It is no good saying: I have been in this job for twenty years. The Revolution cannot go into your long record. We repeat that if you cannot do the job of the Revolution, someone else will be found to do it.

However, we recognize that some devoted public servants may be inefficient simply because they have not received the right and adequate training for what they are required to do. In this respect, our Revolution will do one of two things. Either move them to a job they can do, or provide the right training-on-the-job if this is likely to produce worthwhile results.

TRAINING AND EDUCATION

Our experience during this struggle has brought home to us the need for versatility. Many of our citizens have found themselves having to do emergency duties different from their normal peace-time jobs. In the years after the present armed conflict, we may find that in the defense of the Revolution the general state of mobilization and alertness will remain. One of the ways of preparing ourselves for this emergency will be to ensure that every citizen will be trained in two jobs–his normal peace-time occupation and a different skill which will be called into play during a national emergency. Thus, for example, a clerk may be given training to enable him to operate as an ambulance-driver during an emergency, or a university lecturer as a post-master or a Signal Sergeant in one of the Armed Forces.

We realize here that the problem is more than that of providing narrow technical training. It has to do with re-orientation of attitudes. It has to do with the cultivation of the right kind of civic virtue and loyalty to Biafra. We all stand in need of this.

It is quite clear that to attain the goals of the Biafran Revolution will require extensive political and civic education of our People. To this effect, we will, in near future, set up a National Orientation College (N.O.C) which will undertake the needful function of formally inculcating the Biafran ideology and the Principles of the Revolution. We will also pursue this vital task of education through seminars, mass rallies, formal and informal address by the leaders and standard-bearers of the Revolution. All Biafrans who are going to play a role in the promotion of the

Revolution, especially those who are going to operate the institutions of the New Society, must first of all expose themselves to the ideology of the Revolution.

The full realization of the Biafran ideology and the promise of the Biafran Revolution will have the important effect of drawing the People of Biafra into close unity with the Biafran State. The Biafran State and the Biafran People thus become one. The People jealously defend and protect the integrity of the State. The State guarantees the People certain basic rights and welfare. In this third year of our independence, we re-state those basic rights and welfare obligations which the revolutionary State of Biafra guarantees to the People.

THE RIGHT TO WORK

In the field of employment and labor, the Biafran Revolution guarantees every able Biafran the right to work. All those who are lazy or refuse to work forfeit their right to this guarantee. "He who does not work should not eat" is an important principle in Biafra.

Our Revolution provides equal opportunities for employment and labor for all Biafrans irrespective of sex. For equal output a woman must receive the same remuneration as a man.

Our revolutionary Biafran State will guarantee a rational system of remuneration of labor. Merit and output shall be the criteria for reward in labor. "To each according to his ability, to each ability according to its product" shall be our motto in Biafra.

Our Revolution guarantees security for workers who have been incapacitated by physical injury, old age or disease. It will be the duty of the Biafran State to raise the standard of living of the Biafran People, to provide them with improved living conditions and to afford them modern amenities that enhance their human dignity and self-esteem. We recognize at all times the great contributions made by the farmers, the craftsmen and other toilers of the Revolution to our national progress. It will be a cardinal point of our economic policy to keep their welfare constantly in view. The Biafran Revolution will promulgate a Workers' Charter which will codify and establish workers' rights.

HEALTH AND WELFARE

The maintenance of the health and physical well-being of the Biafran citizen must be the concern and the responsibility of the State. The revolutionary Biafran State will at all times strive to provide medical service for all its citizens in accordance with the resources available to it; it will wage a continuous struggle against epidemic and endemic diseases; and will promote among the People knowledge of hygienic living. It will develop social and preventive medicine, set up sanatoriums for incurable and infectious diseases and mental cases, and a net-work of maternity homes for ante- and post-natal care of Biafran mothers. Furthermore, Biafra will set great store by the purity of the air which its People breathe. We have a right to live in a clean, pollution-free atmosphere.

CULTURE AND HIGHER EDUCATION

Our Revolution recognizes the vital importance of the mental and emotional needs of the Biafran People. To this end, the Biafran State will pay great attention to Religion, Education, Culture and the Arts. We shall aim at elevating our cultural institutions and promoting educational reforms which will foster a sense of national and racial pride among our People and discourage ideas which inspire a feeling of inferiority and dependence on foreigners and foreign interests. We must produce the kind of manpower that will nurture the Biafran Revolution. It will be the prime duty of the revolutionary Biafran State to eradicate illiteracy from our society, to guarantee free education to all Biafran children to a stage limited only by existing resources. Our nation will encourage the training of scientists, technicians and skilled workers needed for quick industrialization and the modernization of our agriculture. We will ensure the development of higher education and technological training for our People, encourage our intellectuals, writers, artists and scientists to research, create and invent in the service of the State and the People. We must prepare our People to contribute significantly to knowledge and world culture.

Finally, the present armed struggle, in which many of our countrymen and women have distinguished themselves and made numerous sacrifices in defense of the Fatherland and the Revolution, has imposed on the state of Biafra extra responsibility for the welfare of its People. Biafra will give special care and assistance to soldiers and civilians disabled in the course of the pogrom and the war; it will develop special schemes for resettlement and rehabilitation. The nation will assume responsibility for the dependants of the heroes of the Revolution who have lost their lives in defense of the Fatherland.

In talking about the rights of the Biafrans and the welfare obligations the State owes to them, I have had cause to refer to our limited resources. These limitations are particularly severe at the moment as a result of the war. But even without the war we would be short of adequate resources for putting into effect all the principles and policies for transforming our society. This is partly because of the wrong economic policies of the past, policies that we must immediately tackle if the Revolution is to fulfill its promise to the People; for the Revolution is also the servant of the People.

SELF-RELIANCE

One of the key problems of the economy of under-developed countries is the fact that they are controlled and exploited by foreign monopoly interests. Under-developed countries cannot advance unless they break the strangle-hold of the foreign monopolies. The only hope of success lies in the state pursuing an active policy of self-reliance in putting its own economic house in order. But it cannot do this unless it takes control of the main springs of the economy–the means of production, distribution and exchange. This will ensure central mobilization of the national economy through proper planning and control. This is what Biafra must do; this is what African countries must do; this is what the under-developed world must do, if they are to save themselves.

As primary producers, we are economically at the mercy of the industrialized countries. We are obliged to sell our products cheap to them and to buy their manufactures dear from them. Like other under-developed countries, our economy is fragile, and because we do not earn enough for what we produce we remain poor and cannot improve the standard of living of our people. And because we are poor we cannot develop our economy. How then can we break this vicious circle? If we try to unite with other primary producers to obtain better terms of trade, we find that because of our poverty we cannot hold out long enough against the aggressive policies of these rich industrialized countries.

Here, as in all other spheres of our Revolution, the answer must come from within, from ourselves. We must pursue an enlightened dynamic policy which will concentrate on employing our primary products in various domestic manufactures. The present war has already opened our eyes to what we can do by relying on our own resources in material and men. It is unthinkable that after the war we shall return to the old system of selling our primary products to someone in Europe at his own price so that he can turn them into manufactured goods and sell back to us, again at his own price. Our primary products shall henceforth be used mainly to feed Biafra's growing industries.

Another economic goal of the Biafran Revolution is self-sufficiency in food production. Our experience during the present war has emphasized to us the importance of this. The work of the Biafra Land Army has also shown us the tremendous possibilities that exist for a major agrarian revolution. The Biafran Revolution will intervene actively to end the exploitation of the countryside by the town–a baneful process which is often easily lost sight of. The Biafran Revolution will encourage farmers, craftsmen and tradesmen to form co-operatives and communes, and will make them take pride in their work by according them the recognition and prestige they deserve. The program for industrial progress in revolutionary Biafra will achieve balanced development between industry and agriculture, between regions or provinces within Biafra, between town and country and finally between Biafra and other African countries who desire to do business with us.

Again and again, in stating the Principles of our Revolution, we have spoken of the People. We have spoken of the primacy of the People, of the belief that power belongs to the People; that the Revolution is the servant of the People. We make no apologies for speaking so constantly about the People, because we believe in the People; we have faith in the People. They are the bastion of the Nation, the makers of its culture and history.

THE QUALITIES OF THE INDIVIDUAL

But in talking about the People we must never lose sight of the individuals who make up the People. The single individual is the final, irreducible unit of the People. In Biafra that single individual counts. The Biafran Revolution cannot lose sight of this fact.

The desirable changes which the Revolution aims to bring to the lives of the People will first manifest themselves in the lives of individual Biafrans. The success of the Biafran Revolution will depend on the quality of individuals within the State. Therefore, the caliber of the individual is of the utmost importance to the Revolution. To build the New Society we will require new men who are in tune with the spirit of the New Order. What then should be the qualities of this Biafran of the New Order?

- He is patriotic, loyal to his State, his Government and its leadership; he must no do anything which undermines the security of his State or gives advantage to the enemies of his country. He must not indulge in such evil practices as tribalism and nepotism which weaken the loyalty of their victims to the state. He should be prepared, if need be, to give up his life in defense of the Nation.

- He must be his brother's keeper; he must help all Biafrans in difficulty, whether or not they are related to him by blood; he must avoid, at all costs, doing anything which is capable of bringing distress and hardship to other Biafrans. A man who hoards money or goods is not his brother's keeper because he brings distress and hardship to his fellow citizens.

- He must be honorable; he must be a person who keeps his promise and the promise of his office, a person who can always be trusted.

- He must be truthful: he must not cheat his neighbor, his fellow citizens and his country. He must not give or receive bribes or corruptly advance himself or his interests.

- He must be responsible: he must not push across to others the task which properly belongs to him, or let others receive the blame or punishment for his own failings. A responsible man keeps secrets. A Biafran who is in a position to know what our troops are planning and talks about it is irresponsible. The information he gives out will spread and reach the ear of the enemy. A responsible man minds his own business; he does not show off.

- He must be brave and courageous: he must never allow himself to be attacked by others without fighting back to defend himself and his rights. He must be ready to tackle tasks which other people might regard as impossible.

- He must be law-abiding: he obeys the laws of the land and does nothing to undermine the due processes of law.

- He must be freedom-loving: he must stand up resolutely against all forms of injustice, oppression and suppression. He must never be afraid to demand his rights. For example, a true Biafran at a post office or bank counter will insist on being served in his turn.

- He must be progressive: he should not slavishly and blindly adhere to old ways of doing things; he must be prepared to make changes in his way of life in the light of our new revolutionary experience.

- He is industrious, resourceful and inventive; he must not fold his arms and wait for the Government to do everything for him; he must also help himself.

CONCLUSION

My fellow countrymen and women, proud and courageous Biafrans, two years ago, faced with the threat of total extermination, we met in circumstances not unlike today's. At that August gathering, the entire leaders of our people being present, we as a people decided that we had to take our destiny into our own hand, to plan and decide our future and to stand by these decisions no matter the vicissitude of this war which by then was already imminent. At that time, our major pre-occupation was how to remain alive, how to restrain an implacable enemy from destroying us in our own homes. In that moment of crisis we decided to resume our sovereignty.

In my statement to the leaders of our community before that decision was made, I spoke about the difficulties. I explained that the road which we were about to tread was to be carved through a jungle of thorns and that our ability to emerge through this jungle was, to say the least, uncertain. Since that fateful decision, the very worst has happened. Our people have continually been subjected to genocide. The entire conspiracy of neo-colonialism has joined hands to stifle our nascent independence. Yet, undaunted by the odds, proud in the fact of our manhood, encouraged by the companionship of the Almighty, we have fought to this day with honor, with pride, with glory so that today, as I stand before you, I see a proud people acknowledged by the world. I see a heroic people, men with heart-beats as regular and blood as red as the best on earth.

On that fateful day two years ago, you mandated me to do everything within my power to avert the dangers that loomed ahead, the threat of extermination. Little did we, you and I, know how long the battle was to be, how complex its attendant problems. From then on, what have been achieved are there for the entire world to see and have only been possible because of the solidarity and support of our people. For this I thank you all. I must have made certain mistakes in the course of this journey but I am sure that whatever mistakes I have made are mistakes of the head and never of the heart. I have tackled the sudden problems as they unfold before my eyes and I have tackled them to the best of my ability with the greater interest of our people in mind.

Today, I am glad that our problems are less than they were a year ago; that arms alone can no longer destroy us; that our victory, the fulfillment of our dreams, is very much in sight. We have forced a stalemate on the enemy and this is likely to continue, with any advances likely to be on our side. If we fail, which God forbid, it can only be because of certain inner weakness in our being. It is in order to avoid these pitfalls that I have today proclaimed before you the Principles of the Biafran Revolution.

We in Biafra are convinced that the Black man can never come into his own until he is able to build modern states based on indigenous African ideologies, to enjoy true independence, to be able to make his mark in the arts and sciences and to engage in meaningful dialogue with the white man on a basis of equality. When he achieves this, he will have brought a new dimension into international affairs.

Biafra will not betray the Black man. No matter the odds, we will fight with all our might until Black men everywhere can point with pride to this Republic, standing dignified and defiant, an example of African nationalism triumphant over its many and age-old enemies.

We believe that God, humanity and history are on our side, and that the Biafran Revolution is indestructible and eternal.

OH GOD, NOT MY WILL, BUT THINE FOREVER.

Ahiara Village, Biafra.

1st June 1969.